THE DRAGON'S SHADOW

BALAKRISHNA KAMATH

Srishti
PUBLISHERS & DISTRIBUTORS

Srishti Publishers & Distributors
A unit of AJR Publishing LLP
212A, Peacock Lane
Shahpur Jat, New Delhi – 110 049

editorial@srishtipublishers.com

First Published by Srishti Publishers & Distributors in 2025

10 9 8 7 6 5 4 3 2 1

To my sons and their spouses,
Pramod-Nandini and Atul-Padmapriya.

I sincerely thank my friends Sasang, Jeevan and Gokul for their valuable support and guidance while writing this book.

In present-day hybrid warfare, attacks are as unpredictable as they are devastating. Bolstered by innovative technologies, 'cold fire' has become an ominous weapon that can engulf you before you even realize it's there. The only defence is to be ever-vigilant, anticipating the threat at every turn, and ensuring your assets are shielded in an efficient and perpetual protective barrier.

This is the world you are about to enter – a world where the line between man and technology is blurred, and survival depends on your wits and instincts.

Preface

Since the Indo-China War of 1962, which was the result of blatant Chinese aggression on an unsuspecting Indian nation, China has been viewed as a difficult adversary and an escalating threat to its security. An unsettled border and China's unrelenting claim over vast swathes of Indian territory have only intensified tensions. China has continuously pressured India by rapidly building roads and upgrading its military infrastructure close to the Line of Actual Control (LAC). Over the years, several standoffs, showdowns, and skirmishes have brought both countries to the brink of war. Consequently, the mechanisms both countries established over the years to prevent the accidental triggering of war are now resting on thin ice.

In the context of India and China's chequered relations, the absence of war does not mean peace prevails. Both countries know the precarious nature of their relations and are busy keeping their powder dry. Over and above, China was seen pursuing what can be termed as a wholesome hostile policy that entailed not just indulging in espionage, working on raising its potential for sabotage and subversion, but encircling India by spreading its influence among India's immediate neighbours. As technology advanced, China started taking the lead in exploiting it to keep adversaries tied down and keep their cyberspace and sensitive data safe. It is a sinister game that China stealthily plays. In recent years, with a clever mix of conventional techniques and new technology, China has acquired an edge and capacity to target countries that it perceives as its adversaries.

The Dragon's Shadow is a fictional portrayal of an episode of confrontation between Indian and Chinese intelligence. It shows how India's Counter Intelligence Agency is trying to safeguard India's assets and cyberspace from the mounting challenges of the sophisticated tech-aided furtive Chinese gameplans aimed at crippling India at any time of its choice. One has to remember that while the spy and intelligence operations are fundamentally alike, the Chinese prefer to adopt a distinct tactic and pace. To make it look natural, the book sticks to a near-real portrayal of the events and action rather than the usual pomp-and-show depiction. Thus, the readers can feel the situations intelligence operatives genuinely live through.

Like in the author's two earlier books, *The Velvet Gloves* and *The Ace of Shadows*, the protagonist of the current story is Intelligence Operative Yashwant Narayan Godbole. Although Godbole's retirement was dealt with in one of the author's earlier books, he had to be pulled out from the cold, respecting the feedback and pressure from Godbole's fans.

Prologue

October 12, 2020
8:00 a.m.

Mumbai – India's financial capital and premier megalopolis – experienced a power outage like never before. The local trains stopped, road signals failed, and flights from the city's airport could not take off. Biometric and chip reading machines at the office entrances stopped working, blocking the employees' entry into their offices. Hospitals and their patient services were paralyzed. The lifts in skyscrapers and air conditioners stopped working. Online transactions did not work, and ATMs stopped dispensing cash. Automated systems and innumerable machines in the factories in Mumbai's industrial zones stood frozen. The authorities did not know how it happened or how it could be fixed quickly.

At the Western Navy Headquarters, an emergency meeting was in progress. The Commanders were worried because even after two hours of the power failure, there was no information about when the power would be restored. To make matters worse, the electric company's special alternate power lines to handle emergencies were also dead. The Navy's own standby power supply system was activated, but it couldn't power the vast defence facility forever. What would happen if the sensitive radar stations, communication equipment, missile control and launch facilities stopped working? The entire western region was in danger of becoming vulnerable to enemy attacks. The worried Commander picked up the hotline to his headquarters in Delhi.

A similar situation was unfolding at Bhabha Atomic Research Centre (BARC), fearing the disastrous situation. The BARC Chief called the PMO and spoke to the PM's secretary.

The experts did not see any plausible snag that could have triggered a power crisis of such enormity. It was unusual, since Mumbai is painstakingly protected against power failures. Theories started floating, and many saw a cyber-attack as the most likely cause of the blackout.

Pakistan and China were the natural suspects. However, the timing of the outage turned the focus on China. The tensions created since May 2020 by the aggressive standoffs and bloody clashes between the Chinese People's Liberation Army (PLA) and the Indian Armed Forces along the Sino-Indian border in Ladakh were nowhere near an end. Was the cyber breach China's way of signalling to India how deep it could strike, without firing a single bullet? The war games were changing radically. The new era of hybrid warfare had suddenly reached India's doorstep.

In June-August 2017, the Doklam standoff between the PLA and Indian Army at the India-China-Bhutan trijunction had made the Chinese hostile intentions abundantly clear. Then India's Internal Intelligence Agency raised 'NES-17' (North and East Security – 2017). NES-17 is a close-knit group of selected intelligence operatives to deal with the emerging security and counter-intelligence challenges posed by China's covert operations targeting India. The Agency entrusted the command of NES-17 to Operations Director Anand Kumar Das, with Senior Operative Yashwant Narayan Godbole, aka Yash, as the field team leader. Godbole's team had three Field Operatives – Ashok Talreja, Vilas Pande, and Abdul Riaz. Amit Rao acted as the team coordinator and handled the communication and desk work for the group. Kamini Dube and Sneha Kumar, two newly-trained operatives, ran a tiny but sophisticated cyber cell for the group. The team had their job well cut out; they had to prevent China from turning India's cyberspace into a minefield.

Chapter – 1
Droplets from Far and Wide

TG-2 camp near the LAC in Arunachal Pradesh
12 October, 2020
10.30 a.m.

Despite the cool breeze at eleven thousand feet above sea level, Major Prashant Bakshi felt uncomfortable. His eyebrows furrowed with worry as he entered the barracks and quietly sank into his chair. Subedar Rameshwar Gupta was aware of his officers' disappointment over their aborted patrolling exercise. He hesitantly followed the Major into the tent. He would have left the Major alone, but the patrolling party waiting outside had to be given instructions.

Maj Bakshi was trying to figure out how the Chinese PLA patrol had suddenly appeared in the vicinity, just ahead of his patrol party, forcing him to abort his team's patrolling exercise. He had tactfully ordered his soldiers to change their tracks and return to the TG-2 camp. Given the volatile situation, he wanted to avoid the rival patrol parties coming face to face on disputed territory.

Maj Bakshi's concern was not just that his soldiers had to abandon the planned patrol, but that it happened for the second time in quick succession in the same PP-6 (Patrolling Point-6) area. They had faced a similar situation just twelve days ago.

He refused to believe that it was just a coincidence.

Were the Chinese trying to deliberately prevent them from patrolling the PP-6 area? How did they know the Indian Army's patrolling plans? The nearest PLA base to PP-6 was over thirty-five kilometres north in the Shannan part of Tibet. There was also no direct road connection to PP-6. Without advance information, it would be impossible for the Chinese to arrive there around 8 a.m., travelling through the treacherous route. Perhaps the Chinese had come and camped in the area the previous afternoon, walking through a narrow valley well-hidden from the Indian side.

Maj Bakshi finally looked up and gestured for Sub Gupta to sit. As the Subedar settled on a narrow bench, Maj Bakshi asked, "Subedar saab, do you think today's incident was just a coincidence?"

"No, sir. I have my doubts. It's difficult to guess how the Chinese got there twice in perfect time to thwart us from proceeding ahead." The Subedar briefly stopped and added, "Except the old man, Tashi Norbu, and the boy, Tenzin Lote, nobody had any wind on our trip to the village. They regularly serve us and are trustworthy. Even they thought we were on our bi-weekly visit to the village to maintain these tents and replenish the stocks. There was no chance of them knowing about our patrol plans."

Maj Bakshi again fell silent. Tashi Norbu, the village head locally known as *Gaonbudda*, was influential, and Tenzin, a hardworking young man, was well-known for his helpful nature in the village. Questioning them would be a delicate matter, so the Major decided it would be best not to discuss it with them at this stage.

After a pause, the Major pointed at the small wooden box on his desk and asked the Subedar, "Can you open this? I need to speak to the Corps HQ."

The Subedar fished out a key from his pocket and opened the box, revealing a telephone. Maj Bakshi reached for the phone, but hesitantly glanced at Sub Gupta. He got the hint and quietly left the tent. The Major picked up the receiver and asked the operator to connect him to the CO.

*****

Rameswaram sea-face, Tamil Nadu
The intervening night of October 12-13, 2020

Tech Officer Manoj Raghavan sat in his chair on the top deck of a lighthouse, sipping the strong, black coffee brewed by his colleague Varghese John. The coffee felt like a lifeline due to the gloomy atmosphere, caused by intermittent rains, strong winds, and a rough sea. The storm's fury seemed magnified from their room on the top deck of the lighthouse. Each gust of wind and crash of waves echoed ominously.

The old lighthouse standing tall in the secluded part of Rameswaram was a beacon for fishing boats and ships at sea. It also housed a secret listening post run by India's Internal Intelligence Agency. Within its walls, sophisticated equipment tirelessly monitored the communications that crisscrossed between the shore, boats, ships, and aircraft. Few voice intercepts existed that stormy night, since most boats had not ventured out.

Suddenly, at 11:48 p.m., Raghavan's computer screen flashed with a beep and a pop-up. He quickly leaned over the screen, his fingers deftly manoeuvring the controls of the equipment, which was kept close to the computer.

Looking at the computer screen, his eyes narrowing at the data, Raghavan said, "John, a satellite phone just became active. It may be trying to dial. It looks like an Iridium Satellite phone..."

Raghavan gently tapped on a few keys. As he adjusted the equipment's controls to zero in on the source of the intercept, the speaker crackled to life, and a burst of chatter filled the room. The conversation lasted only 18 seconds. The conversation ended as abruptly as it started, and the signal vanished from the screen. Raghavan downloaded the voice file quickly and played it to listen once more. It was a quick conversation in a foreign language, making it difficult to decipher. So, he fed the voice content into another computer and waited for the result. After a tense minute, the computer labelled the 18-second interaction 'Language –Mandarin'.

Raghavan sat down to look for the coordinates, determined to find the exact location of the satellite phone when the chatter was initiated. He entered the coordinates, and moments later, the computer pinpointed the location—9.351182 to 81.291530 in the Bay of Bengal, about fifty kilometres east of Mullaitivu in north-eastern Sri Lanka. The other details confirmed that the chatter was from an Iridium Satellite phone.

"This isn't a normal shipping route," Raghavan muttered, frowning. "Could it be a boat? But locals in the coastal regions of India and Sri Lanka don't speak Mandarin."

In his four years at the listening post, he had intercepted numerous Chinese messages from vessels on the high seas. But this one was the briefest and was marked by a strangely calm tone. This chatter appeared suspicious. As a rule, the listening posts were not equipped with translation software. Hence, Raghavan promptly forwarded the voice file to the Agency's control room in Delhi for further analysis and necessary action.

Meanwhile, Raghavan kept an eye out for further signals or chatter from the same phone. He hoped to map the vessel's route by tracking the locations from where further calls would be made. Raghavan also tried to find the location and details of the phone equipment on which that call was received. The call was to a cell phone in Sri Lanka.

"Who could this Mandarin speaker in Sri Lanka be?" Raghavan wondered aloud.

Nevertheless, Raghavan and John maintained a vigil for further communication from that source.

At 00:35 a.m., an urgent message arrived from the Agency's Delhi office:

'Request high alert. Maintain a close lookout for any further chatter from the same source. Work out the locations of the originator

and recipient of the satellite call. All details are needed urgently. Send your further reports directly to NES-17.'

Raghavan understood the gravity of the message. Especially with the ongoing standoff between the Indian Army and PLA in eastern Ladakh, anything involving the Chinese assumed extreme urgency. He quickly gathered all the details and started preparing his reply to NES-17.

*****

New Delhi
October 13, 2020

Yashwant Narayan Godbole struggled to come out of vacation mode. Summoned in the middle of his family vacation in Goa, he faced his family's lingering disappointment over the unfinished vacation. As he entered the office, his colleague Amit Rao handed a thick file folder to Godbole, tactfully urging him back into the fray. Godbole reluctantly opened the folder and started turning the sheets.

"I know switching from vacation mode is tough, but Yash, you need to get up to date before meeting Das," Rao said.

Godbole sighed, slumping into his chair. "Amit, please sit. Before I dive into this, give me a quick brief if you can."

Rao settled in a chair opposite him. "Things are hectic as ever. This unending tussle, which the Chinese are forcing along the LAC, is getting worse. You know, yesterday's power outage in Mumbai has brought things to the fore."

"Yes, indeed. I read some experts' views in today's press and electronic media. The Chinese seem to be playing it hard. Well, anything interesting caught in our net so far?" Godbole interrupted, sitting up.

"How could we... with you missing in action?" Rao laughed loudly, then turned serious. He said, "Jokes apart, things are heating up. Kamini and Sneha are already neck-deep in this. Our cyber cell is buzzing with activity. We have also roped in Professor Singh and Professor Farook from the National Technical Institute. Das wants you to join them."

"It's a highly specialized area. I'm not sure how I can contribute."

"Yash, they have noticed some faint pug marks. While they've made progress, they need some technical data and details from the electric company. Then your turn will come to pursue the case in the field."

Godbole leaned back, taking it in, "Well, I need to get a clear picture. Tell me, Amit, is there any other clue about their larger game plan? Any clandestine activity within our boundaries?"

"Nothing major, but we have some input... what Das describes as droplets received from far corners of the country, within the last twenty-four hours. There's been an unusual movement of a Chinese vessel in the sea off the coast of north-eastern Sri Lanka. Our listening post in Rameswaram detected it. This morning, Das packed off Riaz and Talreja to Rameswaram to track the vessel's route in that area," Rao said.

"Das is always meticulous."

"He's got some other work lined up for you, too."

"Something new?"

"Well... yesterday morning, something cropped up at the LAC in the Tawang district of Arunachal Pradesh. Das has you in mind for this work. Better keep your bags packed," Rao said with a chuckle.

"That is one thing everyone masters after joining the Agency. Nowadays, I don't bother unpacking my bags any longer," Godbole, too, laughed heartily. "Who's looking into the Mumbai blackout?" he added.

"Das is on that. Anyway, we'll have to wait for the electric company's technical data for experts to analyze and confirm a cyber-attack. Now, get set to go, buddy," Rao said, heading out of the room.

*****

In the afternoon, when Godbole reported to Anand Kumar Das, he found his boss without his usual smile.

Das glanced up from his desk, a deep frown creasing his forehead. "Sorry, Yash... I called you back from your vacation."

"Well, sir, I understand. Only my wife and daughter were a tad upset," he replied.

"Naturally."

"I reported about four hours ago, but I feel the vacation I availed was ages ago," Godbole said with a weary smile.

Das nodded, "Again, sorry I am not giving you breathing time. Things are tough. The sudden power failure in Mumbai has changed our priorities. But, you know, the electric company has to give us all the information, so that we can start working on it. Professor Singh said that even if the data is available today, its scrutiny will take at least a few days. They must study the data to conclude how it happened. For now, everyone says China did it remotely."

"That's what the media says," Godbole said.

"You know the blackout isn't the only thing that happened yesterday. There were two other incidents, too, that happened miles apart. They might be mere coincidences. However, since they took place in the same time frame, while the standoff at the LAC is on, there's a natural suspicion. Are the Chinese up to something?"

"I know," Godbole muttered.

"Amidst all this, the Army has brought up another issue."

Das pushed aside the files on his table and leaned forward. "Actually, I am just back from a meeting with Brigadier Kedar."

"Brig Kedar of the Military Intelligence?"

"Yes, Bhupinder Kedar, the number two man in the DGMI. These challenges are unique, especially since most are AI-driven and too technical."

"Naturally... unlike the Pakis, the Chinese have a disadvantage operating in the field in India. Their language and facial features work against them. Therefore, they exploit technology and try to manage things remotely, making it more difficult for us."

"True, Yash. That's why we are probing even the slightest purr and the tiniest droplets of information trickling from far corners of the country."

"I have just finished studying the file Amit gave—"

"Anyway, the probe into the power disruption can move forward only when the power company and our cyber experts come up with leads. Meanwhile, you will have to go to Arunachal. Brig Kedar wants us to look into the issue as quickly as possible. The PLA has shown great sensitivity to our Army men patrolling the PP-6 area. Why this undue attention near the PP-6 area? Are they gathering their troops there?"

"It is a matter of concern..."

"To further complicate matters, the Army feels that there's a leak on our side. Maybe someone from the village where the TG2 camp is situated is alerting the Chinese about our Army's patrolling plans? So, they want us to investigate this leak. The village is small, with just sixteen to seventeen houses. I'm confident you can handle this well." Das handed Godbole an envelope containing the case details received from the Army.

Since Amit Rao had already hinted at the Arunachal assignment, Godbole was prepared, but still had some anxiety.

"What if I get stuck there for longer?" Godbole asked.

"You see, the officer in charge of that Army camp, Maj Bakshi, has done good work. He has quietly investigated and seems to know how it could have happened. The Army is keeping us in the loop. The Army suspects civilian involvement. I think with the Major's help, you'll be able to deal with the matter easily," Das reassured him.

"I'll do my best. When do I leave for Tawang?"

"Tomorrow morning. The details are in the envelope. The Army has made all the arrangements."

"Well... let me study the case," Godbole said, rising to leave.

"Yash... wait. Now, you'll be gone for a few days, but you're the one I look for when I want to speak my mind."

It was evident that Das had something more to discuss.

"Frankly, Yash, all this work is like firefighting. We've received the intercept in Rameswaram and are sending our men to enquire; we have the LAC incident and will investigate that, too. I'm not satisfied with our responses yet. Take this power disruption in Mumbai. Why didn't we see it coming? We believed all the precautions taken to protect the power grids and the distribution system would work perfectly well, right?"

"You're right. Our job is to foresee and forewarn."

"Yash, I'm not saying that we've been napping. On the diplomatic and trade war fronts, India has made significant strides. We also made good contributions to strategic matters. However, our performance on some security-related issues remains less than desired. We are too Pakistan-focused. Why are the Chinese manipulations escaping our attention?"

"One of the answers... rather the excuse... is what you already hinted at a while ago – the Chinese rely more on technology than men in the field."

"I agree, but as we all know, avoiding human involvement altogether is impossible. Somewhere in the process, they will need human help. We have to look for that..."

"You're right," said Godbole. "It is hard to believe the power disruption was done remotely. After all, the electricity supply, control, and monitoring system remain isolated, without being linked to the internet or other power supply networks."

"Exactly! This morning, when I met Professor Singh and Professor Farook in our lab, they said they were inclined to look into the possibility of a modus operandi assisted by a semi-remote hand and an on-site intervention."

"In that case, we must be proactive, not wait for the tech report on the incident."

"Yash, that's what I am working on. Our record section and fielders have been on the job for the last twenty-four hours. Amidst all this, I've stumbled upon something linked to the Chinese network in India."

"Oh, what is that, sir?"

"Well, I didn't include an input I discussed with Brig Kedar in that file. As I said, I went to him to discuss the Tawang-LAC matter. After that discussion, we discussed a pending matter about a young left-liberal, Kanak Mohan, who has been masquerading as a defence journalist lately."

"Kanak Mohan? The name doesn't ring a bell."

"It won't; he's just popped out of nowhere. He is bugging Pankaj Banerji to get one of his articles published in his monthly journal."

"Sir, as far as I know, Banerji's journal carries articles from only top commentators and experts... Banerji maintains the decades-long reputation of his journal as one of India's respected publications, both nationally and internationally. After all, even the government consults him on security and defence matters."

"You're right, and that's why this matter landed in my lap."

A couple of days ago, Pankaj Banerji, the seventy-year-old veteran editor of the *Strategic and Defence Journal of India*, spoke to Das about an article Kanak Mohan forwarded him for publication.

"Initially, Banerji was not inclined even to read Mohan's article because Mohan had no notable credentials," Das said. "However, one of Banerji's junior staff members from the editorial board read the article and recommended that Banerji examine it. Banerji found the article relevant to the ongoing Sino-Indian military standoff in eastern Ladakh. He is inclined to publish it."

As Godbole listened patiently, Das continued, "However, Mohan's article highlighted the inadequacies of a weapon system deployed by the Indian Army to counter the Chinese belligerence. Since Banerji was wary of risking his reputation by carrying speculative observations in the journal, he wanted to verify the information before publishing it. Given the rapport we shared, he showed the article to me for my opinion."

"Well, I felt it's a sensitive piece," Das informed Godbole. "I was not in a position to comment about the accuracy of his reporting. Nevertheless, from a security point of view, it could have repercussions. The problem is that Banerji wants to publish the article if it has some truth. So, I thought it better to consult Brig Kedar."

"Sir, what was it that raised your concern?"

"The crux of what Mohan has reported is that a certain category of missile systems deployed at LAC has an unproven guidance system. He says the problem is because of the wrong choice of technology, while the market had a better choice. His article has labelled the missile system as defective because of inferior electronic circuitry and software used in the guidance system."

"Such information is difficult to access. How did Mohan come to know of it?"

"Exactly. You know, Yash, Brig Kedar was livid after reading the draft."

"Did he mention anything about the veracity of Mohan's information?"

"He didn't, but what if Mohan's reporting is correct? You know the consequences of such information going public and China finding out..."

"Sir, I know, and Banerji's journal publishing it will add to its authenticity."

"That's why the Brigadier is upset. Today, when I met with him to discuss the LAC leakage issue, he requested that I stop Banerji from publishing it. He said the Military Intelligence cannot handle it, but our operatives can!"

"How do we stop Banerji? He is a hard-boiled editor. No one can intimidate a man of Banerji's stature," Godbole voiced his concern.

"I am conscious of this, Yash, some journalists look for brownie points. National security can take a backseat. Banerji is no different. He would say he's trying to tell the truth so that authorities can rectify mistakes."

"Can we do it the other way around, sir? I mean, why not try to approach Kanak Mohan instead of Banerji?"

"Yes, indeed, that could be a better way. After all, we, too, must know how he receives this sensitive information. We also need to know the alternate choice of technology that he said the Army ignored. Is his article an attempt to push for that technology? We have to examine this quickly."

"I feel Mohan could only be a pawn, sir. Can a junior journalist like him have high-placed contacts to gather such information? Something isn't right. There must be someone behind him."

"We will probe him thoroughly, Yash. I'll have it done as soon as possible."

"Will Banerji wait till then?"

"You see, the November edition of the journal is already planned, and it's too late to accommodate Mohan's article. It would be possible only in the December edition. So, we have a thirty-day window," Das said.

"That's enough time."

"But stopping Mohan's article from publishing is only one part of what I have in my mind. Something tells me it has a Chinese angle... an attempt to misinform and demoralize our Army."

"If it's what you are saying, then Mohan is being propped up by someone," Godbole said, gently tapping the table. "We have to pursue Kanak Mohan, and this could be an opportunity to get close to the Chinese network."

"Yes, that's what I wanted to share with you." Das briefly stopped and added, "Yash, you see, I have already asked Vilas Pande to conduct a thorough background check of Kanak Mohan. When you return from Tawang, things will be ready for you to take over."

Chapter – 2
The Mantle of Calm

Tawang district, Arunachal Pradesh
October 15-17, 2020
2 p.m.

Godbole trudged through the Army camp in the southern part of Tawang district, Arunachal Pradesh. The mandatory two-day acclimatization halt felt like a prison sentence rather than a necessary precaution. The mountains loomed around him, silent and indifferent. His mind was restless and yearning for action. On the second day, as the sun began its slow ascent over the peaks, a sudden stir of activity caught his attention. A tall figure, radiating authority and warmth, strode into the camp. With his easy smile and engaging demeanour, Maj Prashant Bakshi approached Godbole, cutting through the monotony like a breath of fresh air.

"Mr Godbole, I'm Maj Bakshi. I'll escort you to our forward post in Zemithang tomorrow," he said, shaking Godbole's hand firmly.

Relief washed over Godbole. Finally, something was happening.

The next morning, Godbole was up with the lark. He was ready to go as soon as Maj Bakshi arrived at 6.30 a.m.

"The journey in this terrain is challenging, but the breathtaking landscape will make up for any discomfort you might experience," Maj Bakshi assured Godbole as they boarded an Army vehicle. "And one more thing, this was the same route the venerable Dalai Lama had taken when he escaped from Tibet to India in 1959. Feel the history, feel the moment."

The vehicle rumbled to life, and as they wound their way through the twisting roads, the Major's words sank in. Godbole gazed at the rugged landscape, imagining the Dalai Lama's arduous journey through these very paths. A sense of reverence and awe filled him. Moreover, Godbole was aware that during the 1962 war, Chinese troops had come upto these areas in the Tawang sector. The local population had fled to escape the PLA's high-handedness. Even today, the scars of the war remain in the hearts and minds of the older generation.

Maj Bakshi peppered the trip with tales of the region. He pointed out every hairpin bend, waterfall, lake, and other landmarks that dotted their path with an uncanny familiarity. Despite his engaging conversation, the Major tactfully avoided discussing the purpose of Godbole's visit, perhaps because the driver and the other staff were travelling in their vehicle.

By noon, after more than five hours of driving, they reached Zemithang. Before entering the town, they passed by Gorsam Chorten, a centuries-old Buddhist *stupa*, its towering structure a testament to the region's rich heritage. It was said to be one of the largest Buddhist structures in Asia. Zemithang was a peaceful town nestled in a valley surrounded by tall mountains. The River Nyamjang Chu ran along Zemithang, and the dense greenery tracks enhanced its tranquil beauty. The Army camp was in a scenic location on the town's outskirts, surrounded by thickets of bamboo, rhododendron and pine trees. A board near the camp's entrance proudly displayed: '8500 feet above sea level'.

After a quick lunch, the Major showed Godbole his accommodation in a barrack. "You can relax here for some time. Hope this will be comfortable."

"Major, this looks good."

"It is a tough life here, but we, the soldiers, are trained for such harsh conditions. It could be a challenge for others to get used to.

The high altitude, extreme cold, hilly terrain, and snow-covered barren landscape at the LAC can make others a bit nervous. That's why I kept you engaged in conversation along the way. Otherwise, Mr Godbole, I am not that talkative." The Major smiled and added, "In places like this, talking to one another is the only way to come out of the gloom and maintain sanity."

"I can understand. I had a two-year posting in North Sikkim bordering Tibet in similar harsh conditions. But that was some years ago," Godbole said.

"Oh, good! That'll make your assignment here much easier." The Major briefly halted and added, "We must kick-start our business. If it is fine with you, we may meet in my barrack by 3.30 p.m."

Godbole wanted to take a quick nap, but his mind was racing with thoughts of his new assignment. Despite their efforts, his team had made little progress beyond the few droplets NES-17 had managed to collect. Meanwhile, the PLA continued with the standoff at the LAC in eastern Ladakh. The Indian Army had responded commendably and put up stiff resistance. However, the problem was that the Chinese were not looking to limit the conflict to the LAC alone. The blackout in Mumbai implied that the Chinese were waiting to strike India through non-military means. The Chinese actions were increasingly disturbing.

Zemithang was only a stopover for Godbole. His work awaited him in Janung, a small village where the Army's TG-2 camp was located. Janung was about thirteen kilometres northeast of Zemithang, accessible by a relentlessly winding, steep, rough track. It would take about two hours to get there by an Army vehicle. Located roughly three kilometres from the LAC, Janung had only seventeen houses. Due to the harsh winter, many families would lock their homes and temporarily relocate to Zemithang or other places with their livestock. However, the Army encouraged the villagers to stay by providing provisions and other necessities, as a deserted village so close to the LAC was not in India's security interest.

At 3.30 p.m., a soldier led Godbole to Maj Bakshi's office in a barrack. As he walked, for Godbole, the dreariness was evident. Zemithang, surrounded by tall mountains, received sunlight for three or four hours between 11 a.m. and 3 p.m., thus creating a perpetual gloomy atmosphere for newcomers.

After tea, the Major briefed Godbole about Janung and the security issue he had encountered. At an altitude of ten thousand feet above sea level, the tiny village had just eighty-six people. Nevertheless, Janung was vital as it was the only village close to the LAC. It had an advantage because the village and the TG-2 camp remained hidden from the Chinese side due to the terrain's elevation on the northern side. Since the Army's permanent camp was at Zemithang, the TG-2 camp served as a vital overnight stopover for patrols heading to the LAC. It allowed them to patrol the sensitive PP-6 area and return before the afternoon winds and chill worsened.

The TG-2 camp, a semi-permanent structure, provided lodging for up to twenty patrol members. This small barrack was used only during patrolling assignments. Tashi Norbu, the Gaonbudda or headman of Janung, and the local boy Tenzin Lote maintained the accommodation. Whenever a patrolling exercise was planned from Zemithang camp, the headman would be informed a day prior. He and Lote would clean the accommodation, arrange firewood, and fill up water cans for the use of the patrol party.

The Major recounted how he had to call off the planned patrolling at PP-6 twice. He said, "Mr Godbole, I firmly believe that the Chinese had advance information. Otherwise, it would be impossible for them to reach PP-6 on time to thwart our patrolling. Someone from this village may have leaked the information."

"You mentioned that the Gaonbudda was being informed about the patrolling party's arrival in the village. How do you inform him? Is it via personal messenger, call, or wireless message?" Godbole enquired.

"I know what you mean. We avoid wireless communication here, knowing the Chinese can pick up wireless signals. Instead, we provided the Gaonbudda with a landline connection from the Army exchange. Let me add... he is a trustworthy man."

"Maybe he's clean... but he receives your information. So, he becomes the source from where the leakage could start."

"Yes, theoretically."

"Another thing, Major, Janung is remote and isolated without cell phones or other communication facilities. Therefore, the leakage has to happen by word of mouth, I mean... in person. It means that the Chinese, or the receiver, is within walking distance from Janung."

"You're right. You see, there's a tiny Chinese village about four kilometres from the LAC, within walking distance of Janung. It was set up recently by the Chinese, roughly around seven years ago."

"Oh, I see. So, this village across the LAC is the only Chinese-inhabited area closest to Janung?"

"Yes, but our villagers avoid going anywhere near the LAC, fearing the Chinese may abduct or even kill them. Some such incidents happened in the past."

"With such a small population in Janung, finding the culprit shouldn't be too difficult."

"You're right. I could have made the enquiries myself, but the Army has pretty close relations with the villagers. So, I don't want to make the enquiries myself. The villagers are a sentimental lot. I don't want to risk damaging that trust. If an outsider like you does it, the impact won't be as damaging."

"I get it, Major. I have a plan. Tell me, when can we go to Janung?"

"Day after tomorrow, by 7 a.m."

"If it is not a big issue, can we go tomorrow?" Godbole asked.

"I thought a one-day halt here would help you acclimatize yourself to the conditions. Otherwise, there is no issue tomorrow except that I informed the Gaonbudda. No problem, I will speak to him again."

"No," Godbole said. "No. Let's give him a surprise."

"Fine, we'll do it. Please be ready."

"Thank you, Major."

*****

The following morning, the Major, Sub Rameshwar Gupta, and Godbole left for Janung. Four soldiers accompanied them in another vehicle with provisions and essential items required for a few days' stay at the camp.

The uneven gravel road, steep climb, sudden hairpin bends, and the vehicle's whirring noise made the journey progressively uncomfortable. They halted on the way a few times to let the engine cool down and catch their breath. The silence of the mountains, punctuated only by the occasional chirping of Himalayan birds, made the stopovers refreshing. During one of the halts, the Major took Godbole aside to discuss Godbole's plans in Janung.

"I wouldn't like to question the villagers. It will be the last resort," Godbole said.

"Oh, good. That takes care of some of my concerns, too," a relieved Major said.

"Major, I was going to request you to take me to the LAC today itself. You said it was only three kilometres away from Janung. I want to have a look to understand things."

"Well, it's three kilometres all right... but it's a two-hour uphill trek as there's no motorable road there. The steep climb is challenging."

"I am prepared for the trek..."

"In that case, if the weather permits, we will go. We're lucky because there's no snowing yet." The Major paused, then reluctantly asked, "After this tiring journey, are you sure you want to go to the LAC today?"

Gently raising his head, Godbole replied, "I think we should go today. I fear postponing the visit may not serve our purpose."

"I did not get you."

"You see, I am working on a calculated guess." Godbole took a deep breath and continued, "Look, you told the Gaonbudda about this trip yesterday afternoon. If someone in Janung wanted to tip off the Chinese in person, he wouldn't have had enough time yesterday to walk to the village on the Chinese side and return before nightfall. Logically, if it is an in-person tip-off, the person should have left this morning. From what you told me, it is three kilometres from Janung to LAC and four to the Chinese village. It should be, at most, an eight-hour trek back and forth. A seasoned local could complete this trek in an even shorter time. So, if we are at the right place at the LAC by early afternoon, we can spot this person returning from his errand. Major, we should take this chance."

An impressed Major exclaimed, "What a postulation!"

He added, "Then we must leave for the LAC before noon. Since we are not crossing the LAC, you, my Subedar, and I need to go forward. The four soldiers in our team will follow us at a distance. But first we have to reach Janung... hurry."

The vehicles kept moving slowly and steadily. The sight of the prayer flags signalled their arrival in Janung. While Zemithang had large tracks of cultivable lands, meadows, and lakes, Janung differed. With only tiny plain space available, most houses were perched on slopes. As they alighted from the vehicle, around 9 o'clock, a few apple-cheeked children appeared from nowhere. Tashi Norbu, the Gaonbudda, too, came rushing.

"I was away with my yaks when I noticed the Army vehicles coming this way," he said. "I was expecting you tomorrow, or did I hear incorrectly?"

"No, you heard me right, but we came today as we have work coming up in two days. Hope we did not inconvenience you," the Major said.

"Saheb, we are always happy to see you. Your presence here is like a celebration for us. I will have the tents cleaned now. Luckily, I filled a few water cans this morning."

"Thank you."

"This time, you have a guest too!" he said, looking at Godbole, who was in civilian attire.

"Yes," the Major said without giving any explanation. "Where is Lote?" he asked.

"I think he has gone out with his yaks... he'll be back by the afternoon."

The soldiers and the Gaonbudda got busy cleaning and preparing lunch in the barracks. Meanwhile, the visitors donned protective clothing and windcheater jackets. Around eleven, carrying backpacks filled with the necessary equipment and food, they embarked on the journey to the LAC.

"Saheb, where are you going without even resting?" the curious headman enquired.

"Our guest wants to have the feel of the LAC. We will have our usual chatting session in the evening when we return."

The Major was not sure if he was satisfied with his response.

The uphill trek was treacherous as expected. On the way, the Major and Subedar encouraged Godbole to take small breaks. He was also advised to keep chewing hard cheese cubes locally made from yak milk. In an hour, the worst was over. Although the ground remained uneven, the remaining route was relatively easy.

"We have crossed twelve thousand feet, but this place is the lowest in this area. That makes crossing into China from here easier. The LAC and the PP-6 are still further away. From this place onwards, it is a long-stretched, open and plain barren land; any movement is visible from the Chinese positions kilometres away. We have a safe place behind the elevated ground. We can hide and keep a vigil for anyone coming from the other side."

"Where is the Chinese village?" Godbole enquired.

"The village is right there," the Major said, pointing in the northwest direction. "It is hidden from our view because it is in a valley-like depression."

The team settled on a rocky patch and had their refreshments. All the while, taking turns, at least one from the team kept scanning using binoculars to spot any movement from the direction of the Chinese village. After an hour and a half, Sub Gupta spotted three persons from the other side of the LAC, steadily progressing towards the Indian side. The Major and Godbole, too, pulled out their binoculars. Soon, after pausing on their track for a while, one of the three men started walking towards the Indian side, and the other two returned to the Chinese side.

The Major looked at Godbole and exclaimed, "How accurate your hunch was! Someone is helping the Chinese. Right under my nose!"

The Subedar shuffled his feet a few times and said, "The person is coming straight to our position. I still can't figure out who he is. The traitor! Feel like pulling the trigger."

"You know we can't do it. You better keep your cool," the Major instructed. Then he turned to Godbole and asked, "When do we make our move? Now?"

"No," Godbole said firmly. "What if he runs back to the Chinese side, seeing us approaching? We wait here till he is well within our side. Then we can approach him from behind."

"That sounds fine."

"One more thing. Let him come out with his story. We will begin our exchange as if we do not know he had been to the Chinese side. I will request that you do the initial talking. It would be ideal if we tactfully took him along to your barracks for questioning."

"I got it," the Major said.

The person was walking forward steadily, braving the strong, cold winds. He was wearing a fluffy cap and had wrapped himself in a shawl. The bulge on his back meant he was carrying something. In about half an hour, when the person was sufficiently inside the Indian territory, the team moved towards him. Soon, the team caught up. Hearing the sound of boots behind him, the person turned and stood startled.

"Major Saheb? You were to arrive tomorrow!" The person said in disbelief. It was Lote.

"Yes, but I had to come today on urgent work. But how are you here, Tenzin?" Instantly, Godbole remembered the Major mentioning Tenzin Lote, who, along with the Gaonbudda, helped them in Janung.

"Saheb, I had come to collect some items," Lote replied without elaborating.

The Major did not insist on knowing further, as he did not want to give the impression that he suspected Lote. It was worrying as Lote knew the workings of the Army. He introduced Godbole as his friend from Delhi, who was on official duty in the Zemithang division. They chatted on the way back.

Maj Bakshi walked close to Godbole and briefly spoke about him, "Lote's father is no longer there, which puts the burden of caring for his mother and two sisters on his shoulders. His primary occupation is tending yaks."

When the trekking party entered Janung, it was 4:30 p.m. and daylight had already faded. Maj Bakshi led Godbole and Lote straight to his barracks. Before entering the barrack, the Major instructed Sub Gupta to keep the Gaonbudda engaged in some work in the other barrack so that he would not interrupt them.

After an almost day-long journey and trek, they were exhausted. However, Maj Bakshi was not in the mood to rest. He stretched open two folding chairs for Godbole and himself. He then asked Lote to sit on a wooden stool.

"Saheb, I'll quickly prepare some tea for all," Lote said, rising to leave.

"Tenzin, I have already asked my men to do so. Please sit and relax. After all, you went for a long trek," the Major said.

With the bulging bag on his back, Lote stood there as if he did not hear the Major. When he repeated his words, Lote sat down gingerly. All the while, Godbole's attention was on Lote and his bag. Lote was clearly nervous, fidgeting with his bag.

Maj Bakshi turned to Godbole and said, "Mr Godbole, the trek was a bit tough, but I am happy you managed it well. And you, Tenzin... why is the bag still on your shoulders? Keep it down and relax."

Despite the Major's best efforts to be casual, Lote sensed the attention he was drawing from the Major. He quietly removed the bag from his shoulders and kept it close to his seat. Meanwhile, tea and snacks were served. Soon, Maj Bakshi exchanged glances with Godbole, hinting to him to take over.

Godbole glanced at Lote's bag. Hoping the bag's contents would cue him to what Lote was doing, Godbole began slowly, "Major, being new here, I am curious about things one can collect from the LAC area. Maybe some exotic things are found there."

He paused briefly and added, "Lote mentioned that he went to collect certain items. It would be nice to see what he has collected."

Then, Godbole turned, "Tenzin, can we see the items in the bag?"

Lote's face fell. His discomfort was evident. He just sat still in silence.

"If you don't want to show us, that's perfectly fine, but you seem shaken. Please let us know if something is bothering you," Godbole said.

"Tell me, Tenzin, what's troubling you?" Maj Bakshi leaned forward.

Lote didn't respond. Instead, his eyes welled up, and tears rolled down his cheeks. The boy seemed to be cracking. Maj Bakshi stood near Lote and put his hand on his shoulder.

"We are here to help you," Maj Bakshi repeated.

A tearful Lote kept biting his lower lip, trying to control his tears. Perhaps he was a simple tribal boy manipulated by the Chinese, Godbole thought. Anyway, they had to find out what damage he had caused. It was also essential to know how he got into the undesirable activity and what he was getting in return.

Godbole pulled his chair close to him, "Look here, Tenzin, we all make mistakes at some stage. We do not mean any harm. It would help if you cooperate with us. Let us first understand what you have done."

Since Lote did not respond, Godbole continued, "See, Tenzin, I know you will tell us everything. Be sure we will not get you in any trouble. We also will not let anyone in the village know. This is an assurance."

Lote nervously took his bag and kept it on his lap. He untied the securely tied knot of the bag and emptied its contents on the floor, as Maj Bakshi and Godbole quietly watched. There were three medium-sized transparent plastic pouches containing some white powder, one large plastic bag containing rice, neatly tied dry meat pouches, and one cigarette lighter. Still, Lote did not utter a word. Godbole examined the plain cloth bag to ensure that it was empty. Maj Bakshi also scrutinized the items. The items looked harmless and were given to Lote for personal use, but what was the white powder?

It was time for Godbole to entice the reluctant Lote into a conversation.

"Tenzin, was it snowing on the other side... the Chinese side?" Godbole asked. It was a simple but loaded question.

Lote answered instantly, "No, Sahib." Godbole was happy that Lote answered and what his answer implied.

"Wasn't it difficult to carry this heavy bag from there? I think the rice alone is about five kilos."

"No, Saheb."

"What is the white powder in those three pouches?"

"Sahib, milk powder to make tea."

"Have you brought anything else? A letter... a message?"

"No, Saheb. This is all I brought back from Tangma."

"Tangma... is that the name of the village?"

"Yes"

"Well... who gave you these items?"

"I do not know his name, but the villagers call him Haao. He is a Chinese man, not a Tibetan."

"How does Haao communicate with you? In Hindi?"

"No, Saheb. Tsering Dorjee helps to translate my Monpa to Haao's language."

"How does this Dorjee know the Monpa dialect?"

"Saheb, Dorjee said he was from Zemithang. He was living in Zemithang with his wife and daughter. About seven years ago, he lost his way at the LAC and went missing. The Chinese caught him and sent him to some place in China, where he underwent training for five years. There, he married a Chinese widow much older than him. I gathered from him that it was a forced marriage. For the past two years, Dorjee and his wife have settled in Tangma."

"Anything else you know about Tsering Dorjee?"

"Not much. When others are around, Dorjee will not speak freely. However, if he gets a chance, he will enquire about Zemithang. Once, he requested me to go to Zemithang to look for his family."

"Did you go to Zemithang?"

"I had gone there a month ago, but I gathered that his family left for Tawang a couple of years ago looking for livelihood."

"How old is Dorjee?"

"He had told me he's forty years old."

The talk was taking an exciting turn, especially with the new character, Tsering Dorjee. It needed further probing, Godbole thought. Planned interrogation would be necessary to learn about Lote's trips to Tangma and what the Chinese wanted from him.

After around an hour, Godbole felt Lote was getting impatient to return home, so he decided to take a chance and make Lote feel at ease.

"Tenzin, you must be exhausted. Please go home, freshen up, and come back in a while. Have dinner here. By the way... take the rice and the dried meat and give it to your mother," Godbole said. Lote's face lit up instantly. He picked up the rice and meat and left.

After Lote left, Godbole said, "Major, I am sorry. There was no chance to take your concurrence before letting Lote go home."

"No issue, Mr Godbole. I can figure out why you did it. What is important is we get to the root of this whole episode. This apart, I have a soft corner for Lote. I believe he is a simple boy struggling to make both ends meet. Maybe that pushed him into this."

"It may be so. Meanwhile, could you please verify whether anyone by the name of Tsering Dorjee has been missing from Zemithang for the past seven years?"

"Will do. We have records of the missing men from the border villages."

"The moment Lote mentioned Dorjee's background, it kindled a ray of hope in me. Now, before the Gaonbudda gets nosey, could you please tackle him? It is not that I don't trust him, but it's better to be cautious."

*****

When Lote returned, he was in good spirits. Maj Bakshi, Lote, and Godbole huddled in the Major's cramped office space and chatted over a simple dinner. Lote was more forthcoming and readily answered Godbole's questions.

Lote's trouble began with his habit of collecting *Yarsagumba*, the valuable caterpillar fungus called Himalayan Viagra. It was in demand and fetched quite a price in the Tawang market. It provided much-needed income for his struggling family. Lote had discovered a deep gorge near the LAC, where it was found. The Army men and the villagers never ventured there as the chasm was deep and serpentine. Lote occasionally risked descending into the gorge to look for the fungus. One fateful day, a year ago in August 2019, when Lote was collecting the fungus, he was suddenly circled by five Chinese men.

The Chinese took him to Tangma village, where Lote first met Tsering Dorjee and Haao. Initially, their questioning was intense and hostile. They enquired about Indian Army camps, the number of vehicles, details of roads, and other things. Lote's vague responses revealed little except for the Zemithang camp and a temporary Army facility in Janung. After an hour, Haao's demeanour softened. He suddenly left only to return with dried meat, rice, and milk powder for Lote as a 'token of their love'.

Dorjee informed Lote that he would be released as they understood he meant no harm. Dorjee said they liked him and invited him to visit them every month for more gifts, but warned him to keep the visits secret from Indian authorities. He was shown a safer route to the Indian side. Although Lote was welcome to visit Tangma every month, he went there only on four occasions when times were desperate for his family. On his second trip in October 2019, the Chinese asked the same questions about the Indian Army deployment and gave him similar gifts. A few days after the trip, Maj Bakshi and his team came to Janung. Lote treated the Army men with tea, which he made using the milk powder he had brought from Tangma. Maj Bakshi had given him one thousand rupees as a token of appreciation. Lote realized that if he could treat the visiting Army men with tea and refreshments, he would get big tips.

"You know, Tenzin, after October 2019, I visited Janung with my team at least eight times," Maj Bakshi said, "We patrolled the LAC without any issues, but during our last two patrolling trips in September and the current month, October, the Chinese confronted us."

"Saheb, you are right. You have come often, but I could not go to the Chinese side to get things. From December to April, the route remained covered by knee-deep snow. After that, the rains made the route slippery and prone to landslides."

"Okay. When did you go there last?" Godbole asked.

"Mid-September... last month. I learnt from our Gaonbudda that Major Saheb and soldiers were coming, so I made a quick trip. Likewise, early this month, I went there when I learnt that the Army team was visiting. The Chinese gave me the usual items, and I told them I was taking the items to treat the soldiers visiting our village the following day."

Godbole and Maj Bakshi exchanged a look, realizing how the Chinese were tipped off in advance.

"So, Tenzin, you've gone five times in total?" Godbole confirmed.

"Yes, Saheb. Twice last year and thrice this year."

"Every time they gave you only the usual items – milk powder, rice, and so on – nothing else?"

"Saheb, once they gave me... a small package. In October last year, during my second visit."

"What package?"

"A small package," Lote said, demonstrating its size with his hands, a rectangular package about ten inches by six inches and barely four inches thick. "The package was in a small blue... light blue cloth bag."

"So, a new gift?" Godbole asked.

"No. Dorjee wanted me to travel to Guwahati to hand over the package to someone. I refused because I had never travelled beyond Tawang. They kept me waiting there for almost one hour. At last, they said I could hand it over in Tawang. They instructed me to reach the Tawang monastery on the fifth day from that day. I was told to wait near the entry door of the library in the monastery by 11 a.m. with the cloth bag. I was to wait until someone came and offered me a tin of Amul milk powder. That would be the signal to hand over the cloth bag to him. After receiving the bag, that person was to give me two thousand rupees for my efforts."

"Did you go to Tawang?"

"I was tense, but I did it just to earn money. As promised, I received the money."

"Do you know that person? Can you describe him?"

"Sahib, the person looked like he was from the plains. He wore a cap and a muffler around his neck that covered his chin, too. He did the business quickly and went away. I don't think I can recognize him now."

"Did he converse with you in Monpa?"

"No, he spoke Hindi... not like the Army men here speak... a little different."

"Do you know what was in that parcel?"

"No, Saheb. But I remember Dorjee telling me repeatedly that it should not get wet."

"Was the parcel heavy?"

"It was about a quarter kilo... I guess."

This information about the package was disturbing. Godbole wondered if the package contained electronic items. He paused, then he leaned forward.

"Tell me who the two people were who came to see you off today from the Chinese village?"

"One was Dorjee, and the other a villager."

"Did Dorjee and the other person accompany you every time?"

"Yes. They accompany me to ensure my safe return to our side."

"Tenzin, it's getting late. Thank you for all that you've told us. Do not discuss this with anyone," Godbole said as Lote left.

"This is getting far more serious than I thought," Maj Bakshi said. "Lote's visit, Dorjee's presence there, and the parcel... well, how do we know what was in the parcel? Who was the man who received the parcel, and for whom?"

"Major, we need to get that Dorjee. Encouraging Lote to stay in touch with him could be key. We should explore whether we can get Dorjee back to Zemithang. After all, Lote mentioned he was unhappy. With five years' training and two years' stay in Tangma, Dorjee would be a goldmine for us. Given the situation at the LAC, I know it is difficult... even risky to get him back, but we have to try. And for this, we may have to prepare Lote proactively. What is your take, Major?"

"It is a brilliant idea. You can count me in. But the problem is that we may have to cross the LAC to get him."

"I am certain that getting Dorjee is key to further progress in this case. About the LAC, we will see if we can do without crossing it. We will discuss this later. For now, I think you must plan a trip to the PP-6 area with some soldiers tomorrow."

"Anything special, Mr Godbole?"

"Nothing special. Lote's reliability needs to remain intact with the Chinese. Since Lote had gone there today, the Chinese might expect your men at the LAC tomorrow."

"I haven't brought the full patrol team here, though. But my four soldiers, Sub Gupta, and I could go there tomorrow."

"That'll do; at least Lote will prove his worth to the Chinese. Make sure the Chinese spot your team."

"Done."

"One more thing: after ascertaining about Tsering Dorjee from the missing person's records in Zemithang, can you help me trace his family? Lote says the family shifted to Tawang. I'm certain Dorjee's old neighbours in Zemithang might be in touch with his family."

"I'll do my best. Well, it's been a long day for us, and tomorrow, our hands will be full too. Shall we call it a night?"

"Yes, Major. But I want to say that tomorrow, when you are away at the LAC, I will spend some time with Lote to prepare him for Mission Dorjee." Godbole laughed.

"By all means. You are already on the fast track," Maj Bakshi replied. Before walking away, the Major added, "Mr Godbole, your timely decision to go to the LAC was spot on. You solved the leak."

"Thank you, Major. In matters of security and intelligence, it is not the one who solves the problem; it is the one who smells it first that matters the most. So it was because of your hunch, Major. Great job!"

Chapter – 3
Mission Dorjee

Janung
2 p.m.

Godbole spent nearly three hours with Tenzin Lote, discussing the intricate details of Mission Dorjee. Initially, Lote was hesitant, fearing the repercussions if Dorjee revealed the truth to the Chinese. However, Godbole subtly hinted at the underlying possibility, explaining what Dorjee's persistent questions about his family and Zemithang signified. He also briefed Lote about Maj Bakshi's efforts to trace Dorjee's family and bring them back to Zemithang. Eventually, Lote agreed to convey the plan to Dorjee if he found an opportunity during his upcoming trip.

It was inconceivable for anyone other than Lote to venture into Tangma. The plan had other challenges, too. The only window of opportunity to rescue Dorjee was when he would, as usual, accompany Lote to the LAC. However, the Chinese man who always shadowed Dorjee posed a problem. If Lote could persuade Dorjee and the other man to come up to the deep gorge, the intricately winding deep ravines there could potentially simplify the mission. The rescue team could lie in wait, concealed in the gorge, for the opportune moment to strike. Godbole was eager to discuss it with Maj Bakshi.

As Godbole jotted down notes, Maj Bakshi entered the barracks, looking tired but determined. "Mr Godbole, the Chinese were already there near PP-6. We remained far away as if we were surprised by their presence. After waiting for over thirty minutes, we returned. I think our purpose was met."

"Good! Our job is done, Major," Godbole said, his voice tinged with relief.

"I am exhausted from the trek, but I am keen to know your discussions with Lote."

"Well, it took a bit longer to convince him, but he's on board. When do you think we can send him to Tangma?" Godbole asked.

"I think we should wait at least a week," the Major advised. "My concern is that our frequent visits might alarm the Chinese, leading them to think we're increasing our presence, and in retaliation, they might scale up their presence."

"You have a point," Godbole agreed.

"However, we can't delay too long. It's almost November, and although snowfall usually starts after mid-December, it sometimes occurs earlier. And if it snows, we won't be able to send Lote."

"So, we have a limited window?" Godbole said thoughtfully.

"Yes, let's aim for next Monday. It's the 26th of October. Could we assume that Dorjee would take this risk, that too without any prior notice?"

"I have considered this aspect. We know that Dorjee is unhappy and misses the family he had left behind. Lote has been tutored to paint this as a once-in-a-lifetime opportunity for Dorjee, and if this opportunity is lost, Lote is not sure when he'd go to Tangma next. It could create a now-or-never situation for Dorjee."

"My staff has confirmed that Dorjee is on the missing list. He had gone missing in August 2013. We've shared the available family details with my counterpart in Tawang. Let's hope for the best."

"Anyway, Major, we have a week to prepare. So, should we go back to Zemithang till then?" Godbole asked.

"No, we need to stay here. Although getting supplies here is quite a task, we must prepare well for this operation. We also need to monitor the conditions at the LAC," the Major concluded.

*****

Godbole strolled into Maj Bakshi's enclosure, glancing at his watch. He was early for the call expected from his boss, Anand Kumar Das, at 9 a.m. Two days had passed since his trip to the LAC, and he still hadn't briefed Das. Das might have needed time to coordinate with Brigadier Kedar to secure an Army line for the call. Sharp at 9 a.m., the phone rang. Maj Bakshi passed the receiver to him.

"Yash, I know you made a wonderful breakthrough, and things are fine there," Das's voice crackled with enthusiasm. "You know, I got a briefing from Brig Kedar. Maj Bakshi had kept his unit head updated on the developments. But I wanted your assessment."

"Just a few points," Godbole began, "I think... I should start from the Chinese village, Tangma. Undoubtedly, the Chinese set up this village seven years ago with a specific aim. The village is at a vantage point close to the LAC, close to PP-6, so it should concern us."

"I agree. Brig Kedar shares the same view."

"Tangma is crucial. A Chinese man named Haao seems to be the key person. His handling of Tenzin Lote and his attempts to collect information on the Indian Army suggest that Haao is not an ordinary villager. They have also detained Tsering Dorjee for a long time. And, of course, the parcel Lote delivered in Tawang originated from this village," Godbole said.

"Yash, I wonder if Tangma is only a mere village. It could be a masked Chinese post!"

"Sir, there are many questions. Only Dorjee can provide the answers. That's why I want to bring him back to our side."

"Look, Yash... there could be repercussions. If anything goes wrong, things could escalate. We might need permission from the higher echelons before venturing into this."

"Sir, Dorjee is our citizen; there's nothing wrong with rescuing him."

Das thought for a minute, then said, "If we undertake this operation, it should look like Dorjee has escaped... without our intervention."

"Certainly, I will try to make it appear that way, but you know how unpredictable the field can be. If Dorjee hesitates at the last moment, I'd use force rather than let the opportunity slip away."

Das inhaled deeply and asked, "How will you execute this? Before I approach the authorities, I need to know your plans."

"Maj Bakshi and I have discussed this. We plan to send Lote there on Monday, five days from now. It is the safest window before the weather conditions start turning tough. Lote will try to gain Dorjee's confidence. We'll hide in the deep ravines near the LAC. When Lote arrives with Dorjee and the Chinese man, we will create a minor commotion to separate the man from Dorjee. If Dorjee comes with us, great; otherwise, we'll use force. This is the plan, but we're prepared to adapt as the situation develops."

"You plan to go up to this stream... the ravines? Do the Chinese come up there often? Will this amount to any provocation? What's the Major's take on it?

"The Chinese don't. However, they seem to be familiar with the place. They showed Lote a shortcut from there to our side. Anyway, the ravines are a natural barrier preventing easy crossing to either side; some as deep as twenty to forty metres. We'll plan carefully to ensure there's no scope for trouble."

"Yash, I have worked with you long enough, and I know how determined you become when you plan something. You said you want to do this on Monday? I will get back to you after consulting the top brass."

*****

Maj Bakshi and Godbole spent three days finalizing the details for executing Mission Dorjee. That Saturday, Godbole had just finished lunch when Maj Bakshi rushed in, his face lit with excitement, "Mr Godbole, there's good news."

As Godbole looked up with anticipation, the Major continued, "Tsering Dorjee's family has been traced in Tawang. They're overjoyed... excited to know that Dorjee is alive and they may see him one day."

"Wow! That's timely. Now, it will be easier for Lote to approach Dorjee," Godbole replied.

"I know Dorjee will feel compelled to come over," Maj Bakshi said confidently. "Dorjee's family will arrive in Zemithang in two days."

Godbole's expression shifted slightly. "This is good news, of course, but, Major, I have not yet received the go-ahead signal from my boss. Yesterday, when he spoke to me, he said the request for permission is pending with the Ministry. Any directions from your officers?"

"I have been asked to give you full support as long as the operation is clearly on our side of the LAC. They hinted at providing manpower, and told me to decide based on the situation. A final clearance message is expected but hasn't come through yet."

Godbole nodded, understanding the unspoken challenges. "Oh, I see... I hope you will receive the message soon. Regarding manpower, just two of your men will do without their Army uniforms. I will manage the rest."

"You'll have two of my best men. Besides, I also want to join you as an additional hand."

Godbole looked at the Major, seeing the resolve in his eyes. "Very kind of you, Major, but you are the Commander of this unit, having greater responsibilities to shoulder. Please give two of your men and leave this to me."

"You'll lead the operation, of course. You know, Mr Godbole, the leakage episode was a challenge thrown at me. So, I *have* to be there with you at work."

Seeing Maj Bakshi was determined, Godbole did not try to dissuade him. Taking the discussions further, he said, "Today is Saturday. We have only a day left. In anticipation of the clearance, we better start preparing."

"We should go ahead with the preparations?"

"Yes, Major, our establishments cannot be insensitive and delay such an important matter. I sense they want us to proceed. If we succeed, it's fine. If we fail, they can say the operation wasn't pre-planned; it just happened owing to a sudden development at the LAC. My boss knows that I am inclined to carry out this operation. If he is against it, he would have told me by now."

"Are they playing safe?"

"No, Major. Maybe they're trying to be technically correct. Besides, they know we'll be extra cautious when we venture into this without formal permission. It's a tactic played rarely but played in good faith," Godbole said with a chuckle.

"Mr Godbole, I can easily relate to this. We, too, have similar situations at times. There are unwritten rules and norms, and we play it subtly."

"Those of us in the field can differentiate a tactical delay from a systemic one. Let's meet with Lote to finalize our plans."

"By all means. We meet after tea," Maj Bakshi confirmed.

*****

October 26, 2020
6 a.m.

In remote forward posts like Zemithang and Janung, on Sunday or Monday, all days were alike. There would be no relief from the challenges or the state of alertness to be maintained at the sensitive border. That Monday, Maj Bakshi had an additional worry gnawing at him. He was about to embark on a risky operation based only on oral clearance. He knew Godbole was also similarly burdened that morning.

At 6 a.m., the chill cut through the air like a knife. Tenzin Lote was adequately dressed in his local attire – *khanjar* and *chupa*. Draped in a thick woollen shawl, he was ready to embark on his journey across the LAC to Tangma, a path he had trodden before. Godbole had already briefed Lote, yet wanted to give some last-minute tips.

"Tenzin, try to act normal, just like your previous trips. Dorjee will be busy interpreting your conversation in Monpa to the Chinese. Amidst that, look for the right moment to convey our plan to him. Start by informing him about his family. Let him know that this would be the best chance if he wanted to return."

"Okay, sir, noted."

"Now... don't whisper to Dorjee. Speak naturally to avoid raising any suspicion. One last thing, while coming back with Dorjee and the Chinese man, try to lead them up to the ravines. The rest we will manage," Godbole instructed.

An hour after Lote's departure, Maj Bakshi, Godbole, and two soldiers disguised as locals collecting medicinal herbs headed to the chosen spot near the LAC. Meanwhile, Maj Bakshi stationed Sub Gupta and the other two soldiers at their usual observation site near the LAC.

"Is there any chance of our presence near the LAC being noticed by the Chinese?" Godbole asked, keeping pace with Maj Bakshi.

"Always a possibility. Since the Ladakh standoff, the PLA and our Army have been on high alert. The Chinese use high-altitude, long-endurance drones, HALEs. They can spot even tiny Himalayan hares, while the drones are nearly invisible to the naked eye," Maj Bakshi replied.

"So, we need to be cautious," Godbole said.

"The drones are meant to serve as a deterrent. The place we are heading to is well within our side but dangerous because of the deep gorges and winding ravines," Maj Bakshi added.

"Surprisingly, the Chinese knew of a shortcut to our side through these treacherous ravines, indicating they've explored this area. We have to be mindful of that," Godbole said.

Upon reaching the stream, they identified the crossing point Lote had used a week prior. They chose a spot in the ravine to wait, hidden from the Chinese side. The steep, slippery slope, colder than anticipated, was unsettling. Despite the unease, the team settled down, scanning the area with binoculars for Lote, Dorjee, the Chinese man, as well as any suspicious Chinese movements. The open, barren plateau on the Chinese side gave the team good visibility from their position.

Time ticked by, and by noon, six hours had passed since Lote's departure. Maj Bakshi's mind raced with worries. What if the Chinese have caught Lote? How would I face his family?

"It's time for Lote to show up. Mr Godbole, do you think they are holding up Lote? You see, he is an untrained civilian. And, we are on a mission with only oral sanction."

"I understand your concern, but we would've seen some signs if the Chinese got wind of our plans. The fact is that the Chinese would know only if Dorjee disclosed it to them. With his family at stake, Dorjee wouldn't. Let's wait."

Anxiety grew with each passing moment. Finally, at 1:20 p.m., they spotted three figures approaching the LAC. Maj Bakshi estimated they would take at least forty minutes to reach the ravines. Since there was no well-set walking track, it wasn't easy to anticipate where precisely the team could meet the three men. Therefore, the team had to keep changing positions to align with their progress. Apart from a couple of stopovers, the men were making steady progress. Lote seemed to have successfully coaxed the other two men to come closer to the Indian side than usual – a positive sign from Dorjee. When the men were about 200 metres away, Godbole leaned from his position and signalled Maj Bakshi, who responded with a thumb-up.

Godbole emerged from the ravine and quietly advanced, taking a roundabout path through a precarious slope, and he positioned himself much ahead of his team. Though he knew Maj Bakshi wouldn't approve of the risk, he feared Dorjee changing his mind at the last minute and running back to the Chinese side. He planned to let the three men pass him and spring up behind them. As for the Chinese man, Godbole would be happy if he ran away. The other team members would intervene only if force became necessary.

Godbole saw the men passing by his position. As they walked some distance, Godbole crawled forward. Once he reached behind them, he calmly got up and started walking. The alert Chinese man heard him and instantly turned around. The man was stunned to see Godbole. Then, in a flash, he pulled out a square object with an antenna from his jacket and pressed a button repeatedly before tucking it back in his jacket.

The very next moment, the Chinese man charged towards Godbole. A fight broke out as he tried to hold Godbole down. He sought help from Dorjee and Lote, but saw them running away. By then, Maj Bakshi and his soldiers rushed to help Godbole. Realizing he was outnumbered, the Chinese man dashed back. That was all Godbole and the team wanted.

Back in the ravine, Maj Bakshi and Godbole welcomed Dorjee, who was overwhelmed with tears. There was no time for a detailed conversation as they needed to leave quickly. Maj Bakshi embraced Lote, praising his excellent work. "Tenzin, I got worried when you took so long to return."

"Saheb, I managed to convey our plan to Dorjee, but he did not respond for a while. I thought he did not like the idea and might tip off the Chinese," Lote said.

Just then, Dorjee intervened, "I was dying to return to my family. So, there was no way I could reject Lote's proposal. But the problem was that Tashi was sitting there when Lote spoke to me. Tashi speaks another dialect of Arunachal but can pick up Monpa words," Dorjee said.

"Who is Tashi?" Maj Bakshi asked.

"He is Rinchin Tashi from the eastern part of Arunachal. We were the only two Indians there. He, too, was captured near the LAC many years ago. He is a mysterious, reserved old man over seventy."

"Then, how did you manage to come?"

"Before I agreed to Lote's plan, I watched how Tashi reacted. After waiting a while, I decided to take this chance when I was sure Tashi wouldn't alert the Chinese. Tashi may not have heard Lote, or maybe he let me escape, because as we left, I saw a smile on Tashi's face."

"I want to know more about Tashi, but later. Right now, we have to get out of here quickly," Maj Bakshi said.

The group made their way back. Despite successfully getting Dorjee back, Maj Bakshi was anxious about the Chinese reaction. Although there might not be any chance for skirmishes between the two armies, the Chinese would not take losing Dorjee lightly. In such situations, settling scores through symbolic actions was a tradition the Chinese and the Indians followed. Maj Bakshi knew that once the man returned to his village, the Chinese would investigate.

"Anyhow, it'll be over an hour before the man reaches the village. So, we have time to get away from. But Mr Godbole, you may have seen the man using that gadget. The Chinese could land sooner than we expect. We have to hurry."

"You are right, Major. That man was trying to alert his masters using that wireless gadget. They won't waste any time coming to investigate if they received his signal. That chap didn't seem like a villager, considering how he charged at me. First, that Haao and now this man with the gadget... is Tangma a village or a PLA camp?"

"Thankfully, now we have Dorjee with us. But I'm worried. Though we're dressed like the locals, the Chinese could suspect us of being Indian Army men. We should be on guard. I've already instructed Sub Gupta and the two men at the observation site to keep observing the LAC until dusk," Maj Bakshi said.

"Anyway, Major, we have succeeded in giving them a message that in this battle of wits, we do not intend to lag behind. We can't let them take our villagers and play them against us," Godbole said.

The successful mission provided a brief moment of solace in their arduous journey, providing respite from the constant tension and uncertainty.

"Mr Godbole, it's a relief. But let's wait and see how this pans out."

"Saheb!" the soldier called out suddenly. "I see a small group from the Chinese side heading in this direction. They're far but moving fast."

"They have powerful binoculars and cameras to capture and compare our figures with the data they might already have. They may deploy their surveillance drones too. Move fast!" Maj Bakshi shouted urgently.

*****

The Army tent enveloped them in warmth after the biting cold of their long trek. The team savoured steaming mugs of tea, accompanied by biscuits and dry fruits. Dorjee's eyes sparkled with undiminished excitement, contrasting with his otherwise weary demeanour. Godbole, sensing the importance of this moment, decided not to delay their conversation. He was keen to capture Dorjee's fresh impressions of his homeland. With Maj Bakshi sitting by his side, Godbole sparked a conversation with Dorjee to put him at ease.

"I'll address you as Tsering..." Godbole smiled and continued, "We are so happy you are back. You are safe now."

Dorjee instantly folded his hands into a namaste, his face contorted as tears trickled down his cheeks. Godbole got up and gently patted Dorjee's back to calm him down.

After a few seconds, Dorjee said, "Sir, I never thought I would be able to return to my village and see my family. Lote told me that my family is waiting for me in Zemithang."

"Yes, not just your family, but the entire village," Godbole said.

Maj Bakshi added, "Tsering, we will leave for Zemithang early tomorrow."

Dorjee wiped his tears. "How do I thank you, sir? I will always be grateful to you all."

Maj Bakshi said, "This is what we are here for... to protect our citizens."

"Please feel free and relax," Godbole told Dorjee. "Soon, you can have dinner and go to bed. We're just chatting."

"I don't think I will be able to sleep tonight," Dorjee said. "That is the state of my mind. Talking to you will keep me occupied and happy."

Seeing Dorjee's willingness to talk, Godbole asked him about the Chinese side of the border. Dorjee began to explain, painting a vivid picture of the Chinese village and his life there. His detailed account of Tangma revealed its significance. The town, established three years before the 2017 Doklam standoff, was cleverly concealed from Indian positions due to its location on a slope. Tangma's proximity to the Tawang sector and the Bhutan border posed new concerns.

With about 200 inhabitants, including a few PLA platoons and their families, Tangma operated under the command of Haao, both the PLA Commander and village head. The PLA men typically wore civilian clothes, blending in with the villagers, except during operations when they donned uniforms. Half of Tangma's living quarters housed the PLA. Two large cabins in the PLA area, equipped with machinery running day and night, drew power from a generator housed in a sound-muffled trench. Dorjee also noted a long power cable extending from the generator to a distant location.

As Dorjee recounted his traumatic experience, he paused frequently, overwhelmed by emotion. After he was captured at the LAC, he endured extensive questioning. When nothing worthwhile yielded from him, they jailed him. After eight months of solitary confinement, he was sent to a labour camp-cum-rehabilitation centre, where he was taught Mandarin and trained to adopt the Chinese way of life. He was also forcefully married to an abusive widow, much older than he was. Four years later, just after the Doklam standoff, he was moved to Tangma to serve as an interpreter for the Chinese, interrogating intruders from Arunachal, ascertaining details about infrastructure development and Indian Army deployments.

Before interrogating Lote, Dorjee had helped the Chinese question three other trespassers, two from Arunachal and one from Bhutan. In an apparent change in strategy, the Chinese would allow the trespassers to return. The returning men were presented with gifts to encourage them to come again, with information on the Indian Army. In Lote's case, under the watch of a Chinese man, Dorjee was allowed to accompany and see him off near the Indian border to instil confidence in him. That worked. Lote was the only one from Tawang who had returned to Tangma at least five times.

Meanwhile, the Chinese brought Rinchin Tashi to Tangma to speak to those crossing over from the eastern part of Arunachal, where a different dialect was spoken. Tashi was over seventy years old, and his arthritic problems made it difficult for him to walk. The Chinese called him Rex. Tashi and Dorjee were kept isolated from each other and away from others. Yet Dorjee had the opportunity to speak with Tashi occasionally. Thus, Dorjee learnt his real name and gathered that he belonged to the eastern part of Arunachal. He had been with the Chinese since 1982.

On all five occasions when Dorjee interpreted Lote, Tashi was present in the room. Probably, the Chinese were using Tashi to double-check Dorjee's translation. This made Dorjee cautious when Lote mentioned the rescue plan, but he ultimately trusted Tashi, who seemed to support his escape silently. Tashi's smile as they left Tangma confirmed his suspicions. In a one-and-a-half-hour-long discussion with Dorjee, Godbole got a fair picture of Tangma and the Chinese activities there. Soon after dinner, Dorjee was taken to Sub Gupta's tent to rest.

By midnight, Godbole had compiled a detailed report of Dorjee's information. His mind raced with the implications of Dorjee's revelations. Tangma's proximity to the border and the presence of PLA men in civilian disguise were particularly troubling. What was the significance of the parcel the Chinese sent to Tawang? Godbole also pondered Rinchin Tashi. Who was this man? If he could have prevented Dorjee from escaping to India, why did he not do that? Dorjee could not answer the other vital question about the parcel the Chinese had sent to Tawang through Lote. Would it ever be possible to identify and trace the one who came to receive the parcel? He could be an essential link to the Chinese espionage and subversive activities in India.

Unable to sleep, Godbole sat up, contemplating whether to resume the debriefing with Dorjee. Eventually, he decided against disturbing him and reluctantly settled into his sleeping bag, thoughts of Tangma and Tashi swirling in his mind.

Chapter – 4
The Red Route

Zemithang
October 27, 2020
6 p.m.

The Zemithang camp buzzed with joy, the celebratory mood lingering well into the second day of the team's return. After seven long years of painful separation, the sight of Dorjee embracing his family brought an overwhelming sense of joy to the entire village. This heartwarming reunion, a testament to the villagers' resilience and unity, earned the Army their goodwill. Evening bonfires crackled as villagers danced and shared special meals. Away from home, on challenging duties at the faraway borders, the soldiers cling to even the smallest pleasures. So, Maj Bakshi did not mind his men indulging a bit longer. Besides, the Chinese reaction was muted, at least for now. However, Maj Bakshi refused to believe that the Chinese were taking things lightly. Therefore, he had instructed his men to keep their guard up at the LAC.

Twenty-four hours after their arrival in Zemithang, Godbole pulled Dorjee aside, seeking privacy.

"Tell me about the generator the Chinese installed," Godbole urged, his voice low and intense.

Dorjee described the massive generator, tucked away in a noise-muffled trench, powering an equipment room and a few homes. Initially, he couldn't recall the details about the long cable extending from the facility to an unknown location. Godbole's persistent questioning finally jogged Dorjee's memory, revealing a year-old digging operation along the Lhasa-Cona-Tangma Road.

"The road from Lhasa to Cona was already tarred. However, the portion of the road from Cona to Tangma was tarred only last year," Dorjee explained.

"So, Tangma is now connected by a tarred road," Godbole said.

"Yes, sir. The digging site is along this road, just two kilometres before Tangma village. The digging site was heavily restricted. Strangely, civil trucks, not military, were used to remove the debris."

Dorjee described how he and other able-bodied villagers were conscripted to clear the soil and rocks. They returned to the village once the debris was gone, only to be summoned months later to unload heavy equipment into newly constructed trenches.

"After a few months, we were sent to the site to unload heavy equipment packed in large wooden crates. I saw the trenches closely. There were four trenches, all interconnected. The trenches had tin-sheet roofs barely a foot and a half above ground, covered with stones and sand for camouflage. Then, I noticed a power cable stretching from the village to the site. I also saw two medium-sized dish antennae lying in one of the trenches, yet to be installed."

The concealed nature of the trenches and the equipment's strategic placement hinted at a meticulously planned operation. As Godbole pieced together the details – newly tarred roads from Cona, strategically hidden equipment and antennae, power cables leading to the trenches, and the Chinese efforts to befriend Indian trespassers – his suspicion grew. The packet Tenzin Lote delivered in Tawang, combined with the Chinese sensitivity to Indian patrols near PP-6, only confirmed his fears.

It all pointed to a significant Chinese operation in Tangma. With the Chinese claiming all of Arunachal Pradesh, was this part of their larger strategy? Amid the current stand-off, was a new front about to open at the LAC?

"Saheb, you have a call from Delhi. Please come to Major Saheb's cabin," a soldier suddenly came up to him and said.

Godbole was expecting that call. A day ago, he had sent his initial report to Das using the Army's secure intranet system. Eager to ascertain Das's reaction to the developments, Godbole hurried to Maj Bakshi's cabin.

"Good work, Yash, I am happy that you rightly read my silence and went ahead with the operation," Das said.

Godbole expected a more excited reaction from his boss. Das was usually generous with praise when an operation concluded with reasonable success. Something was worrying him.

"Thank you, sir, but is there anything amiss?"

"Why do you say so?" Das asked.

"Well... maybe I did not meet your expectations. Yet, did we not get Dorjee back and some good information from him, too?"

"Yash, as always, you did a marvellous job. Dorjee and his information are exemplary work. But you know the news about Rinchin Tashi has dwarfed all your other aces, truly."

"Is he anyone of significance?"

"Well, Tashi was from our field cadre... an able operator. After receiving your report, I sent the details to the special cell for verification. For the special cell, the name Rinchin Tashi was enough to know who he was because he was legendary, and one of the few accomplished operatives on the missing list. Tashi's age, mentioned as seventy-plus, and the year of his disappearance in 1982, helped further to confirm his identity. We thought he was not alive. Sadly, his wife passed away about two years ago."

"Oh God, this is something to know!"

"Yash, it may be good news that Tashi is alive, but we at the headquarters are also distressed by his plight. Please think of the scale of his suffering... thirty-eight long years in captivity! Records say Monpa was among the dialects Tashi knew. He might have understood what Lote was telling Dorjee!"

"Incarcerated so long by the enemy and still steadfastly loyal to the motherland! I think of Tashi's smile when Lote and Dorjee departed from Tangma. Sir, he knew they were escaping."

"I read his record. Tashi was a brave and skilful operator; he used to go on assignment to the other side up to Tsona Dzong, the capital of Cona County in Tibetan Shannan. Just imagine. It is over thirty kilometres to Cona from the nearest point on the LAC. Even if it was in the late seventies and early eighties, it was risky. Sadly, the Chinese caught up with him."

"Sir, I shudder to think how the Chinese might have dealt with him. He might have been tortured or even drugged. That is why he is in such poor health. Can we ever rescue him?"

"Here in Delhi, we examined all the angles. It is just not possible to send a team crossing the LAC. It would be a huge risk, especially in the prevailing situation. Even a Dorjee-style civilian rescue attempt is difficult."

"Yes, that would be difficult. Lote stands compromised; he can't be sent there anymore. Besides, after Dorjee's escape, the Chinese would be cautious."

"Yash, in our profession, there are moments like this. An operative is hopelessly stuck in a hostile land. It may look like we are leaving Tashi to his fate. It is painful, but is there anything to be done?"

"I can understand. I think even Tashi is aware of our helplessness. He is brave, taking it stoically. What a sacrifice... unsung and unknown!"

"Yes, no one will ever know about him. These are our professional hazards." Das sounded gloomy.

"But sir... Rinchin Tashi will remain in my thoughts."

As Godbole said that, his last words tapered off.

There was a long silence. Das was not sure what was going through Godbole's mind. It was better to stop discussing the touchy subject to avoid further stirring Godbole's mind. Since the leakage issue was successfully resolved, Das thought it better to move on.

Das said, "Yash, our work has to go on. You see, now that the Zemithang operation is over, it is time for you to return to Delhi. I know the follow-up work on the information provided by Dorjee and the mystery parcel delivered in Tawang is there. But this can be taken up from Delhi."

Godbole was still silent. So, Das added, "Yash, we are left with very little time to tackle Kanak Mohan. The deadline for publishing his article is fast approaching, and Brig Kedar is getting impatient."

"I understand, sir. I am sending a follow-up report on a technical installation that the Chinese have built near Tangma. I think it is a serious development..."

"Send it over. We will discuss it when you return."

As the call ended, Godbole felt enveloped by gloom. Being an operative, he could feel the pain Tashi was undergoing. The irony was that Tangma was close to the border, yet there was no easy way to get Tashi back. Now that it was time to go to Delhi, Godbole feared the thoughts about Tashi might start fading.

Chapter – 5
A Trail Opens

New Delhi
October 29, 2020
9 a.m.

Godbole was excited about meeting his entire team after a long break. When he returned from his Goa vacation on 13th October, Ashok Talreja and Abdul Riaz were away in Rameswaram, and Vilas Pande was busy checking Kanak Mohan's background. Now that they were all back in the office, they could cushion the impact of the crushing challenges of each other's fieldwork.

The meeting called by Das with the team was at 11 a.m., but Godbole reached the NES-17 office almost two hours early. He was eager to brief his team on the work he completed at the LAC and to review Pande's report on Kanak Mohan.

Amidst all the pressing issues, the primary focus was on uncovering the Chinese clandestine network in India responsible for covert tech attacks. Of all the leads they had, Kanak Mohan seemed the most promising. After reading Pande's report on Mohan, Godbole couldn't shake the feeling that Mohan's background was cloaked in mystery. Mohan owned a motorbike, an old Maruti-Suzuki car, and a one-bedroom apartment in a Mumbai suburb. With personal assets amounting to about ninety-five lakh rupees, nothing seemed amiss–until one considered that Mohan had no regular employment. Documents accessed by Pande revealed Mohan worked as a freelance journalist, writing columns for a left-leaning digital publication in Singapore, earning up to

$300 monthly. He recently moved to Delhi, renting a one-bedroom flat, while his Mumbai apartment was leased for twenty thousand rupees a month.

Godbole reread Pande's report and noticed a curious detail: Mohan's bank records showed he had renewed his membership at the Delhi Public Library by paying a hundred-rupee fee. Pande's preliminary inquiries at the library confirmed that Mohan visited the library on Thursdays around 3 p.m. to borrow books. Thursday! Godbole squirmed in his seat. By sheer luck, it was a Thursday. Why not try to find Mohan at the library? After the meeting with Das, he decided he would visit the Delhi Public Library near Old Delhi Railway Station that afternoon.

Well before 11 a.m., the team assembled in the conference room. Everyone's joy at getting together was evident. After hugs, shaking hands, and brief chit-chats, Das started the meeting. First, Das gave a quick overview of Godbole's LAC work, Talreja and Riaz's Rameswaram trip, and Pande's findings about Kanak Mohan's background.

"The situation looks challenging," Das said, his concern evident. "What has shaken our organization is Rinchin Tashi's plight – our man, trapped in China for decades. Our options are severely limited, but the matter isn't closed. The top brass is still deliberating on this issue."

Das removed his glasses, cleaned them with a tissue, and seemed to ponder what to say next. The impact of Tashi's story weighed heavily on everyone. Das continued, "I know it is painful, but we cannot sit brooding over it; let the department take a call on this. Our hands are full with pressing matters."

The room fell silent, everyone relating to Das's feelings. Breaking the silence, Das said, "Godbole's report about the concealed technical installation near Tangma is under serious review. It is rather an odd installation. We need more input on this to have a meaningful discussion."

"The voice intercept in Mandarin we picked up that stormy night has a worrying angle. Possible Chinese involvement in this matter, especially in the current situation at the LAC, warrants serious attention. You'll soon get a detailed report on what Talreja and Riaz found in Rameswaram. For now, I'll brief you." Das opened a file and flipped through a few sheets.

Initially, we had no clue about the sea liner or the person in Sri Lanka involved in that Mandarin call. We decided to monitor the skies, hoping for another communication from the ship's sat phone or the Sri Lankan phone. Our patience paid off. Three days after the Mandarin call, at 3 a.m., we intercepted a call from an Indian cell phone in Rameswaram to the Sri Lankan phone. This time, it was in Tamil, cryptically indicating a consignment was handed over safely to a party," Das explained.

"That means they smuggled something to India," Godbole said.

"Yes, it suggested illegal smuggling," Das confirmed. "Riaz and Talreja quickly identified the Indian phone user, a smuggling gang member operating between Rameswaram and Talaimannar in Sri Lanka. While typical items were local agricultural products and handicrafts, this consignment was different. It consisted of eight securely packed cardboard boxes weighing about fifteen kilograms. Not a large shipment."

"Any information on who received it and where it was being taken to?" Godbole asked.

"Fortunately, we have some information. In the past year, two such consignments arrived in Rameswaram, usually picked up by a mysterious Hemant from Mumbai, who died a few weeks ago. The packages were now handed to a new person, who took away the consignment in a Karnataka-registered SUV, the number of which we lack," Das said.

"Another challenge," Godbole noted.

"Well, it is difficult, but we are still working on getting a breakthrough. We're checking records at road toll booths in

Rameswaram and Madurai for Karnataka-registered SUVs that passed between 3 a.m. and 8 a.m.," Das concluded.

"Next, let's discuss Kanak Mohan," Das continued. "What's your plan?"

"Well, sir, as you will agree, we are looking at Mohan not just to stall his article from publishing. He could be far more important. We believe he might be our entry point into the Chinese network."

"You're right, Yash. Unlike the Pakis, the Chinese can't have a large network in India. They always work with a limited number, and Mohan could be one of their key operatives."

"Exactly," Godbole said. Luckily, it's Thursday. I intend to start our surveillance on Mohan this afternoon at the Delhi Public Library. I may want all three of my team with me."

"It was smart of Pande to dig up his membership details and photograph. Hope it's a lead."

"I hope so. Today, we'll observe from afar and assess him. We may film him too. In the coming days, we might trail him until we find something," Godbole said.

Das glanced at his watch, "Oh... it is already twelve-forty! You need to be at the library well before 3 p.m. I'm winding up the meeting. We'll reconvene tomorrow morning."

*****

Godbole and the team parked their car in the Old Delhi Railway Station's crowded parking area to remain inconspicuous. As Abdul Riaz stayed behind in the car, Godbole, Talreja, and Pande walked towards the library. "Vilas, your report says Mohan sticks to the Tibetology and Near-East sections of the library," Godbole said as they walked.

"Yes. All the books he takes are also from that section only," Pande informed.

Godbole frowned. "That's strange! His online articles focus on social issues and leftist topics. Could he be retrieving these books from the Tibetology section for someone else?" He paused, his brow furrowing deeper. "And there's another thing. Sticking to such a strict routine could mean more. We need to move carefully."

At the library entrance, Talreja offered to stay outside and keep watch for Mohan. Godbole and Pande entered the reception area at 2:10 p.m., noting the sparse crowd. The receptionist's face lit up with recognition when she saw Pande. "Sir, your friend will arrive in about an hour," the lady said with a broad smile.

"What does he do after coming here?" Godbole asked.

"Oh... you brought a friend this time," the receptionist said without answering Godbole's query.

Pande approached the lady and whispered, "Ma'am, I briefed you last time. This is confidential. We need your help."

Her expression sobered, "Sorry, sir. After you spoke to me, I checked with the assistant librarian in the Tibetology section. He remembers your man well; it's been nearly two years. He heads to that secluded area and spends about ten minutes picking out books, making entries, and leaving. That's his routine, almost every visit," the receptionist informed.

Godbole and Pande thanked the receptionist and moved inside, eyes scanning for the Tibetology section. They found it – a quiet corner at the end of the right wing, precisely as described. The area was deserted, with only three rows of book racks.

"Keep an eye out for anything suspicious," he instructed Pande before heading towards the racks.

It was 2:20 p.m., and Godbole knew he had to work fast. He moved quietly among the book racks, his eyes scanning the shelves. His fingers brushed over the books and slid under the shelves, a habit from years of covert inspections. Suddenly, he felt something sticky under a waist-level plank of the last rack. He pulled his hand back, grimacing at the lump of chewing gum now stuck to his fingers. A small piece of butter paper peeked out as he tried to flick it off. Carefully, he extracted it, revealing a tiny memory card wrapped inside. His heart raced; someone was using this spot as a dead-letter box.

Godbole's initial impulse was to take the card, but he quickly reconsidered. Who had done it? Was the person still around, watching? And most crucially, was the card meant for Kanak Mohan?

Deciding to wait and observe, he carefully replaced the card and the chewing gum. It was 2:30 p.m., and he needed to move swiftly. He walked back to Pande, standing guard five racks away, and discreetly informed him of the find. As they spoke, Pande's attention was drawn to a well-built man in a grey T-shirt and blue jeans heading towards the Tibetology section. The man walked past it, moving on to the English fiction section. It was 2:50 p.m., and his appearance didn't match Kanak Mohan's photo. Still, he was the only person to approach the Tibetology area since their arrival. Pande saw the man exit the library without looking at any books. The timing was suspicious, but with Mohan expected any moment, Pande returned to his post.

"What was that man doing in the hall?" Godbole asked.

"He just passed through and left," Pande replied.

Godbole nodded. "His movements were odd. I could tell you considered following him. But for now, let's focus on Mohan. Find a good spot to set up the hidden camera. We need a clear record of Mohan's activities."

Godbole paused, pulling out a page from his pocket notepad to clean his fingers. "If Mohan is here to collect that chip, I want to catch him in the act," he said.

"Without formalities and permission from Das?" Pande questioned.

"No time for that. We need the card and Mohan. We can't miss this chance," Godbole stated firmly.

Minutes stretched into what felt like hours. At 3:05 p.m., a message from Talreja lit up Godbole's phone: *'Mohan entered the building'.*

A few minutes later, Godbole saw Mohan walking in. Mohan returned a hefty book before heading towards the Tibetology section. He browsed the shelves, flipping through a few books before moving to the last rack. Glancing around, he extracted a small plastic sheet from his wallet and retrieved the chewing gum lump. Hidden from view, Godbole saw him wrap the lump in plastic and securely keep it in his wallet. Mohan then headed for the exit. Godbole signalled Pande and discreetly trailed Mohan. Meanwhile, Pande alerted Talreja and Riaz, who were waiting outside in the car.

Mohan left the library building and crossed the road. It was apparent that he had not come in his car. Sensing that Mohan was about to hire a taxi, Godbole approached him.

"Mr Kanak Mohan?" Godbole asked.

Mohan was momentarily jolted. "Who are you?" he asked after a few seconds.

"I am from the Defence establishment."

"What do you want?"

"Mr Mohan, I know you are writing a story on defence matters."

"Who told you all this? Please leave me."

"You see, I have more inside information that could add credibility to your article."

"But what's your interest?"

"All that I can tell you... But we need to sit somewhere to talk."

Godbole pressed on, "Mr Mohan, I know that Pankaj Banerji is showing some hesitation in publishing your article. My information could convince him."

Mohan remained silent, but Godbole could figure out that Mohan was in two minds. Godbole signalled Riaz to bring the car.

As the vehicle arrived, Godbole said, "This is my car. Please come... You are safe with a defence officer; do not worry."

Mohan scrutinized Godbole. He looked respectable, but was he genuinely from the Defence, as he claimed? However, the offer was tempting. Banerji's fifteen-thousand fee for the article meant a lot to Mohan. Besides, the article could become a defence scoop and help him earn a name.

After some more persuasion, Mohan boarded the car with Godbole.

"Driver, to my house," Godbole told Riaz, who nodded and started the car.

Godbole quickly texted Pande:

Get a memory card reader and come to the house. We will be there.

"Mr Mohan, please make yourself comfortable."

"I am confused. How do you know about my article?" Mohan asked suspiciously.

"Banerji wanted to corroborate the information in the article. After all, it is about the credibility of his reputed magazine. He approached us. We have more information to add, and since you are the writer, we thought of speaking directly to you."

"But why do you want to do all this?"

"You wanted to reveal the truth to the public, right? So do we for the greater good."

"I hope this stays confidential."

"Please don't worry."

The car pulled into the compound of a building through a nondescript gate. Godbole led Mohan into the building, taking the lift to the fourth-floor apartment.

"This building is a bit weird. You stay here?"

"Government buildings are like this... tasteless," Godbole replied with a smile as he rang the doorbell. A person opened the door, and Godbole promptly led Mohan inside.

Chapter – 6
Phantoms in the Shadows

New Delhi
5.30 p.m.

Kanak Mohan sat wearily in the sofa chair, his eyes darting around the room, not knowing what to expect. He hoped to unearth sensitive information to stage a journalistic coup and earn a name and money.

"Mr Mohan, you have not yet sipped the tea. Please be comfortable," Godbole said, his voice smooth but firm.

"What is this place? What is your name?" Mohan's voice trembled slightly.

"First, have your tea, then we can talk."

Mohan swallowed hard and finished the tea in a few hurried sips. Then, he pulled a writing pad from his pouch.

Godbole settled into the chair opposite him. "Before we speak, please switch off your cell phone as a security precaution," Godbole said, his tone leaving no room for argument.

"My phone is already switched off. Before I could switch it on, you met me outside the library," Mohan said, handing his smartphone to Godbole.

"Why is your phone switched off?" Godbole asked, his eyes narrowing.

Mohan shifted uncomfortably. "It's my habit; I don't want to disturb anyone in the library."

Switching off the phone is an act followed by professionals to cover their tracks. By now, Godbole knew he would have to handle Mohan with caution.

"Mr Mohan, now please listen.... I am from the National Security Division. I brought you here because we need your cooperation in an important matter."

"I don't understand what you are saying." Mohan appeared genuinely surprised. "You did not bring me here to provide information? Were you misleading me?"

Mohan's voice rose in anger, his irritation evident as he continued, "This is against the law, and I am a journalist. This will prove costly to you."

"If you do not cooperate, this will prove costly to you instead."

"I should have known that you are a thug. National security, my foot!" Mohan thundered.

"Calm down. You have a house in Mumbai, an asset of over ninety lakh rupees. We also know about your other assets. All disproportionate to your income."

"Don't cook up stories and try to scare me. I file my income tax returns."

"Yes, indeed. Your file returns to cover the few dollars you make from your articles in foreign digital media, isn't it?"

"I am a clean person; I have nothing to hide." Mohan asserted.

"Then why are you indulging in something stealthy?"

"What do you mean?" Mohan looked annoyed.

"Mr Mohan, can you please take out your wallet? I want to see that chewing gum lump tucked in there."

"What?" In the room's stillness, Mohan's voice sank to a whisper.

"*Take out your wallet*!" Godbole shouted.

Mohan's face suddenly fell. He was dazed and instantly started sweating. On cue, Talreja, Pande, and Riaz appeared in the room from another door.

Godbole signalled Pande, who opened his laptop and played the video clip of Mohan collecting the gum.

"Mr Mohan, we have come to you well prepared. We have material against you. If you don't cooperate, you'll end up in more trouble. I want to see the chip... the card."

A despondent Mohan sat there looking utterly miserable. When Godbole insisted, he nervously took his purse and placed the plastic wrapping in Godbole's hands. Godbole gave it to Talreja.

"Who was the one who left this lump there for you?" Godbole continued the questioning.

"I don't know," Mohan said.

"I cannot believe that. You will have to come clean."

"Believe me, sir, I don't know who he is... I have not yet seen him. It has been so for the past two years. I have never met or spoken to him, not even on the phone."

"Remember, if you deliberately hide and mislead me, the repercussions will be severe. I want to avoid putting pressure on you... including physical pressure."

Mohan's defences crumbled. Godbole knew Mohan needed only a little nudging to talk.

"Look here, Mohan. If you open up, it might save you from a lot of trouble. We know... You are an important link in the subversive network that the Chinese are running in this country. Are you aware of the consequences of such a crime?"

He panicked and looked at Godbole pleadingly.

Sensing an opportunity, Godbole said, "I will not promise you anything, but perhaps I might be able to lessen the impact of the legal action awaiting you. Maybe I can help you more if you tell me everything honestly."

Straightaway, Mohan responded, "Believe me, sir, I'm telling you the truth... I'm not a criminal; circumstances have pushed me to do this...” Mohan abruptly stopped and sobbed. “Sir, I do it for my family–my aged parents, wife, and one son. How long can I manage without a well-paying job?” Mohan’s eyes were moist.

Godbole always avoided being distracted by the subject’s emotional behaviour. Yet, something about Mohan appeared to be genuine.

Godbole continued to pursue his point, ignoring Mohan. He remarked, “It is hard to believe that you are doing this risky business with someone whom you have not seen or spoken to.”

“But it is a fact,” Mohan said.

Before Godbole could respond, Talreja entered the room with the memory card and said, “Sorry to interrupt, sir. The message on this card is not readable. It is ciphered.”

“If the message in the card is coded, how do you read it?” Godbole asked Mohan instantly.

Mohan said reluctantly. “There’s an app on my phone, ‘Chess-1’. If the message is opened using that app, it can be read.”

Godbole handed Mohan’s phone to Talreja and said, “Ensure that the SIM and the phone’s Wi-Fi are disabled before you switch on the phone.”

Godbole continued the questioning. “So, you say you neither speak nor meet each other. Then how do you report to your Chinese master? Is it that you also stick a memory card in that library to convey what you have to say?”

“Normally, I have nothing to report to them in detail. They assign tasks that I receive via the memory card. The only occasion I communicate with them is when I need clarification about the task or inform them about the progress of my efforts.”

“Mr Mohan, how is that done?”

“Well, sir, there is an online mechanism to do that.”

Hiding his surprise, Godbole asked, “What is this mechanism?”

"Whenever I have to ask them or report something to them, I have to log in to the booking website of Rose Valley Resort in Thailand. Like a customer who wants to book accommodation at the resort, I fill in a form that pops up on that website. After filling in a fake name 'Anil Dev' and typing fake details, I proceed to the comments box, which can take up to 250 words. This space is meant to write the family's special requirements during their stay there. I begin with a normal sentence and then write all that I want to know from them or pass on to them. Once I click the 'post' button, the form disappears from the website and gets forwarded to the desired person on their side."

What an inimitable way to communicate, Godbole thought. No personal meetings, no phone calls, or no emails! He was sure that the website through which Mohan communicated might be hosted from a foreign location without easy access for the Indians. No doubt, the Chinese took all precautions to safeguard their network effectively. Godbole realized how challenging the work ahead was going to be! If the Chinese fortress had to be breached, it could only be through the Chinese cogs. For now, Mohan was the only cog Godbole had, maybe the weakest link in their chain.

Godbole looked sharply at Mohan. He wanted Mohan to know that the matter was grave and had severe implications for him. In an attempt to mollify his interrogator, Mohan said, "Sir... what I told you is factual. I am honest with you. I shall reveal all I know, but please, for my family's sake, have mercy on me."

"Let me first hear you out," Godbole said. "If I am convinced, I can see what I can do for you. Besides, you will have to do some work for me. Are you ready?"

"Sir, I am ready to do what is ordered, but please take care of me. I want you to know that if I am exposed, they might eliminate me."

Godbole paused briefly, saying, "We will work carefully and ensure you do not get exposed. Now... I want to get a complete picture of your role and how you are operating – with details. I have no patience for cock-and-bull stories."

"Okay sir"

"Okay, do you visit the library every Thursday at 3 p.m.?"

"Yes, those are the instructions. I keep going to the library at 3 p.m. every Thursday."

"Well, that means you get instructions in a memory card every Thursday."

"No, sir. They will keep the memory card only when they assign me some work. Sometimes, I get only one card in a month. But I must keep going there every Thursday, so I do not miss the card. Since I go there every Thursday, they do not need to schedule an appointment separately."

"I get it. Then what happens to the books you take from the library?"

"Sir, it is only a ploy to keep visiting the library."

"Have you ever tried to know who planted the card there?"

"No. I have been warned not to try to see who does this. I was told not to visit the library before 3 p.m."

"The card is always stuck in the Tibetology section?"

"Yes, sir, since it is less frequently visited," Mohan explained.

"Okay. Now tell me about your background. I want to know how they recruited you."

Mohan looked up momentarily and took a deep breath. It was seven years since Mohan began sliding into the Chinese trap. With just a few articles published in a small left-leaning local fortnightly in Andhra Pradesh, Mohan struggled to establish himself as a journalist and social commentator. Then, someone spoke to him about *Social Endeavour*, a fortnightly digital publication from Indonesia. He was impressed by the periodical's efforts to bring the focus of the readers to social issues of global relevance.

Soon, he started sending his writeups, covering the lives and struggles of marginalized sections in India. His articles were accepted, and he received payments for his contributions through legal banking channels. Some of the editorial staff became friendly with Mohan. Initially, he received requests for details of some persons and places in India via emails and chats. He was paid to send the details, too. Their requests started growing. Soon he realized he was in the grip of some people he had not seen or talked to.

About two years ago, *Social Endeavour* wound up, and the emails and chats stopped too. Mohan was worried that his source of income would dry up. However, one fine morning, Hemant from Mumbai landed at Mohan's residence and gave him an envelope containing a new set of instructions. That was when the Delhi Public Library rendezvous was fixed. He was also asked to contribute his articles to the digital fortnightly '*Man and Nature*' published in Cambodia. In some months, Hemant arranged funds to purchase a new apartment for Mohan in Mumbai. Hemant stayed in the new apartment and paid Mohan rupees twenty thousand monthly rent. It was a great relief for Mohan, and he was willing to ignore the illegality of acquiring the apartment.

The knots were opening up, but Godbole knew he had to cover a long distance.

"Where is Hemant now... in Mumbai?"

"Sir, about two months ago, he was murdered in his Mumbai residence."

"He is no more!" Godbole's disappointment was evident in his tone. Investigating Hemant could have led Godbole's team to the doorstep of the Chinese network.

"Sir, with his death, I have stopped getting my rent. It is difficult for me to pull on."

"Can't you rent it out to someone else?"

"The problem is that Hemant's murder has not yet been solved, and the police have sealed his house. Hemant was living alone. One night, somebody entered the house and killed him."

"Hemant was a valuable ally of the Chinese. They might be worried too."

"I have a hunch the Chinese have got him killed."

Godbole was astounded. He asked, "Why do you think so?"

"Because a few days before he was murdered, he had come here..." Mohan explained.

One afternoon, Hemant came to Delhi from Bangalore. After meeting someone in Delhi, he was to proceed to Mumbai the very night. However, he missed his flight and came to Mohan's home for the night. Hemant wasn't his usual self and looked worried. After probing, he said he was supposed to deliver some parcels to certain people in Bangalore, but some mix-up took place, and he delivered them to the wrong people. He said his bosses were extremely upset. It was challenging and even risky to retrieve the wrong deliveries. Before leaving, Hemant cryptically said that he feared the worst.

"Sir, I am badly entangled. If they ever discover I have spilt something to you, it might be my end, too." Mohan looked worried.

Noting that Mohan was scared, Godbole wanted to reassure him. Keeping a hand on his shoulders, Godbole said, "Look here, Mohan, if you have decided to cooperate with us, we will do everything to protect you, but you must act as I say. If I'm sure you are cooperating, I will not detain you. We will let you go home. You must act normally and follow your routine as always, including your Thursday trips to the library. We will devise a way to remain in touch with you. Okay?"

"As long as I'm not harmed, everything is acceptable to me, sir."

"Good. Now, let me check the instructions you received via your memory card because you should be carrying out their instructions," he said turning towards his colleagues.

"Talreja was examining it. I'll check," Riaz said and went into the adjacent room.

Godbole turned his attention to Mohan. "Meanwhile, can you recount the assignments entrusted to you so far?"

"There hadn't been many. The current task is to get the article published in Banerji's *Strategic and Défense Journal of India*. I have been running around to have the article published. Somehow, Banerji is taking his own sweet time."

"You wrote that article?"

"No. The article was in the memory card. I was to study it thoroughly and get it published under my name."

"What was your previous assignment?"

"I was sent to Rameswaram in Tamil Nadu a few weeks ago. I was to tie up with a smuggler there to get some items smuggled from Sri Lanka to India."

"So, you handle those smuggling operations at Rameswaram?"

"No, sir. It was my first trip. I guess Hemant was doing it.

"Who was that smuggler?"

"I don't know the real name, but we call him Rolex. His details and contact phone number were sent to me through the memory card. When I addressed him as Rolex, he understood I was Hemant's man."

"Oh, I see. Any other place you visited?"

"I had been to Mumbai on a few occasions, but that was for the purchase of the apartment."

"Have you been to Bangalore?"

"No, sir. A year ago, they had sent me to Arunachal Pradesh."

"Where in Arunachal?"

"Tawang... Tawang monastery precisely. I had to collect a parcel from a local there."

It was getting interesting. Godbole asked, "What was that parcel, and to whom did you deliver it?"

"It was a small cardboard box to be delivered to Hemant in Mumbai."

Finally, things were falling into place. It seemed that Hemant was the one who distributed those parcels. Only Hemant could have revealed details about the parcels and to whom those were delivered. Could some tell-tale things be lying in Hemant's home in Mumbai, Godbole wondered. A dead Hemant couldn't speak, but his home might.

Soon, Talreja came and handed over the memory card and a typed sheet. He said, "This is what is on the memory card. We also did the mandatory checks and forensic examination of the card. It appears to be clean, otherwise."

Godbole slowly ran his forefinger over the typed matter. The text had some oblique words and expressions. However, those who knew the context could figure out the matter dealt with in the message.

The message for Mohan read:

> *Double up your efforts to get 'it' published. If the editor wanted any clarification, that could be addressed.*
>
> *A special and essential requirement exists* in the *'South' where 'you' had been a few weeks ago. We learnt that someone from the 'Law' had come there enquiring about movements from the sea a few days ago. We must be cautious because we are preparing to use Rolex's 'services' again, but this time from 'here' to 'there'. However, we will hold that plan till you visit that place and give us an all-clear signal. We wouldn't like to come if the 'Law' is still camping there. Remain prepared to go there in a few days. Next week's message may tell you when to go.*
>
> *We know you are not getting your rent, but we have no one there in Hemant's place to make the payment. Please bear with us. If it takes too long, you may send some writeups.*

As remuneration, some funds can be transferred to your bank.

After reading the message, Godbole felt concerned. Wasn't the mention of 'Law' an oblique reference to his team, which had made inquiries in Rameswaram? The one, his team, had approached in Rameswaram could be Rolex himself or someone from Rolex's smuggling ring. Ultimately, the ruffian smugglers proved loyal to their shady customers. The message also indicated that the Chinese were preparing to carry something out of India. What could that cargo be? Now that the Chinese side had been alerted, the team must deploy a different strategy for any operation in Rameswaram.

Godbole returned the memory card to Mohan and said, "Please keep it with you and store it as you do. Frankly, it is disgusting to handle the lump somebody had chewed."

"Do not worry, sir. They had assured me that it was not chewing gum. It just looks as if people will be deterred from picking it up."

Godbole silently admired the Chinese ingenuity. Showing a business-like attitude, he said, "Go through the instructions on the card and follow them fully without giving room for any suspicion. Act normally, as if this episode did not happen at all. One of us will drop you near the library; you can go home from there."

Initially, Mohan was in disbelief. As the fact sank in, he sighed as though a heavy burden had gotten off his shoulders.

Meanwhile, Godbole continued, "The officer coming to drop you off will explain what is expected of you and how to communicate with us. He will also give you other detailed instructions tomorrow."

"I will do all that you want me to do... but..." Mohan stopped abruptly.

"But what?" Godbole asked.

"Sir, please take care that I am not seen with you or your

people in public. I feel that one person keeps a watch on me at random times."

"Mohan, have you noticed anyone?"

"Yes, sir. In the past two months after Hemant's death, I have seen a tall and slightly stout person at the library on three occasions. He comes to the library before me and leaves as soon as I enter. He must be making sure that I collect the card. He is not Chinese, maybe a local man."

"Oh, I see."

"Sir, he was there today. I met him near the main gate of the library."

Godbole was taken aback. Was the person Pande tried to check the one Mohan was talking about? "What was he wearing today?"

"Sir, I think a T-shirt and blue jeans."

A chill passed through Godbole's spine. If that person had been watching Mohan, he would have been more critical than Mohan. Trailing him would have yielded vital information on the Chinese ring. The team lost an excellent opportunity. However, Godbole believed in the saying, 'You cannot get all the eggs you find in the field.' Since they were focused on Mohan, it would not have been possible to go after that man merely on suspicion. Even then, Godbole felt relieved that the person had not noticed him checking the Tibetology section and examining the chewing gum lump.

"Don't worry, Mohan," Godbole said.

"I am grateful, sir. I do not know how to thank you."

"Mohan, tomorrow at 10 a.m., come and stand near Counter No.5 of the ticket reservation centre at the Old Delhi Railway Station. The same officer will meet you there and take you for a detailed briefing. We will provide you with a simple cell phone... not a smartphone. This phone is programmed to dial only one number – our phone number. Please note that anyone on my team will answer your call because we will get the alerts when you call.

Text messages can also be sent. Please cooperate. A last point – switch on your phone only after you cross the library area."

"Okay, sir."

"Do you have a set of spare keys for your Mumbai apartment?"

"I do."

"Then bring them tomorrow. When you come tomorrow, be prepared to tell us all you know about Hemant and Rolex. Also, call Banerji at your convenience today or tomorrow and tell him to hold back your article. Tell him you will submit a revised article with more information. This is priority. I hope you understand."

"Yes, sir. The apartment keys, details on Rolex and Hemant, and speaking to Banerji... I will not forget."

"Good. One more thing... be conscious that you will be under our constant watch. If you attempt to double-cross us, we will know... and we'll not be forgiving."

"I'll never do that, sir."

Godbole signalled Riaz, who escorted Mohan out of the room. After they left, Godbole leaned back in the chair and thought of the tall person they had seen at the library. They would have to catch up with him as soon as possible.

Godbole turned to his team and said, "Please wind up. Tomorrow, after Mohan gives us the spare keys, three of us will proceed to Mumbai. I will request Amit to book our flight tickets for tomorrow afternoon. We can start our work by Saturday morning," Godbole continued. "I know the police have sealed that apartment, but we will explore how we can avail ourselves of an opportunity to search it. Riaz will wait here to keep an eye on Mohan."

As Pande and Talreja nodded in approval, Godbole added, "We have to be back before Thursday. There is a high probability of that person coming to the library on Thursday to stick a new memory card." Godbole gave final instructions to his team as they left the room.

Chapter – 7
The Vacant Home

Mumbai
October 31, 2020
10.30 a.m.

It had been almost half an hour since Godbole had been waiting at the police station in eastern Dahisar, a northwest suburb of Mumbai. Since Hemant's apartment fell under the jurisdiction of that police station, Godbole had taken an appointment to meet the station-in-charge, Inspector Ghorpade. Talreja and Pande were left to recce the area where Hemant's apartment was located.

The atmosphere at the police station was thick with activity, suffocating under the weight of officers bustling in and out, detainees in handcuffs, and a crowd of people awaiting various official procedures. The air buzzed with conversations, punctuated by the occasional shrill ring of telephones. It was evident that the station's resources were stretched thin, leaving little room for the meticulous investigation of cases like Hemant's murder.

At last, when Godbole was called in, it was half past noon. Despite his stout figure and impressive uniform, Inspector Ghorpade looked tired and harassed. Before Godbole could take his seat, the Inspector's phone rang. For the next ten minutes, he was on the phone explaining to someone the progress of a case.

"My apologies for waiting, Mr Godbole. Here, things are so tough that sparing even a minute becomes difficult," Ghorpade said and laughed wryly.

"No issue, Inspector. I know how difficult it is," Godbole said.

"So you are here to know details of the murder case in Sunflower Apartments. When you called this morning, I wanted to tell you it was a dud case.It has become a headache for me. We cannot have a murder case unsolved for months, and bosses are unhappy."

"Why is the case difficult to solve?"

"This fellow... Hemant Khanna... no one claimed his body. We're unable to locate any of his relatives. He stayed in that flat for almost two years. Yet, no one in the neighbourhood knew him well. He kept himself aloof. Neighbours say he had no regular visitors. To top it all, we didn't find his cell phone."

"I see," Godbole said.

"There were no break-in signs. That night, Hemant seemed to have opened the door for the killer. He died of a single shot just above his right ear. None of his neighbours heard the sound of the gunshot. Nothing from the house was robbed. The small almirah, a wooden shelf, and a couple of travel bags in the house were not tampered with. It's a complete dead end, but my seniors are at my throat. They want me to solve the murder case soon. And... you know how busy we are with all sorts of work," Ghorpade said, throwing up his hands.

"I can understand," Godbole said.

"By the way, is there any chance this case will go to your central agency?"

"I don't think so, Inspector."

"Then, why is this enquiry? Anything special?"

"We have no interest in this murder case. We are only checking about this person... you said he is Hemant Khanna. Wanted to know if he has any connections with any of the cases we are probing."

"We have no details about this man's background. Not even a basic clue. But the case keeps festering. You know, after we sealed the apartment, there were two attempts to break into that empty house. Somehow, they failed."

Godbole found it disturbing. If there were attempts to break into that empty house, there was surely something valuable inside. Were the Chinese trying to retrieve something left behind in the house? He asked Ghorpade, "Can we have a look at this apartment?"

"I wonder what you can dig up from there!" Ghorpade said. "Anyway, I may need permission from above to break the seal. Besides, an officer of the Deputy Superintendent rank must be present when someone inspects the sealed premises. A week will be the shortest time to meet these formalities in these busy times."

Godbole was disappointed. As he was trying to explore a way to get access to the apartment, Ghorpade said, "You, the central agency guys, have more time and resources than us and can do a good job. You see... if it were in my power, I would have helped you. I badly need this case to be solved."

"I understand. In my case, too, it's important. I need to inspect the apartment, but as I said, it is not to solve the murder. It is solely to determine the linkages of the dead man. It is essential to do it as quietly as possible and without attracting attention. If I can enter the apartment, I believe it can help both of us."

"But how?"

"You may have to play a role... just a passive role. It would be helpful if you tackled the seal, including your signature, on the attached paper. Rest, I'll do... discreetly."

As Ghorpade debated the offer, Godbole tried to reason, "We are circumventing a minor rule for the larger good. Remember, our intentions are morally correct. We are not looking to manipulate evidence. That is how I look at it."

Ghorpade sat blankly, tapping his fingers on the file on the table. Then he got up from his chair, crossed the table, and came and sat near Godbole. "Mr Godbole, I guess this is a high-profile case... otherwise, you wouldn't be insisting."

"You're right, Inspector, but I cannot explain things now. You have waited for two months already. Please wait for two more weeks. I shall see to it that you get due credit."

"I get it. I hope you'll manage this operation at your own risk. My role begins after your work in the apartment is over. I have to place a new wax seal with my signature, appending the original date."

"Yes. That's what I want."

Glancing at the calendar on the wall, Ghorpade asked, "When do you intend to do this?"

"Tonight... late tonight, positively. Tomorrow is a Sunday, and that suits us. People tend to sleep longer into the morning."

"That's true. So, tomorrow early morning, I will go there as part of a routine check and quietly set up the seal."

"Yes. That's all."

"But the issue is that you will need the apartment keys. The keys are sealed and kept in the station locker."

"Do not bother. I have a duplicate set."

Ghorpade looked at Godbole with admiration. "Well, Mr Godbole, in that case, it looks okay. Now, I need not tell you to do a clean job without alerting the neighbours."

"Be assured," Godbole emphasized.

"Just one question. You could have done it if you had been confident about doing it quietly. Why involve me?"

"We can do it, but it will become newsworthy if the seal is not found intact. The tabloids and newspapers will report the break-in, and the culprits will be alerted. We don't want that to happen."

"Yes, indeed. That's smart!"

Ghorpade went back to his chair and ordered tea. While having tea, Ghorpade briefed Godbole about every detail of the apartment, security, and neighbourhood. Ghorpade asked, "We were strangers. How did you gather the confidence to put this proposal before me?"

"Frankly, I always do some homework. I had enquired about you with one of my contacts. I was satisfied with what he said about you," Godbole said with a smile.

"Good luck, friend," Ghorpade wished Godbole with gusto.

*****

Godbole studied the maps and Pande's charts of the area where the Sunflower Apartments building was situated. The structure, a modest ground-plus-seven-story tower nestled in a middle-class neighbourhood, revealed itself in his mind's eye. He visualized the stilt parking area, the quaint garden, and the lively children's play zone, all enclosed by a modest six-foot compound wall. Inspector Ghorpade's intel painted a picture of minimal security – just two guards stationed, one at the gate and the other multitasking in the lobby and lift operation. There were twenty-eight apartments spread over seven floors. Mohan's apartment was on the third floor. While recceing the apartment area, Pande and Talreja shortlisted two points along the compound wall from where the team could attempt to enter the premises.

At about 1:15 a.m., the team carrying their backpacks arrived in a rented SUV and parked it about two hundred fifty metres away. The team walked towards the building through the poorly lit street. As they reached a sprawling tree that blocked even the available light, Godbole and Pande waited there in the darkness. The tree, being close to the compound wall of the Sunflower Apartments, was one of the spots they had selected to get into the compound. Just opposite that spot, on the other side of the road, was a parked truck.

Meanwhile, Talreja stealthily walked along the compound wall and came close to the locked iron gate. Talreja stretched to peer into the security guard's cabin. Looking through the glass window, he saw a security guard relaxing in a plastic chair with his feet on the table. Whispering into his microphone, Talreja said, "The guard is in the cabin... relaxing. All clear."

"Okay, be there to ensure the guard is in the cabin till we enter the compound."

Godbole and Pande were geared up in seconds with hand gloves, a hood, and a cloth mask. As Pande sat leaning against the wall, Godbole kept his foot on Pande's shoulder and climbed the wall. He then assisted Pande in climbing by pulling him up. Both touched down inside the premises.

"We're in," Godbole softly said into the microphone.

"The guard is still in the cabin," Talreja whispered back.

"Now come... quick," Godbole said.

Talreja returned to the spot near the tree and prepared to scale the wall. Suddenly, he saw the headlights of an approaching vehicle. He instantly hid behind the tree trunk. He saw a car stopping to find a parking place. He waited with bated breath. Soon, the vehicle was parked in a poorly lit area on the opposite side of the road. After a while, a tall figure alighted from the car and walked towards the gate of the Sunflower Apartments. The man approached the security cabin. He gently tried to wake the security guard, but the guard did not notice the visitor.

Talreja wanted to alert Godbole and Pande to wait inside the compound. Before Talreja could speak, Godbole asked over the wireless, "What's the delay?"

"There's a person at the gate who just arrived in a car," Talreja whispered.

"At this time! He cannot be a visitor. Maybe a resident," Godbole said.

"But he has parked his car on the other side of the road. I did not see the confidence of a resident in him. He is trying to wake up the security guard. We need to be alert and hidden till he goes away."

"We will manage that. You, too, remain out of sight. But keep us informed of his movements," Godbole said.

Godbole and Pande took position in the stilt area facing the lobby and waited there for the danger to pass.

Talreja saw the guard approaching the gate while talking to the visitor. The guard kept looking around while talking. Possibly, the guard knew the visitor. In a short while, the visitor put his hands in his pocket and gave something to the guard, who just shoved it into his pocket without checking. Was it money? Did the visitor bribe the guard to enter the building? There was something fishy. Godbole had mentioned two robbery attempts in Hemant's flat. Was that person also on a mission to enter Hemant's flat? Would the team be forced to abort the operation? Talreja did not want that to happen. He quickly crossed the road and stood behind the parked truck.

Meanwhile, the guard hurriedly entered the cabin and returned to the gate with something, probably the keys. As the guard tried to open the gate lock, Talreja stood behind the truck and momentarily flashed his torchlight at the gate. The visitor suddenly turned and ran to his car. Strangely, the guard did not venture to check the source of the light. Instead, the guard rushed into his cabin. It was enough to conclude that something illegal was taking place. By that time, the visitor had sped away in his car. Since his team was inside the compound, Talreja could not have ventured to follow the visitor. With the guard now alert, their operation was in jeopardy. Talreja briefed Godbole and sought his instructions.

"What if the visitor returns? Please be there to keep a close watch and alert us in case of danger. I am reluctant to call off the operation... not as yet. We will wait for a while and see if we can proceed... even if it is risky," Godbole said.

The guard remained in his cabin. The flashlight might have rattled him. Probably, he thought it was the police on patrol duty. Godbole was getting impatient. Since the visitor did not return by 1:50 a.m., Pande and Godbole proceeded with their plan.

First, Pande tried to look for the second guard in the lobby. The guard's chair was empty. When he quietly moved towards the entrance, he saw the guard sleeping on a sheet of cloth on the floor near the lift. He signalled Godbole to join him.

Soon, the team tiptoed towards the staircase and reached the apartment door on the third floor. In the gloomy light from a tube light in the lobby, they could see the wax seal stuck on the door with a signed paper covering the keyhole of the door latch. Pande knelt, swiftly broke the seal, and tore the signed paper. Godbole collected the broken wax and bits of paper in his palms to ensure there was no sign of a break-in. When the keyhole was exposed, Godbole inserted the key. The two quietly entered the apartment.

Since switching on the lights was out of the question, they wore night vision goggles and used tiny flashlights whenever required. The five-hundred-and-fifty-square-foot apartment had a drawing room, a bedroom, a kitchen area, and a washroom. It was sparsely furnished with an ordinary sofa set in the front room and a cot in the bedroom. The bedroom also had a wooden shelf, a five-foot steel almirah, and two travel bags. On the front room floor, there were white markings made by the police denoting the spot where Hemant's body was lying. As the Inspector had said, nothing in the house was disturbed. It was apparent that the person had only one aim that night – eliminating Hemant.

Godbole and Pande spread out and quietly combed every inch of the apartment. They looked for documents, photographs, electronic equipment, or other items that could explain who Hemant was and what he was doing. The open wooden shelf and the two travel bags had nothing incriminating. Then, they opened the locked steel almirah using their manoeuvrable master key. The almirah had three racks. The middle and top racks had some personal clothes. On the bottom rack, he found a cardboard box sealed with cello tape. On opening, Godbole found a few rectangular bundles. He removed the night vision goggles and switched on his flashlight. He saw three new bundles of five-hundred-rupee notes and one bundle of one-hundred-rupee notes. Godbole pulled out a five-hundred-rupee note and a one-hundred-rupee note and kept them in his backpack. He wanted to check if those notes were genuine. He replaced the box on the bottom rack.

Godbole was not content. Was that money the only valuable thing in the flat for which the unknown persons tried to break-in? If it were the Chinese cohorts, they would not have tried to get into the apartment just for that money. Godbole decided to scan the premises once again. Before starting the second round of search, he checked with Talreja.

"The guard appears to be restless," Talreja said. "He keeps coming out of his cabin frequently and waits near the gate. He is at his cabin or the gate, not going anywhere else. After all, the visitor paid him something. Maybe he expects the visitor to return. I'm alert," Talreja assured.

Exiting the bedroom to continue the search, Godbole saw Pande examining the kitchen. Standing near the kitchen, Godbole tried to recount the areas they might have missed.

In moments, Godbole's attention fell on the loft over the bathroom. Placed on the loft was a square white water storage tank. He removed his goggles and flashed the light. The water tank occupied the entire loft area, and there was no space to keep anything hidden there. As he stood thinking with the flashlight switched on, he saw an extended cut at the back of the tank. If water were there in the tank, it should flow out. He ran his fingers along the cut portion. The tank's backside opened with a slight pull at the cut portion. Godbole asked Pande to bring the sofa chair. Standing on the armrest of the chair, Godbole peeped in. He saw a box inside. When he pulled the tank, he realized that the tank was just a façade. Through the opening, he pulled out the box.

It was an aluminium chest, two feet long, one foot wide, and one foot tall. The chest was locked with a brass padlock. The face of the padlock had a brand marking – *'Umeed'*. As he turned the lock, he noticed Umeed engraved in Urdu. Considering how the box was kept concealed, he expected something important in the box. Although the team tried to open the padlock, their master key did not fit in the strange keyhole. Finally, they opened the box by removing the riveted screws and taking away the hinges of the top cover. Godbole saw the contents and smiled. The box contained a laptop, its charging cord, a Jio-serviced Wi-Fi device, a USB connector cord, and a used cell phone. He carefully placed all the items in his backpack. He saw a couple of folded sheets of paper at the bottom of the box and promptly stuffed them in his backpack.

Godbole and Pande had spent almost thirty minutes there. They needed to leave before the guard in the lobby got up. They quickly replaced the box in the tank. After ensuring everything in the house was as before, the team rushed out. Godbole hoped Inspector Ghorpade would fix the wax seal before someone took notice of it missing. They tiptoed down the stairs towards the ground-floor lobby. Pande leaned to check on the guard. Luckily, the guard was still deep in slumber.

In the hotel room, Godbole sighed in relief. It had been a tense operation. He was happy that despite the incident at the gate, he had gone ahead. However, had the mysterious visitor succeeded in entering the building, the team would have been in trouble. Luckily, Talreja spotted the person and saved the day.

While Pande and Talreja retired for the night, Godbole was not yet ready to rest. He wanted to check the items. Since the laptop, the Wi-Fi device, and the phone needed forensic examination, Godbole did not venture to examine those items. But he was eager to glance through the folded sheets of paper to see if they were valuable.

As Godbole opened the folded sheets, a photograph fell from them. The photo had a woman wearing a headscarf and two children, both girls, probably aged between seven and nine years. It seemed like a Muslim family. How was Hemant connected to them, Godbole wondered. He then opened the folded paper. It was a handwritten letter in Urdu. He was unsure if he still had the mastery over Urdu he had had during his training days several years ago. Yet he was confident of understanding what was written in the letter.

He started reading the letter. Even before he completed the first few sentences, he sat up straight. The three-page letter was from a wife to her husband. It was passionate, touching and, of course, had important information. Godbole wanted to underline some portions of the letter that needed to be focused on unravelling Hemant's identity. However, he refrained from doing so since the letter was required to be submitted at NES-17 for detailed analysis.

> *'I know this letter will surprise you, but dear, I wanted to pour out my feelings without anyone in between... Javed is a good boy; he types and sends you everything I tell him. He also reads out your messages to me sincerely. But a letter is different. That is why I took the trouble to chase Abid Bhai when I heard he was going to your side. Initially, he was reluctant, saying it would be difficult to meet Arshad. Somehow, later, he agreed to carry the letter. I am thrilled that I could write to you at least once. But you do not take the risk of writing to me. You keep sending your computer messages to Javed once a month. It is better to have your computer messages than live without knowing anything*

about you. I know how difficult it had been in the first two years when we had no communication from you. At the same time, I am concerned that you are sending the messages to Javed from the computer you have managed to retain without their knowledge. Is there any risk in this? I am always worried about you and will remain so until you return. You had said it was a three-year assignment. If so, you should return to my arms in two or three months. Always think of our two beautiful girls, for whom you took this big risk. May Allah take care of you.'

So, Hemant was the pseudonym of Arshad, a Pakistani in India who was on an assignment. Was he a Pakistani intelligence operative loaned out to the Chinese? Chinese operatives' constraints in India might have forced them to look for a Pakistani to handle open functions like coordinating with different assets. From what NES-17 knew, Hemant, now Arshad, was a crucial link in the Chinese network. Arshad had erred. He was not supposed to communicate with his family. Yet, he did so under emotional pressure, using a laptop provided by the Chinese. Probably, that was why he kept the computer hidden. Godbole thought about Abid Bhai, who had brought Arshad's letter to India. Could he still be operating in India?

Arshad's wife and children eagerly awaited his homecoming, but he would not be returning. The anguish of his family would be unimaginable. But it was a typical tragedy that spies and intelligence operatives of any nationality could end up with. The system would brush aside that collateral damage. Only the concerned family would be left to face the loss. Arshad might have been an adversary, but anyone laying down their life in the line of duty commanded respect. Godbole closed his eyes in prayer.

Myriad thoughts kept Godbole awake. Some details about 'Hemant' emerged from the search at his apartment, but tracing

Hemant's handlers and contacts in his absence would be challenging. Anyway, the laptop and the used phone might hold some leads, Godbole hoped. Just then, the cell phone rang. It was 5:30 a.m., and the call was from Inspector Ghorpade.

"Good morning, Mr Godbole," Ghorpade said. "I went early and fixed the seal."

"Oh, good. Thank you," Godbole said.

"I pretended I was on a surprise check. While my constable kept both guards engaged in the main lobby, I went to the third floor. You seem to have done a clean job, I should say."

"Yes, we were careful."

"Well, I won't ask you what you got from there, but was it worth the trouble?"

"Of course," Godbole said. "I think it was useful. I expect to solve your case, but give me some time. And a big thank you for all the help," Godbole said.

Before ending the call, Godbole briefed Ghorpade about the incident at the gate and asked him to keep a watch on the security guard.

"You are welcome, always. Thank you for the tip on the guard. I shall take care of it tactfully."

Godbole was happy that Inspector Ghorpade had kept his word. Now, no one would know about their break-in. It had been a fruitful day for the team.

Relieved, Godbole wanted to get some sleep, but he had one more thing to do. He texted Amit Rao requesting that he book their tickets to return to Delhi that evening. Finally, he sent another text message to Das, cryptically informing him about the operation and his return journey, before falling into a deep slumber.

Chapter – 8
Flamingo

New Delhi
November 2, 2020
10 a.m.

After a gruelling three-day mission in Mumbai, Godbole and his team returned to Delhi late on Sunday night. The following morning, he was eager to send the crucial evidence for forensic examination and analysis. Upon reaching the office, Godbole promptly met his superior, Das, and handed over the laptop, the Wi-Fi device, the cell phone, the two currency notes, and the letter written in Urdu, all of which held the potential to unravel the mystery they were chasing.

While examining the items, Das said, "Great Yash. Another remarkable operation..."

"Yes, it's been a smooth run so far. But I know that luck can't always be on our side. I'm ready for the unexpected moves the Chinese might make," Godbole replied, his smile masking the underlying tension.

"You think it was just luck?" Das asked in a serious tone. "I know it looked easy because of your brilliant planning, timing and execution. You knew when to go to the LAC to spot Lote and rescue Dorjee. You did not hesitate to think about what to do next when encountering the chewing gum in the library. The visitor at Hemant's apartment had all the potential to endanger your work, but Yash, you and your team can weather the toughest storm."

Was this appreciation or merely a boss's pep talk, Godbole wondered.

Das and Godbole soon began serious discussions. Discovering Arshad, a Pakistani national masquerading as Hemant, was a significant breakthrough. Arshad was probably a trained Pakistani intelligence agent assigned to help the Chinese. The letter from Arshad's wife made it abundantly clear how stringent the security precautions were. The Chinese needed men who looked like Indians to carry out their tasks without arousing suspicion in India.

"Abid Bhai, mentioned in the letter, could also be a Pakistani operator working for the Chinese," Godbole noted. Abid knew Arshad and even met him. It wouldn't have been possible if they weren't working together. Now we need to hunt for Abid..."

Das nodded. "The laptop and other electronic items might hold valuable information. We'll have to wait for the technical team to examine them."

They also discussed the situation at the LAC. Following Dorjee's rescue, the Indian Army observed the Chinese visiting the PP-6 area almost every other day. Godbole speculated that the increased Chinese vigilance was more about protecting their tech centre than Dorjee's rescue. Brig Kedar had mentioned concerns about the tech installation that the Chinese had built close to the Indian side. For now, the Army decided to lie low. Periodic evaluations of developments at the LAC kept the Army ready for action.

As their meeting drew to a close, Das brought up Kanak Mohan. Riaz has spent some time with Mohan. He's cooperating but still scared of the Chinese. He's tense about the coming Thursday."

"I expect the person who planted the memory card to visit the library on Thursday," Godbole said, his voice filled with anticipation. "The Chinese are troubled by developments in Rameswaram. Their last message hinted at giving Mohan some work this week."

After the discussion, Das proceeded to the cyber lab with the electronic items brought from Mumbai.

*****

November 4, 2020

That Wednesday morning, Godbole was unusually busy at his desk. He was preparing to take his team to the Delhi Public Library the next day to tail the man who'd come to plant the gum. The plan was to follow the suspect discreetly and gather intelligence. Godbole knew the field's unpredictability; the person might work alone or in a group. He sketched various scenarios and responses for each situation. Two teams were planned: the first, including Godbole and Kamini Dube, would monitor inside the library. Kamini, fitting seamlessly into the setting, would keep a watch from the reading section. The second team, a three-member unit, would wait outside in a car, ready to trail and house the suspect. As Godbole gave his plan the final touches, Das entered.

"Yash, the lab has made some findings. Firstly, the currency notes are genuine. The money might be for funding their operations."

Godbole shrugged disinterestedly. He was keen to learn about the gadgets. "What about the phone instrument, the Wi-Fi device and the laptop?"

Das said, "The 'cell phone' isn't a phone. It's a device that looks like one but works on Wi-Fi to access the internet. The lab guys charged it and turned it on without an internet connection. The screen showed a picture of a flamingo. It only has two apps: Google Maps and 'Chess II'. Google Maps might work, but Chess II is disabled. Experts believe Chess II might be navigation software. Essentially, it's a dedicated navigation instrument with maps."

Godbole frowned. "A navigation device? Why would the Chinese use it here?"

"Yash, they could not test the app because they feared the Chinese might discover if the device became internet-connected.

They're planning to test it in secure conditions with a lab-designed net system," Das explained. He handed two sheets of paper to Godbole and added, "All details and specifications are here. It is a Chinese-made device with Chinese markings... have a look."

Godbole read the note on that sheet and recalled Mohan's article on India's alleged faulty missile guidance system. Mohan had inferred that Indian missiles were prone to navigation failure. Godbole suspected some uncanny connection between the Chinese navigation device and Mohan's article. But he realized that he was holding back Das from his briefing.

"Sorry, sir, I drifted for a moment," Godbole said.

Das knew Godbole too well to believe that he had tuned off. He sensed Godbole's sharp mind had caught on to something. He continued briefing.

"You know, the Wi-Fi router you found in Arshad's house is active, and the subscription is paid for regularly. It is a Jio Wi-Fi service registered under the name Eastern Rainbow Tours, a Delhi-based travel service."

"Did the lab procure the usage logs of the Wi-Fi?"

"Yes, indeed. The Wi-Fi device was active in Arunachal Pradesh. More specifically, the data was used in some places in the Tawang sector for six days in November 2019, seven days in December 2019, and five days in March 2020. After that, the device was not used for a couple of months. Then, it was used only in Mumbai once or twice a month from June to early September 2020."

Godbole tapped on his desk and said, "The Mumbai part is easiest to understand. Arshad might have used the Wi-Fi in Mumbai to communicate with his wife. The Chinese would not have wanted Arshad to do that, and they might have found out."

"Was he killed for this security breach?" Das asked.

"Perhaps, but the Tawang data worries me more," Godbole said.

"Exactly. We have to figure this out."

"My thoughts are... if the Chinese sent this Wi-Fi device to Arunachal along with the phone-like navigation device, it would be a serious matter indeed," Godbole said. "They may have sent it in three short spells in November, December 2019, and March 2020, but it was a dedicated operation focusing only on the Tawang area. I am uncomfortable seeing this in the background of the tech centre near the Chinese village of Tangma across the Tawang sector. I am thinking aloud..."

"I know what you mean, and I have the same worry," Das said.

"What about the laptop?"

"It is a normal Lenovo brand laptop. Its hard disc was partitioned into two separate sections. The first partition has all the apps and functions a usual laptop has... for everyday use. The second partition has the Chess II app, which might be the same as the one the navigation device had. Another app, Flamingo, appeared to be a navigation data analysis app. But the app is disabled," Das explained.

"Sir, this is rather interesting. Could it be that the Flamingo app was to analyze the data sent from the navigation device? After all, you said the navigation device opened with the picture of a flamingo."

"The lab people are working on this, but there has been no breakthrough... If I may add, the laptop's Wi-Fi connection history showed that it was connected to two Wi-Fi services; one was named 'Walking Friend' and the other 'Cannery'. While we could confirm that 'Walking Friend' was the name they assigned to that Jio Wi-Fi service, we have no clue about 'Cannery'. Now, from what I have explained, do you have any observations to make?" Das asked.

"I have a few hunches: First, this navigation device could be the one the Chinese sent to India with Lote in October last year. The size of the device and the time of its delivery would only strengthen my view. If you remember, Kanak Mohan admitted that he had visited the Tawang monastery to collect a parcel from a local there. He handed over the parcel to Hemant, i.e. Arshad."

"You're right. We are now getting somewhere," Das said.

"I will sum up my thinking. All those Chinese gadgets we discussed are related to GPS and navigation systems. But why? Are the Chinese doing something in that field in a sensitive area of the LAC? Are they attempting to tamper with the navigation and GPS signals at the LAC? Doesn't the Chinese tech centre in Tangma become relevant in this context?" Godbole asked.

Das did not utter a word.

"Sir, there's another point I want to make. I believe the whole issue is also related to Mohan's write-up on the allegedly faulty missile guidance system used by the Indian Army. In all probability, those gadgets and the Chinese tech centre might be intended to manipulate GPS signals to misguide Indian missiles and fighter jets. Mohan's article aims to divert our attention from the problem and make us believe that our missile system is defective. Pretty smart, no?"

"There is substance in what you say. You know, Yash, Brig Kedar disclosed that two of the IAF jets flying near the Tawang area had experienced navigational problems on the day of the power outage in Mumbai last month. We have to work on this ..."

"Sir, I know it is premature to conclude so, but I feel the Chinese are equipped with GPS manipulation technology, and the tech centre in the Chinese village of Tangma near LAC might be the controlling centre of this secret activity," Godbole almost whispered the last few words. He continued, "Flamingos have an accurate navigational capacity to fly across continents to reach suitable climates. I want to see this Flamingo app decoded."

"Yash, you are a master of connecting dots. My line of thinking was similar," Das said. He fished out a piece of paper from his shirt pocket and added, "Here's what I thought of the possibilities, and it's more or less identical."

Godbole eagerly read Das's note.

Continuing the discussion, Das said, "However, we have encountered a difficulty. Our field staff located the Eastern Rainbow Tours, but the company categorically denied subscribing to a Wi-Fi device from the Jio Internet service. Someone had forged their papers to avail of the Jio service. Therefore, knowing who toured the Tawang area to operate the navigation device has become difficult. Maybe it was Arshad because the electronic devices were in his possession."

"Possibly Arshad... I agree. Arshad may have been sent to the Tawang sector in November, December 2019, and March 2020 for testing," Godbole said.

"Anyhow, our technical team is doing their best. Yash, you know it is not the Chess II and Flamingo apps; it is the hardware and the technology in the devices that they find challenging. And then... look at their stealthy working style backed by innovative methods! They avoid direct communication with each other. If they all have to communicate, they do it from foreign locations, assisted by clandestine sites in cyberspace. It makes penetrating their ring tough."

"Well, sir, this is a technology-driven battle... a difficult battle. Their activities in Tawang, Rameswaram, Bangalore, Mumbai, and Delhi may be part of a coordinated effort to hurt India. Yet, I think the Chinese have made a big mistake. The help they are taking from the Pakis can lead us to their underbelly," Godbole said and chuckled.

Das said, "Let's hope so. I'll take my leave. I shall brief you when the lab has more."

As Das left, Godbole pondered the details Das mentioned to him about the three electronic gadgets, and quietly scribbled those critical points on his notepad.

Chapter – 9
The Dead Watch

New Delhi
November 5, 2020
12 p.m.

A week ago, when Godbole picked up the chewing gum from the library around 3 p.m., it was still moist and sticky. It might have been placed there in the early afternoon, suggesting a consistent time that they followed to plant the gum. With that in mind, Godbole and his team arrived at the library by noon, their steps measured and purposeful, yet they delayed taking up their positions until 12:45 p.m., heightening the anticipation. Their mission was clear: identify and tail the target, a task for which they were well-prepared. They were not to stop or detain the target. Godbole wanted his entire team to see the target they would have to deal with in the future.

First, Vilas Pande and Abul Riaz, the surveillance experts, parked their SUV at a strategic spot close to the library gate. Talreja, the vigilant lookout, stood some distance from the main gate, ensuring an uninterrupted view of the entry point. After that, Kamini moved to the reading area in the library. Upon receiving a signal, she was to proceed to the Tibetology section to film the target using a concealed video camera. Godbole, the elusive strategist, dodged the lady receptionist and slipped in. He also kept an eye out for anyone who had unexpectedly appeared in the library during their previous surveillance of Mohan last Thursday.

The team was prepared to communicate via wireless microphones. This allowed Kamini to be ready with her concealed video recorder. The team was confident. There were about fifty people in the sprawling library, and the place was quiet.

At 1:40 p.m., Talreja noticed a lady driving through the gate in a Maruti car. She parked in an open slot, scanned her surroundings from the driver's seat, and stepped out, wearing sunglasses, blue jeans, and a black T-shirt. Considering her features, was she a Tibetan woman? Talreja's curiosity piqued. Her mysterious demeanour and unexpected arrival added another layer of intrigue to the operation. Would she be the one sticking the memory card for Mohan?

Talreja had no time to waste, as the lady was already heading towards the library entrance. He whispered into the microphone, "TGT- F... watch the entrance."

Godbole did not expect a lady to be their target. However, as a matter of caution, she had to be watched. As she entered the library, he softly spoke into his mouthpiece, "TGT... in."

Godbole's message was explicitly meant to alert Kamini. She promptly responded, "TGT in sight."

Meanwhile, Godbole noticed the lady walking towards the Tibetology section. Suddenly, the lady stopped short of the bookshelf where the card was supposed to be placed. She stood there for a second and hurriedly turned back. Godbole noticed that she swiftly walked back towards the exit. Why was she retreating? Did she sense danger?

As the lady crossed the reception, Godbole wondered what had gone wrong. The target would be lost in minutes with the memory card. Godbole had to make a split-second decision: Should he let the target go or stop her? Apprehending her early in the operation would have implications, but the time was too short to debate.

Godbole whispered into the microphone, "Tee... code seven right now."

"Yes, sir... charging!" Talreja almost shouted.

As the lady hurriedly unlocked the car and settled in the driver's seat, Talreja appeared suddenly, opening the other door and landing beside her. Before she could react, Talreja pressed a pistol against her waist. "No shouting, no resistance... if you want to live, do as I say."

Her silence was immediate, though her eyes reflected her internal debate. Talreja continued, "Just drive me to a safe place, and I'll let you go."

The lady, confused, asked, "Who are you? What are you..." Before she could finish, Talreja interrupted, "Be quick. The cops are following me."

The lady's expression changed as she turned on the ignition. As the car started moving, she asked, "Are you sure the cops are after you? I mean, they are chasing you?"

"Do not chatter... You silly woman. I will not hesitate to shoot you. If you don't want to get hurt, drive fast. Their car is already following us... look!"

By that time, Godbole and the team were behind the lady's car. Seeing the rushing SUV behind her car, the lady became fearful.

"Where do I take the car? I am unfamiliar with the roads here," she said, panicking.

"Take the first left, and then I'll guide you. We'll dodge them soon. Drive fast."

Being early afternoon, the road was not crowded. She was sweating as she tried to focus on the road and avoid bumping into other vehicles. The lady was convinced that the cops were chasing the ruffian sitting beside her. Talreja guided her to an internal road off Lalwani Road. The SUV was not behind them anymore, and the lady finally relaxed. In about twenty-five minutes, they reached the gates of a housing complex. He instructed her to proceed and park the car in the visitor parking. She noticed that the security men at the gate did not stop them. She thought they were either negligent or familiar with the ruffian.

"Now what?" she asked after parking the car. Talreja put the gun in his pants' pocket. With one hand on the concealed gun, he said, "Please get down."

"Where are you taking me?"

"We have only temporarily dodged the police. You cannot drive out immediately."

"I will leave the car. It is a rented car."

"Do you think the cops are dumb?"

"But I need to go; I have work to do."

"Look, if you want to be questioned by the police, you can go. They will detain you at least temporarily for questioning. I would suggest you stay here for another hour, and then you can go."

As the confused lady kept looking at Talreja, he continued, "This is my den. I have my men here. You can breathe easy."

Talreja was sure that the lady wanted to avoid the police. He got out of the car, opened her door and quickly led her to the fourth-floor apartment. When the attendant opened the door, she hesitated to enter. Talreja sternly insisted. Ultimately, she entered, and when she settled into the sofa chair, Talreja asked the attendant to serve her tea.

"I'll just have water... You have spoiled my work. I had to complete it before 3 p.m. Now, I can't get to the library before three. All because of you."

" But were you not leaving that place when I caught you?"

"I don't owe you any explanation," the lady said, going silent. Her frustration and anger were evident on her face. Talreja quietly watched her, waiting for Godbole and the team to join them.

"What was your work in the library?"

"It does not concern you a bit."

"You know... I believed you were also running away from the police, right?"

The lady looked sharply at Talreja but did not answer. As Talreja tried to guess her thoughts, she said, "My guess about the police was correct. I still feel that the cops were looking for me."

"How are you so sure?" Talreja asked.

"I have wireless transmission detector pods for my ears, friend. They are not to listen to music. When I got out of the car at the library, I heard a burst of short wireless messages. When I reached the entrance, I heard another message. The third message was when I was about to reach the Tibetology section. All three messages coincided with the progress I made from the time I got out of the car. So, I am sure they were reporting my movements. They were looking for me."

As Talreja tried to conceal his amazement, she added, "That is why I accompanied you to your den. Otherwise, I know how to tackle small gangsters like you; I can do that quite well." She smirked, pulling a sleek six-inch pistol from her pouch and placing it in her palm before returning it to the bag.

"I am happy you underestimated me," Talreja had to say that to show he was not jolted. Realizing how professional she was, he was relieved she did not know he was the cop who had sent one of those wireless messages. He hastily added, "I know you are smart, yet you are prone to errors too."

"That is fine... I want to go now," The lady said.

Godbole, Kamini, Pande, and Riaz monitored the lady's conversation from the adjacent room. Godbole summoned operative Sneha Kumar to assist Kamini if the target became aggressive and violent. Everything that transpired until then was enough to conclude that the lady was going to plant the memory card in the library. So, Godbole decided that it was time to intervene. Kamini, Sneha, and Godbole suddenly appeared in the room, taking the lady by surprise.

"No, lady, I don't think it is time for you to go!" Godbole said. "Now, please hand over all your possessions to my colleague."

As Kamini stepped forward, the lady struck a karate pose. Kamini managed to push her onto a wooden chair, holding her while Sneha tied her hands to the armrests. Kamini swiftly picked up the lady's pouch, which had fallen on the floor during their scuffle.

"Who the hell are you? What are you doing to me?" she yelled. She was upset and pretended to be bristling with righteous indignation. "This is no way to treat a lady."

"This is not the way we wanted either! You are quite unruly," Godbole said. He sat closer to the lady and continued, "Please be calm. We are from the Central Security Division. We routinely check people who move around suspiciously. We want to check your credentials. That is all. If everything is fine, we'll leave you after checking. Tell me your name and why you visited the library."

"You are not a security man; you are a buffoon. Someone should teach you why people go to the library."

Ridiculing was a tactic professionals used to gain mental superiority over the interrogator. The lady might have taken that posture impulsively, but it confirmed that she was trained. Godbole ignored her gibe and said, "I am willing to be tutored, but later. Now, please tell me your name."

"You are unnecessarily harassing a woman. I am Kesang Dolma from Tawang in Arunachal. My Aadhar card with my name and address is in my pouch."

"Okay. Let me see your Aadhar card," Godbole said and turned to Kamini.

By then, Kamini had finished arranging the items in the lady's bag on a side table. There was a small makeup kit with all the essential items like lipstick, eyeliner, and so on. The other items in the pouch included the pistol, a gel pen, a key chain with two keys, and a piece of paper with 1. *Hydroxyurea*, 2. L-*Glutamine powder,*

3. *Diclofenac (injection)* written on it, the lady's Aadhar card, and some currency notes of five-hundred, one-hundred and fifty denominations. Even after a detailed examination of the pouch, Kamini could not find the memory card or the chewing gum. There was no mobile phone either.

As Godbole picked up the Aadhar card, Talreja came up and whispered in his ears, "We already checked this Aadhar card number online. It is fake."

Since the lady's Aadhar ID was fake, Godbole could safely subject her to harsh questioning and intense search. First, he would have to fish out that memory card from her.

Godbole turned to the lady and asked, "So, you are Kesang Dolma from Arunachal?"

"Yes, I am."

"Dolma, we need to subject you to a body search." Although he was unsure about her real name, Godbole preferred to address her as Dolma.

"Why? What is my crime?"

"Why do you worry if you have not committed any crime?"

"Because it is insulting to undergo such a search for an honourable citizen."

Godbole chuckled. "Since when have honourable citizens started keeping fake Aadhar cards for ID?" Dolma did not respond, but her frustration was evident.

Godbole continued, "Mind you... forging an Aadhar card is an offence, and I can start from there. I am ordering your body search."

"So, you are bent upon fixing me. I take the challenge; go ahead."

Godbole noted Dolma's confidence. He had another worry. The memory card was so small that she could chew it down if she chose to. The card would not just hold valuable information; it would be crucial evidence in the case.

"Comb her... complete body search. Take out her chain, studs, rings, wristwatch, shoes... everything. Let her arms remain tied. She is adventurous at times. We'll wait in the other room."

*****

The search yielded nothing additional to what they already found, except for her wireless earbuds. There was no memory card with her. Her face radiated with silent triumph. Godbole was sure it was with her. Where was it, he wondered. He decided to examine all her possessions kept on the side table. He picked up her belongings one by one, scrutinizing each item with meticulous care. After a few minutes, he turned back to Dolma. She smiled confidently.

"Dolma, you said you are from Arunachal, correct?"

"Yes, I am from Tawang town."

"Well, when did you come to Delhi?"

"I came yesterday afternoon."

"Where do you stay in Delhi?"

"At Hotel Chitrakoot, near Khan Market."

"What is the purpose of your trip?"

"I'm enrolled at Delhi University for distance education. I am doing an MA. I came to collect my course material."

"What's your major subject for MA?"

"Asian Civilisations and Religions." Dolma looked curious, wondering where her interviewer was leading her.

"Tell me... what time did you leave the hotel for the library?"

"At around noon."

"What time?"

"I didn't see the right time."

"You didn't check the time?"

"I tried but noticed that my wristwatch had gone dead just when I was to start for the library."

"Yet, you carried the dead watch with you!"

"I carried it because I wanted its cell replaced on my way to the library."

"Thank you. The things may not be as straight as you say," Godbole said and proceeded to the side table. He came back with the thick black square watch. He showed the watch to Dolma. The watch was dead at 10:40, and the day and date displayed were 'TUE 3'.

"The watch was dead on Tuesday, November 3. Today is Thursday, November 5. You say you noticed only today at noon. Tell me, why would you wear a dead watch?

"You are trying to make a mountain out of a molehill," Dolma said contemptuously.

"No, Dolma. I wanted to know why you carried a dead watch for over two days. So, I checked your watch closely and found that its back cover can be opened with a simple nudge. It has a special chamber... for your favourite chewing gum." Godbole laughed loudly.

Dolma's face paled. They had deciphered their communication method. She fell silent, a trapped look in her eyes.

"Probably this chewing gum was placed in the watch on the third. Someone seemed to have done a shoddy job. The excessive moisture from the gum might have seeped in, and the watch would have gone dead. Don't you think so?"

Dolma glared, "I'm not speaking... go to hell!"

"I go to hell with every tough assignment. I don't mind going there again, but I'll take you with me this time," Godbole said, smiling.

He continued questioning. "What's written on that piece of paper?"

"A list of medications."

"For whom?"

"Naturally for a patient."

Godbole changed his tactic, seeing her resistance. Ignoring Dolma's indifference, he said, "Look here, I do not think this gum was fixed in the watch in Tawang, a small place in a remote area. I also do not think your bosses operate from Tawang. Please know that, ultimately, you will have to speak. I will not relent till you come out with your true story."

He turned to Kamini, "Please help her drink water. Just water, nothing else. I am taking a break. Call me if she wants to speak. Otherwise, do not bother me. If she becomes unruly, tie her feet, too." Godbole swiftly walked out.

Godbole entered the adjacent room, where Talreja, Riaz, Pande, and Sneha watched Dolma on the screen. He handed Pande the memory card he had retrieved from Dolma's watch. "Please get this memory card deciphered using Mohan's app."

Godbole then called up Das to brief him on the developments.

"Yash, Pande kept me informed about this lady. She appears quite tough. I know you had to get her, but I hope it isn't premature. It shouldn't alert the Chinese and send them into a deep freeze."

"I am concerned too. This lady isn't just a courier... she's an agent. She's tough to crack."

"How will you proceed from here?"

"I'm waiting for the memory card to be deciphered. We haven't yet permitted her to go to the washroom. I'm waiting for her to request to strike a bargain."

"All the best, Yash."

Godbole looked at Dolma's pathetic state. Hands tied and immobilized for hours, she was in ongoing torment. Yet she showed no intent to relent. Almost two and a half hours had passed since Dolma was brought there. She had said that she left her hotel room around noon. It was 5:15 p.m. She had just drunk water thrice. When would she reach breaking point, Godbole wondered.

He thought it was unfair to a lady. But she was a spy. Man or woman, the rules of the game were unforgiving. If caught, the mental and physical pressure would be unbearably crushing, and most often, it would be the end of the road.

Godbole kept watching the screen, and suddenly, he saw Dolma looking at Kamini, seemingly pleading for help. Kamini was a professional. She pretended she did not understand until Dolma spoke, requesting the washroom. At last, Kamini came over to inform Godbole.

Godbole was waiting for that moment. He promptly explained to Dolma that he could only help if she divulged her role.

"Look here, as I said before, I do not believe you come from Tawang. I repeat, your wristwatch could not have been fixed in Tawang... your master's handling such technology could not operate out of Tawang. I see your discomfort. I do not mind if you want to sit in this condition for days. I have all the time. But it would be best if you came out clean to get help. Where is your base, and where did you come from? Tell me quickly."

"Kathmandu," Dolma admitted, writhing in discomfort.

"Is that your base? You come from Kathmandu to stick this gum?"

"Yes, I fly from there once every month to do this job. Only this month, I came twice, last week and this week."

"Who gives you this gum and memory card?"

"There is a setup in Kathmandu that takes care of the intelligence activity," Dolma hurriedly explained, saying that she was the offspring of a Chinese father and a Tibetan mother. She was born and educated in Lhasa. The Chinese recruited, trained, and brought her to Kathmandu, where she lived for seven years. She was thirty-four years old but not married.

"Once your job is done at the library, do you have to inform anyone?"

"No. I am not supposed to make phone calls to anyone. However, I can send an electronic message if there is an emergency."

"When were you scheduled to return to Kathmandu?"

"I need to go to the washroom; let me...please..."

"Tell me, when were you scheduled to return to Kathmandu?"

"12th November."

"What are your plans in Delhi till then?"

"Nothing."

"Then why stay on for seven days?"

During a trip to Delhi, I normally stay here for up to seven days. So it would look like a business trip... if anyone is watching by chance."

Godbole saw that Dolma was in agony. He signalled Sneha and Kamini to untie her hands, but put a handcuff on one of her hands and take her to the washroom.

Dolma was to return to Kathmandu on 12th November. That meant the Chinese would know of her detention only when she didn't appear in Kathmandu. It was an excellent six-day period for the NES-17 to pursue their work.

After she returned from the washroom, only one of her hands was bound to the armrest using a handcuff. Godbole was satisfied that he had made a good beginning and ascertained some crucial points. Dragging the targets further into cooperating would be easier.

Before resuming interrogation, Dolma was served coffee.

"Dolma, we need to take you to a detention centre for the night. Before that, I have a bargain. Please listen. If you keep cooperating, maybe we may not officially arrest you. You'll be in our custody and could be a candidate for a detainee exchange programme if an Indo-China exchange programme comes up. So, you can hope to return to China one day. However, if we register a case against you, the court, the legal procedure, and even public opinion will come into play. In that case, I'm sure you will rot in an Indian jail for life. The choice is yours."

Dolma resigned as the bargain offered was the best option for her. Godbole continued to probe.

"Is the library visit your only assignment in Delhi?"

"Normally, yes," Dolma said. "But this time, I was asked to urgently speak to someone about sending a driver to Bangalore. I had to do that work because the regular liaison person was unavailable."

After a pause, Dolma continued, "I am uncomfortable meeting people on these trips. It is strictly against our code of conduct. But I had to take that risk."

"What was the risk?"

"This morning, I had to meet this new driver, Rafique Madani, in my hotel room. Although I called him from the hotel phone, it was a risk. I couldn't avoid it because I had to give him money for his train journey to Bangalore."

"You mean you called him to your hotel room just to hand over money?"

"He was hired for the first time. So, I had to brief him and explain how he could contact the Bangalore guy. Otherwise, I would not have met him. It was a bad omen," she sighed.

Godbole understood how shattered Dolma was feeling. Nevertheless, he asked, "Do you know when he is going to Bangalore?"

"He said he is going by the morning 8.30 train – a direct train to Bangalore. He'll reach Bangalore early morning on Sunday."

"Whom is he supposed to meet in Bangalore?"

"I do not know. He has been asked to reach the True Kappi outlet in Sundaram Mall, a little distance from the railway station at 10 a.m. on Sunday."

"Did you report about Rafique's expected arrival in Bangalore?"

"Yes, I sent them a message electronically."

"I want that mail ID and the contact phone number of the person you called."

"It is not a mail ID, but a tourist resort booking address. The phone I called was Rafique Madani's. I don't remember it off-hand. It is written down in my notebook, in my hotel room."

"That is fine, we will get it. Tell me, what is written on that piece of paper?"

"Those are medicines they wanted in Bangalore. I was to purchase them here and send them with Rafique Madani."

"Is Rafique carrying them to Bangalore?"

"No, just before I left Kathmandu, I got a message that they could purchase it locally. But that piece of paper remained in my pouch."

"The medicine was for whom?"

"I think it is for a child having a rare disease."

"Well, is Madani carrying anything else with him?"

"No. The instructions asked him only to carry a copy of his Aadhar card, which he would discard after the train journey. No other identity cards... not even his driving licence."

"What about his cell phone?"

"Since there was no mention of the phone in the instructions, he is carrying his phone."

"Well... it is already 7:30 p.m., and you've had a long day. We'll take you to one of our dens... not a detention cell. You can have dinner and relax there. You are my guest... as long as you cooperate," Godbole said tactfully, reminding her of the bargain he had offered. After a pause, he added, "Please bear in mind that you will be under watch... a relentless twenty-four-hour watch. Your behaviour will decide our response."

Dolma looked dejected and resigned to her fate. The Agency's guards arrived. Accompanied by Sneha, they ushered Dolma out.

*****

Godbole and the team had much to do before they could even think of heading home. First, he read the message in the memory card, which Pande decoded with Mohan's help. There were two instructions for Mohan in the message:

> *Proceed to the south immediately and be in touch with Rolex. He had said central cops visited him. He can describe their appearance. Find out if the cops are still watching that area. Once you're sure the cops have left and there's no trap, please give us an all-clear signal using your usual channel.*
>
> *Then, go directly to the west and make a written application to the police there requesting that they return your house to you. Tell them that you are losing rent, which is your source of income. Once you get possession of the house, look for any electronic equipment that the fellow had kept hidden there. If you find it, keep it secure until further instructions are given.*

Godbole was worried about the Chinese plans to smuggle something to Sri Lanka. He was disappointed that Indian nationals like Rolex were hand-in-glove with the Chinese. Since the Chinese wanted Mohan to go to Rameswaram, the team must send him. Godbole knew the situation would benefit the team if Mohan could play his role well. The message also indicated that the Chinese were frantic about retrieving the electronic items hidden in Arshad's house. Godbole was happy that those items were already in the team's custody.

"Please brief Mohan and send him to Rameswaram with the special phone so he can stay in contact with us," he instructed Pande.

Then, he focused on Rafique Madani's travel plans to Bangalore.

"We must find out the details of the train leaving for Bangalore at 8:30 a.m. tomorrow. Get the passenger reservation list and check if someone named Rafique Madani is travelling to Bangalore. The ticket should be in that name since he's travelling with a copy of his Aadhar card."

The team listened intently.

"I think Talreja can make these enquiries. Now, Riaz... you be prepared to travel to Bangalore. Tomorrow morning, we'll board the train and pick up Rafique Madani based on the pretext of his fake ticket. I suspect Madani is an ISI chap; otherwise, the Chinese wouldn't hire someone from this far to help in an emergency," Godbole said.

"You're right, sir," Talreja said.

"Now listen," Godbole continued, "Once Madani is whisked away, Riaz will take Madani's seat and travel to Bangalore. This is our chance to infiltrate the Chinese ring. Dolma says this is the first time Madani has been hired. So, the Bangalore guys are not familiar with Madani. We cannot afford to lose this opportunity."

Looking at Riaz, Godbole said, "Okay, Rafique Madani, you can go and start your preparations. Let me sit with the rest of the team and plan to put you in Rafique's place."

"How do I communicate with you?" Riaz asked. "After all, can I not carry my phone?"

"Good question," Godbole said and pondered. "Well... before Madani is taken away, get hold of his cell phone. It'll also help if the Chinese decide to check your phone."

"Noted, sir," Riaz said and left.

Godbole continued his discussion. "Pande and Talreja will reach the railway station tomorrow well before 8.30 a.m. Coordinate with the Ticket Examiner of the concerned coach before removing Rafique. Get a fresh train ticket for Riaz. Is the plan clear?"

"We got it," Pande said.

"In the afternoon, Kamini and Talreja will fly to Bangalore to be at the True Kappi outlet at Sundaram Mall at 10 a.m. on Sunday. See who picks up our Rafique Madani and shadow them. Riaz is entering their ring and needs your full backup in Bangalore. Be prepared..." Godbole stopped briefly and added, "Tomorrow morning, Sneha and I will continue our interaction with Dolma. Now, let's disperse to prepare for our roles."

Chapter – 10
The Missing Operative

New Delhi
November 8, 2020
11.30 a.m.

Godbole was preparing a report on Dolma for the Home Ministry. The Ministry officials were briefed orally, but they would have to be informed about the Agency's plans to keep Dolma's detention under wraps as part of a bargain to extract more information. Although he kept writing, he glanced at the watch intermittently. It was 11:30 a.m. He should have received some feedback from Talreja and Kamini. They were to monitor Riaz at Sundaram Mall at 10 a.m. that morning. What was causing the delay?

Godbole completed the report when his cell phone buzzed.

"Sir, Riaz hasn't shown up," Kamini informed.

"Could you have missed him?" Godbole asked frowning.

"No chance. I was hanging around near True Kappi since 9:30 a.m. Talreja was keeping a watch at the entrance of the mall."

"Did you check the train? Sometimes trains get inordinately delayed."

"Sir, his train arrived at 6:05 a.m., forty minutes later than the scheduled time. I am still at the mall. Without waiting any longer, Talreja proceeded to the main Bangalore city railway station, where Riaz was to alight."

"Is there any feedback from Talreja?"

"Yes, sir. He approached rail authorities and accessed the footage from the platform's CCTV cameras covering both the doors of the coach B-7 in which Riaz was travelling. He watched it several times but did not see Riaz. He has now gone to the Bangalore Cantonment Station, where the train stops briefly before proceeding to the Bangalore City Station."

"This does not sound good," Godbole muttered. "Well, you wait there. Let me know if Talreja makes any progress. I need to work on this," Godbole said and ended the call.

This news hit Godbole like a shockwave, threatening to derail the mission.His mind raced. Where was Riaz? He was a thorough professional who couldn't just go missing just like that. Did the Chinese operatives meet him on the train one or two stations before the destination? Perhaps the True Kappi rendezvous was a security measure intended to mislead others. The development was worrying because the consequences of Riaz falling into the hands of the Chinese would be unthinkable. However, Godbole had faith in Riaz, a brave and wise operative. He would know how to handle the situation.

Godbole remembered that Riaz was to use Rafique Madani's phone. It was primarily to ensure the Chinese that he was indeed Madani. However, contacting Riaz on that phone was out of the question. Had it been safe, Riaz would have contacted anyone from the NES-17 team. Riaz might be unable to use his phone with the Chinese nearby.

Just as Godbole was getting impatient, Ashok Talreja called up at 4 p.m. Talreja said, "The CCTV camera has caught Riaz getting down at Cantonment Station. A well-built person was walking with Riaz. As they walked towards the exit, the stranger kept speaking to Riaz. There was no further coverage to know how and where they went."

Godbole exhaled slowly, "Thank you, Ashok. Thankfully, we

know that Riaz is in Bangalore. Who accompanied Riaz? And where did they go from the railway station?"

"There's no clear lead from here."

"Well, Kamini and you stay in Bangalore," Godbole paused and asked, "Is the clip showing them walking towards the exit sharp and clear? Can it help us identify the man walking with Riaz?"

"Unfortunately, no. The clip wasn't sharp enough; they were too far from the camera. But I have downloaded the clip."

"Okay, send it to me. Let our lab enhance the quality. Meanwhile, let me see how we can proceed from here."

*****

Since Riaz's disappearance, the day passed quickly without any progress. Although Das hadn't explicitly said anything, Godbole knew the team had to double their efforts. The Agency brass was likely pressuring Das. The leaders wanted quick results without significant risks – an understandable but often unrealistic expectation. Godbole understood this dynamic well. Quick results demanded bold risks.

Godbole was in a tight spot. Riaz was with the Chinese suspects in an unknown location in Bangalore. To complicate matters, the Chinese operatives would sense trouble if Dolma failed to return to Kathmandu by 12th November. How would they react, Godbole wondered? Until 12th November, there was only a tiny window of just three days. The team had to come up with some aces to catch up with the Chinese and fast. Additionally, Kanak Mohan in Rameswaram was waiting for the team's direction to give the green signal to the Chinese to go ahead with their Rameswaram operation.

Godbole pondered the mounting challenges. He suddenly remembered the scrap of paper with medicine names. Dolma had said it was to treat a rare disease in a child, and her Chinese contacts in Bangalore had purchased the medicine locally. Could that medicine for a rare disease provide a clue or two? But why medicine for a child? Puzzled, Godbole decided it was time to question Dolma, lodged in the 'den'.

*****

Seeing Godbole entering her room, Dolma offered a faint smile. She appeared relieved that she was not kept in an unclean jail cell but in a comfortable room with reading material and good food. Sneha indulged in occasional chats with Dolma to keep up her spirits.

After enquiring about her welfare, Godbole asked Dolma more about the medicines prescribed on the paper in her bag.

"I already told you, those medicines are for a child having a rare disease," her voice tinged with frustration as she asked, "Why are you after a child?"

"If we have not harmed you, do you think we'll target a child?" Godbole replied calmly. "I am asking because we need to know all the details of what we found in your pouch. It's a security requirement."

"You see, what I know about this is from my boss in Kathmandu. He said that an eight-month-old child of a Chinese engineer working in Bangalore was recently diagnosed with a rare genetic disease: Sickle Cell anaemia. When they couldn't get the prescribed medicines easily, they approached us for help. However, they got the medicines from a major store in Bangalore."

"Where and when was the child diagnosed with this ailment?"

"I don't know that."

"Where in Bangalore do the people associated with you live?"

"I told you already, I don't know where they live in Bangalore. They never share these things. Information is shared with us strictly on a need-to-know basis."

Given its rarity, Godbole reasoned that the disease must have been diagnosed at a major hospital. Why not try his luck at the major hospitals in Bangalore? The registration process should have details of the child's parents. Even if they weren't involved, they must have had contact with the people NES-17 was looking for. How else could they have requested medicine from Dolma's boss? Despite the daunting task it would be, Godbole decided to proceed. By noon, Godbole returned to his office. In his cabin, he first asked Amit Rao to prepare a list of prominent hospitals and medical centres in Bangalore. He called Talreja to brief him on what he had learnt from Dolma. He instructed Talreja and Kamini to visit major hospitals and ascertain if they had diagnosed anyone with Sickle Cell disease in recent weeks.

Godbole slumped in his chair. Many things were at stake – identifying the hand behind the Mumbai blackout was still pending. Then, if Dolma failed to turn up in Kathmandu, the Chinese operatives might vanish. Above all, would Riaz be safe in Chinese hands? His thoughts drifted to Riaz's family – his wife, Fathima, and son, Ibrahim. He sent Pande to Riaz's house that evening to check their welfare. It was a practice followed by the Agency to check on the family when an operative was away from home on assignment.

At 6 p.m., Talreja informed Godbole that he could check just four hospitals and Kamini, two. They would have to wait till 10 a.m. the following day to resume their work. It had been almost thirty-two hours since Riaz disappeared in Bangalore. Godbole felt concerned. As team leader, he was also responsible for the safety and security of everyone in the team. He considered joining Talreja and Kamini in Bangalore the following day. He also instructed Pande to head to Bangalore to expedite their hospital checking exercise.

*****

November 10, 2020

The next day, at 11 a.m., when Godbole and Pande reached their hotel, they found Talreja and Kamini waiting for them.

"Why are you guys waiting here? You should have proceeded with your checking exercise," Godbole said.

"We have some information," Talreja said. "Sir, Dr K.R. Rao, whom Kamini had met yesterday at Neela Giri Hospital, has some information. Finding Dr Rao responsive, Kamini shared her phone number with him. This morning, he called to inform her that a case of Sickle Cell disease was diagnosed at Centurian Hospital in Jayanagar a few weeks ago. Dr Ramesh Sheshadri is handling the case and has been discussing the rare disease with his close circle of medicos."

"Excellent," Godbole said, nodding, "I think Kamini and I will proceed to the Centurian Hospital. You and Pande, wait here."

Godbole and Kamini waited nearly an hour at Centurian Hospital before being escorted to Dr Ramesh Sheshadri's consulting room. The balding, bespectacled, middle-aged doctor greeted them. "Please be seated," the doctor said, pushing aside a file on his desk. I only have a few minutes," he said curtly.

"We'll keep it brief. We're from the Home Ministry, Delhi security division."

"I don't know how I fit into the security division's concerns." The doctor laughed.

Godbole quickly explained what he was looking for.

"Look here, Mr Godbole, I don't know how you discovered this rare disease was diagnosed here, but divulging patient details breaches our ethics."

"I respect your view. Please do not give us any details of the ailment or treatment. We are also not asking for the name of the patient or the parents. We need their residential address."

"It still means the same. Do you have a compelling reason for me to break the norm?"

Godbole leaned in and said in a grave tone, "Of course. All I can say is that this is a matter of national security. I request you to please cooperate."

The doctor sat silently as Godbole added, "I assure you, we won't quote you or take action against the targets until their involvement is confirmed."

Seeing the doctor waver slightly, Godbole pursued, "The Chinese are up to some mischief... in our country."

"Oh, so you know they are Chinese nationals?" The doctor's eyes narrowed.

"We have extensive information. We need to act quickly to stop them from doing something highly damaging."

After a tense silence, Dr Sheshadri sighed. Then, opening a cupboard to retrieve a file, he said, "We still have much to learn about this disease." He flipped through the pages and said, "I'll give you the address, nothing more."

"That is more than enough, and we shall be grateful."

When Godbole was ready with his notepad, the doctor dictated, "Dove Villa, Chittaranjan Farms, Chikkaballore Village Road, Devanahalli, Bangalore Rural."

Godbole and Kamini profusely thanked Dr Sheshadri. When they got up to leave, the doctor said, "This ends here; don't come for any further information. Forget that you ever met me; I don't want to get entangled in this."

Armed with the address, Godbole and his team hired an SUV and proceeded to Chittaranjan Farms to recce the target area. As they were leaving, Godbole shared the address with Amit Rao, requesting that they check with the Foreigners' Regional Registration Office to find out the details of the Chinese staying at that address.

Chapter – 11
Dove Villa

Chikkaballore Village Road
November 10, 2020
3 p.m.

A twenty-eight-kilometre drive from Bangalore city took Godbole and the team to Devanahalli, a small township. Chittaranjan Farms was a further three-kilometre ride down the scenic Chikkaballore Village Road. Beginning from Devanahalli, the left side of the Chikkaballore Village Road was lined with small and medium-sized industrial units. However, on the right side of the road was a long stretch of farmland under active cultivation. By 3 p.m., Godbole and his team, travelling in their rented SUV, reached a small junction on the Chikkaballore Village Road. A sign at the intersection read – *'Take a right turn for Chittaranjan Farms'*. The junction of the road and the lane towards the farms appeared to be the hub of that area, with some shops and a few food and tea stalls. Those small businesses served the workers' requirements in the industrial units on the other side of the road. At the junction was Guru Krupa, an eatery looking better than the other food stalls.

Before entering the lane leading to Chittaranjan Farms, the team parked their vehicle and decided to scout the area. Godbole suggested they sit at Guru Krupa for a good vantage point to survey the area and grab a bite. As they entered the eatery, a middle-aged lady greeted them and led them to a table. It served a variety of dosas, vadas, rice preparations, and sweets. They placed their order. Since there weren't many customers, the lady chatted with the team while serving the food.

"You are from the city. How do you find our food?" the lady asked.

"I admit it is tasty," Kamini said.

"You know my husband and I make the food ourselves. We run this place without any helpers."

"That's impressive; great food," Kamini said.

"Yes, our customers are satisfied," the lady said proudly. "Most of our customers are workers from the industrial units across the road. After 5 p.m., this place will start getting crowded."

"I can imagine," Kamini said.

"What brings you here? Have you come to purchase a farmhouse?" the lady asked Pande.

"We're considering," Pande said noncommittally.

"Chittaranjan Farms is a good choice; they are reputed," the lady remarked.

"We also heard so. How far are their farmhouses from here?" Pande asked.

"Just a ten-minute walk from here," the lady explained. "There are thirty-two posh farmhouses with five bedrooms each. Each farmhouse is built on a one-acre plot of land with a separate compound wall. The villas also have outhouses or servants' quarters."

"You know a lot about the project," Pande observed.

"I know so much because the developer comes here regularly. He has requested that we guide prospective buyers to their office," the lady said and smiled. "Most of the villas have been sold. Now, only six or seven villas are there for sale." Her smile seemed to imply an unshared secret.

"Have people started residing in the sold bungalows?" Godbole asked.

"Yes, sir, nearly twelve bungalows are occupied."

"Maybe only locals of this area live here," Godbole probed.

"No, sir, not locals. People from other areas of the country and some foreigners are also there."

"Foreigners?" Godbole asked as if it were a surprise to him.

"Yes, a few Chinese are staying in the fourth bungalow."

"Are the Chinese living there with family, or are they bachelors?" Godbole asked.

"There is a family... I mean, a couple with a baby and three bachelors," she replied.

As the lady talked about the baby, Godbole knew the team was on the right track. "Do the Chinese come here to eat?" he continued.

"The people living in the villas are rich. They do not come here. Some residents order our food, and my husband or I go there to deliver it. But the Chinese do not come here and do not order our food. They don't interact much. A tall and stout North Indian is staying with the Chinese as a helping hand. Sometimes, he comes here to eat dosas. At times, he packs masala dosas and vadas for the Chinese."

"Is that North Indian a new man here?" Godbole asked.

"No, he has been living here for the past year."

Godbole wanted to ask the lady whether she had seen any new person with the North Indian. He also wanted to show the clip of Riaz and a well-built person coming out of the Cantonment Railway Station. But he refrained as it was too early to do so with a new acquaintance. Instead, he asked, "Is this lane the way to approach the farms?"

"Yes, sir," the lady said. "Just walk for ten minutes, and you will reach it. All the farmhouses have separate gates. The unsold bungalows are towards the end of the lane. They have a sales office in the outhouse of the last bungalow."

They did not get any information about Riaz. Yet, the inputs from the lady were helpful. As per her information, there were four Chinese men – three bachelors and one man with his family, along with a North Indian, staying there. They would have to see if Riaz was staying there, too. Could that man be the one who had come to take Riaz from the train? Godbole decided to proceed to the vicinity of Dove Villa along with Talreja.

From the junction, the lane passed through a deserted agricultural farm. Dove Villa, the fourth in a long row of villas, had a high compound wall and a grilled gate. How could they ascertain if Riaz was in the villa in that setting? Since the lane and the adjoining area remained deserted, mounting a watch on Dove Villa was challenging. As they kept walking, Godbole considered taking the lady's assistance at the eatery. He called up Kamini, who was at the eatery. He wanted Kamini to take the lady into confidence.

After touring the area, when Godbole and Talreja returned, Kamini informed them that the lady and her husband had agreed to cooperate. Godbole quickly devised a plan. From the next day, Pande would work at the eatery in disguise to observe people heading towards the farms and look for Riaz. Being right at the junction, the eatery would be ideal for them to maintain a watch. The lady and her husband, relieved to have an extra hand, agreed to say Pande was temporarily helping them.

Before departing, Godbole showed the lady the clip. She watched it several times, but could not identify the person. However, she agreed that the figure and the person's height resembled the North Indian she was referring to.

****

November 11, 2020

The following day, Pande took up duty at the eatery. He opted to cut vegetables and wash dishes so he could keep an eye on the movement of people and vehicles passing through the junction to the farms. Meanwhile, Godbole and his team remained in their hotel room in Bangalore city, eagerly waiting to hear from Pande. After all, Riaz was masquerading as Rafique Madani to help the

Chinese tide over an emergency. If his cover was blown, his life could be in danger.

To add to Godbole's woes, Kanak Mohan called up to enquire when he should give the green signal to the Chinese men to go ahead with their plan to travel to Rameswaram. On instructions from the Chinese, Mohan reported the daily status of the situation through their usual communication via the travel resort website. Godbole advised Mohan to hold on for a few more days, citing two suspicious men roaming the boat jetty in Rameswaram. However, Godbole knew he couldn't ask Mohan to hold on indefinitely. If they failed to trace Riaz within a day or two, he would have to tell Mohan to give the Chinese an all-clear signal, forcing the NES-17 team to concentrate on the Rameswaram operation.

Amidst all the pressure, they received information from the Foreigners' Regional Registration Office confirming that four Chinese men, one Chinese lady, and a child were staying at the Chittaranjan Farms address. The Foreigner Regional Registration(FFR) office provided the Chinese's names, passports, and visa details. While the four Chinese men were on work visas, the lady was on a family-dependent visa. All of them had permission to reside in the state of Karnataka and to visit Mumbai and New Delhi. Two men worked for a Chinese company called *Tinmin Electronics and Instrumentation.* The other two worked for a Chinese-funded Indian startup working on AI systems.

Godbole also received the first report from the cyber cell on the blackout experienced in Mumbai on 12th October. The experts pinpointed the initial malfunction at the Tarapur Substation, which triggered a cascade of failures across eleven substations in the Greater Mumbai Metropolitan Region. The glitch in the automatic system, regulating the power flow from the grid to match the network flow, was triggered externally by a command prompted by an outside electronic signal.

Godbole was already under sheer pressure, with Riaz still missing and a nagging concern about the possible Chinese reaction to Dolma's failure to return to Kathmandu. Nevertheless, Riaz remained a priority, but Godbole had to change his strategy for a faster result. Before going to bed, he called Pande for an update.

"Sir, the eatery was not crowded except for some time in the morning and evening. So, I was relatively free to maintain a watch. At 9:30 a.m., I saw two cars at the junction with two Chinese men in each of the cars. They slowed down to turn onto the village road. The lady informed me that the cars routinely took Chinese men to their workplaces. She also said that the residents of Dove Villa took out a white Benz car in the evenings to purchase fruits from a stall near the junction," Pande reported.

"This confirms that four Chinese men are living in the villa."

"Yes, four of them and a lady with a baby."

"Any other observation?"

"I can watch the pedestrians, but the problem is to spot passengers in the passing vehicles," Pande said.

"I know it's difficult. We are hoping to spot Riaz if he is in that area. Maybe even with a glance, you can pick out Riaz from a crowd," Godbole responded.

"I, too, think so. Today, I got to go to that farmhouse area twice. The State Electricity Department is installing a transformer adjacent to the last bungalow of the Chittaranjan Farms. The junior engineer, who is rather friendly, had ordered food for his team twice. I took the opportunity to go there to deliver the food," Pande informed.

"Could you see the fourth villa... I mean Dove Villa?"

"Nothing... the compound wall and the greenery there obstruct the view. Only the grilled gates offered a limited view of the porch."

"You said the engineer is friendly. Is he likely to be there tomorrow also?" Godbole asked.

"I think so. He had said the work might take three days to complete."

"Okay, I'll visit you tomorrow morning," Godbole said, disconnecting the call.

Chittaranjan Farms remained the team's best lead in finding Riaz. The medicine for the rare disease was meant for the baby living there, and above all, the lady at the eatery had said that a stout man was staying in the outhouse of the Dove Villa. Coincidentally, a tall and stout person had come to pick up Riaz from the train.

Considering all the factors, the possibility of Riaz's presence in Dove Villa could not be dismissed. Godbole knew he had to enter the villa to look for Riaz and establish contact. He pondered on how to do it.

*****

12 November, 2020

Godbole and Kamini entered the eatery at 9 a.m. That morning, the only thought in Godbole's mind was how to find Riaz. He had been missing for the past four days; it was perturbing indeed. As he mulled over various options, an idea struck him involving the junior engineer and his team. He quickly discussed the plan with Pande, assigning the engineer a crucial role. Godbole was confident that the current anti-Chinese public sentiment, fuelled by the ongoing tense stand-off between the Indian Army and the Chinese PLA, would ensure the engineer's cooperation. Soon after the engineer and his team arrived for work, Pande approached him. After some tactful cajoling, the engineer agreed to assist Godbole. At 10:30 a.m., when the four men from Dove Villa left for work, the engineer cut off power to the villa. He then waited for the Chinese lady to register a complaint. After a long wait, around noon, an online complaint was received from the villa. The staff promptly alerted the engineer about the complaint. The engineer, accompanied by Godbole posing as his assistant, headed to the villa.

A Chinese lady, holding a baby, opened the gate after verifying the engineer's identity. Godbole had expected the stout person to open the gate, but he was not around. The villa and its compound exuded a serene and mystic charm, with green trees, a sprawling garden adorned with flowers and water fountains, and a small pond with clear water. A pathway meandered through the strikingly green lawns, adding to the place's elegance. Speaking in broken English, the Chinese lady explained the power issue. The engineer assured her that the power supply from the regional station was intact and that he suspected there was a short circuit in the villa. They checked the main switchboard and then moved to the other junction switchboards in the gangway to the large drawing room. The lady followed wherever they moved.

As they walked towards the drawing room, Godbole was surprised to see a Chinese man moving from one room to another dressed in cotton pyjamas and a matching shirt. His casual attire was enough to conclude that he was not a visitor but was staying there. As per the FRR office record, only four men lived there. No Chinese national had registered with the local FRR office for a temporary visit to the Bangalore-Devanahalli region. So, who was the fifth person?

When the engineer and Godbole approached the drawing room, they noticed the Chinese lady getting concerned. Godbole did not want to add to the lady's anxiety by entering the rooms looking for Riaz. After all, one can't expect the Chinese to accommodate a driver in their living area. Maybe the Chinese accommodated Riaz in the outhouse. So, Godbole led the engineer towards the outhouse. From the corner of his eye, he saw the lady letting out a sigh of relief.

The lady did not accompany them. They passed an open garage with a white Mercedes-Benz car parked. Godbole memorized the car number. The outhouse had a veranda and two rooms with a washroom attached to the room on the right side. Godbole peeped into the room through the open window when the engineer checked the switchboard on the veranda. Although he didn't find anyone there, he observed used clothes hanging on a line, indicating someone lived there. Among the clothes, he spotted Riaz's jacket, which he had seen Riaz wearing on many occasions. He also saw the airbag Riaz had carried from Delhi. Godbole felt a sudden relief. However, Riaz was not there physically. Was Riaz safe? How would he establish contact with Raiz?

Godbole whispered to the engineer to pretend he spotted the hitch and was fixing the problem. Next, he tore out a small piece of paper from his notepad and quickly wrote Guru Krupa. Below that, in the style of a bill, he wrote idli – Rs thirty and vada – Rs forty-five. Total Rs. 75. He placed that piece of paper in the pocket of Riaz's jacket. He hoped Riaz would find the note, recognize his handwriting and understand what the message meant. He signalled to the engineer to wrap up and have the power restored. The Chinese lady thanked them once the electricity was restored. She inquired in broken English what had gone wrong. The engineer explained there was a short circuit in the switchboard.

Godbole returned to Guru Krupa, feeling a mix of satisfaction and anxiety. His foray into Dove Villa had yielded crucial leads about Riaz and revealed the presence of an unaccounted-for fifth person. Despite the progress, Godbole knew he wouldn't be at ease until he physically met Riaz.

Everything now hinged on how quickly Riaz would find the note left in his jacket. Godbole felt the spotting of an unaccountable fifth person in Dove Villa was ominous. With that person in there, closer surveillance of Dove Villa became necessary. He decided to shift the team's base from Bangalore city to Devanahalli town. Reaching Chittaranjan Farms from Bangalore in an emergency would be difficult.

Chapter – 12
The Fifth Man

Devanahalli
November 13, 2020
4.30 a.m.

In his new hotel room in Devanahalli, Godbole tossed and turned until past midnight, worried about the Chinese reaction to Dolma's failure to return to Kathmandu. As he drifted into a light sleep, his phone rang sharply at 4:30 a.m. Irritated and groggy, he glanced at the screen. Seeing Pande's name flashing, he snapped into action and answered it.

"Sir, around fifteen minutes ago, I noticed an SUV turning at the junction and driving towards Chittaranjan Farms. The mosquitoes had kept me awake. I don't know who the passengers were or how many were there. I stepped out and walked to the lane to see where the SUV was heading. I guess they entered the Dove Villa compound. Initially, the vehicle waited in the lane since it took a few minutes before the gates were opened. I did not venture to look closer," Pande informed.

Godbole's mind was filled with questions. What were the Chinese plotting? Why did the vehicle arrive at such an unusual hour? Should the team react immediately and prepare to follow up if the Chinese leave Dove Villa? Or was this all something harmless, and his worries were unfounded?

"I hope you heard me, sir," Pande prompted, breaking Godbole's reverie.

"Well, the SUV arriving so early suggests they have plans. I'm debating whether we should act now or wait. I'll come over soon. Keep an eye out for any movement from Dove Villa. Great work!" Godbole replied.

"The credit goes to the mosquitoes who kept me awake," Pande said and laughed.

Godbole couldn't fall back to sleep. The uncertainty about Riaz's whereabouts gnawed at him. If the Chinese moved, the team would need to follow, potentially abandoning the search for Riaz. The indications suggested the Chinese might head to Rameswaram. With the Chinese now having two vehicles for use, Godbole decided the team should be equally prepared. He called Talreja to hire another vehicle, specifying a car to avoid using two similar SUVs.

At 7:30 a.m., Godbole and Kamini arrived at Guru Krupa. They were eager to meet Pande and hear about any further Chinese activity. Pande led them to a secluded corner table and recounted his early morning observations. He had passed Dove Villa later in the morning and spotted an ash-coloured SUV parked on the porch. The number plate wasn't visible from the gate. Godbole was satisfied that the vehicle spotted in the morning could be traced to the Dove Villa. Godbole ordered a simple breakfast and continued to chat. Before Pande could serve breakfast, Godbole's phone rang. He was surprised to see that it was Kanak Mohan calling.

"Good morning, sir. I'm sorry if I disturbed you so early in the morning," Mohan said.

"That's fine... what do you have to report?"

"I think the Chinese are planning something. For the first time, a person spoke to me on my phone twice, and he sounded disturbed. He said they wanted to bring someone to Rameswaram within two to three days, no matter what. I was told to look for security threats, especially near the jetty where Rolex operates."

Godbole realized it could be crucial if the Chinese planned to move someone to Rameswaram. Swift and decisive action was needed. "Can you share the phone number from which you received those calls?"

"Well, sir... there were too many digits... and different digits for each call. I think he was making VoIP calls."

"I know, but please send me those digits by SMS."

"I'll do that. Now... when can I give them the green signal?"

Godbole thought briefly and said, "You can't hold on for too long. Well, you may tell them that in the past two days, you did not see any sign of the presence of security men there. But say you want to check the jetty area once more. This should buy us one more day. You got it." Godbole's voice was calm, but his mind was racing with possibilities and potential dangers.

"Yes, sir. I'll tell them in case they call again."

"Have they given you any phone number to contact them in an emergency?"

"No, sir. I am still sending my response using the same online method. That person told me that he would call me whenever necessary."

"Please keep me informed of all the developments."

The Chinese strictly avoided using phones, so calling Mohan indicated urgency. Godbole recalled that Dolma was due back in Kathmandu on 12th November. Her failure to return by the deadline likely alerted the Chinese. Sensing danger, they might rush to send the fifth man in the villa back to Sri Lanka. This man was likely key to their plans. Perhaps the SUV brought that morning was meant to transport him to Rameswaram.

Godbole's thoughts shifted to Riaz, who played Rafique Madani's role. Madani had been summoned to Bangalore to serve as a driver for the Chinese. Could Riaz have brought the SUV that morning? Godbole felt a flicker of hope. The note he left in Riaz's jacket needed to reach him soon. He shared his thoughts with Pande and Kamini, hoping Riaz would resurface soon. Godbole and Kamini returned to their hotel as they didn't expect any Chinese movement before dusk. The Chinese might also wait for Mohan's signal. Staying at the hotel seemed wiser than lingering at Guru Krupa. Vehicles from Chikkaballore Village Road had to pass through Devanahalli to reach the interstate highway, railway stations, or airport anyway. Feeling more at ease, Godbole decided to brief Das on the latest developments. He also requested that Das send him a soft copy of the file containing facial recognition features of the four Chinese men from photos available in the records of the FRR office and the visa-granting authority. This would help identify the fifth Chinese man from the other four, who were legally in India.

*****

After Godbole and Kamini left, Pande engaged himself in other activities in the eatery to ward off boredom. It was early afternoon, so Pande sat aimlessly looking at the occasional traffic passing by the Chikkaballore Village Road and the side lane. He saw two men casually walking towards the junction from the Chittaranjan Farms. Squinting, he rubbed his eyes in disbelief. It was indeed Riaz, accompanied by a well-built person, walking towards the eatery. Before they entered, Pande discreetly alerted the lady. She confirmed the Riaz's companion's identity as the North Indian. When they came closer, Pande recognized the tall man as the same one who had visited the library to check on Mohan.

As Riaz and his companion stepped inside, Pande strategized discreetly on how to converse with Riaz. He asked the lady to engage the hefty man in conversation. She promptly welcomed them, showing them a comfortable spot to sit. Addressing the stout man, she expressed her pleasure in serving him again and engaged him in conversation.

Meanwhile, when Riaz proceeded to the washbasin, Pande came close and pretended to adjust the soft drink crates nearby. "Please listen. I will speak at a stretch and finish as quickly as possible," Riaz said, glancing at Pande to ensure he was listening.

"I saw the chit only an hour ago. It took some time to persuade Abid to come here to eat dosas. I know you were worried. Abid boarded my train a few stops before the Bangalore City Station and asked me to deboard at Cantonment Station. He took away all my belongings, including my phone. I am not allowed to speak to anyone, but they are otherwise looking after me well."

Without arousing suspicion, Pande nodded. So, Riaz continued, "After the first two days at the outhouse of Dove Villa, on the morning of the tenth, we went to the Bannerghatta, away from the main city. Abid arranged two vehicles, both Ford Endeavours... both ash-coloured. We then drove off the Bangalore-Tamil Nadu highway to a hilly area in Krishnagiri. Abid has an acquaintance living in Mulla Malai, a small village about ten kilometres from the highway. He mentioned that the Chinese, too, had rented a bungalow there. The road to the village was narrow and ran by the side of the Krishnagiri Dam. We stayed in that village with Abid's acquaintance. Late last night, Abid received instructions to come to the farmhouse, and we came here early this morning in one of the SUVs."

Riaz paused, checking to see if Abid was still occupied, then continued, "Note down the registration numbers of the vehicles, quickly... 3189 and 5428." Riaz briefly stopped to enable Pande to note down the numbers. He then continued, "The vehicle we brought here is 3189. We are now waiting for instructions on how to take a Chinese man to Rameswaram. Abid has considered two routes, one as the first preference and the second as an alternate route in case of any problem on the first route."

Riaz suddenly stopped as he saw Abid coming towards the wash basin. He used his handkerchief to wipe his wet hands and returned to his table.

Pande quietly came to the table as if he wanted to take orders for food. Riaz held the menu card in his hands. Pretending to read the menu card, Riaz said, "From what I understood, a Chinese man is here. He was brought here a few weeks ago to handle some emergency... they're very secretive about this man. Rolex helped them bring him from Sri Lanka; now, with Rolex's help, they want to send him back quickly. Abid and I are responsible for safely taking that man to Rolex in Rameswaram." Riaz again stopped as he saw Abid returning to his seat.

"Oh, I see... You are a new man here," Abid said to Pande. "Come on... get us two masala dosas. Serve us one vada each, and bring some water, too."

"Yes, sir..." Pande said and hurriedly left.

The food was served. By the time they finished, the eatery was getting crowded. Abid finished first and went to wash his hands. Pande came to the table to enquire whether they wanted anything more. Taking that opportunity, Riaz resumed his conversation.

"Abid... the person accompanying me is a Pakistani guy. He is the same one mentioned in Arshad's Urdu letter, which was recovered from his Mumbai house. The Chinese trust Abid, and he knows a lot about their activities. He is the one who killed Arshad aka Hemant."

"Will you be able to alert us when you start your journey to Rameswaram?" Pande asked.

"I have no phone with me to alert you. You may have to keep a vigil," Riaz said.

"Any more details on the Chinese man you will take to Rameswaram?"

"Not a bit. I saw him only once on 9th November at the villa."

"You said Abid hired two vehicles. Where have you parked the other vehicle?"

"It is parked at Abid's acquaintance's house in Mulla Malai village in Krishnagiri. Abid is familiar with Krishnagiri. A right turn from the highway at Krishnagiri junction will lead to a ten-kilometre-long road to the village. On the way to this village, one has to drive through a winding, hilly road along the Krishnagiri Dam. It's beautiful but remote. Abid said the Chinese have rented a bungalow in Krishnagiri."

Their conversation ended abruptly as Abid returned. They paid the bill and left.

Pande was relieved that Riaz was safe. Yet, his ordeal at the eatery would have to continue as the team banked on him for alerts about Riaz and Abid's commencement of their journey to Rameswaram.

Sitting in the corner of the eatery, Pande called Godbole and shared the information revealed by Riaz. He also informed Godbole that Abid could be the tall, stout person they had seen in the library. Godbole received the happy news with great relief. However, in light of the information Riaz reported, Godbole had to hurry to redraw his plans. So, he quickly concluded the call after asking Pande to intensify his lookout for any movements from Dove Villa.

Chapter – 13
The Quiet Getaway

Devanahalli
November 14, 2020
8 a.m.

Thick, dark clouds loomed ominously in the sky. Intermittent bouts of strong winds kept the atmosphere gloomy and cooler than usual. Despite the weather, Godbole and his team were up at dawn and ready for work by 7:30 a.m. The Chinese, their adversaries, were in the advanced stage of their preparations, with a driver and SUV ready and waiting for the all-clear signal from Kanak Mohan in Rameswaram. It was only a matter of time before they launched the getaway operation, a race against time for the NES-17 team.

The team had just settled at the breakfast table, savouring a rare moment of calm before the storm of the impending mission. Godbole's cell phone emitted a sharp beep, cutting through the silence. It was a message from Mohan.

'Signal given. I am with Rolex, so I can't call. I have been asked to be with him until the work is completed. They are coming as soon as possible.'

The time for the Chinese to smuggle out their man was fast approaching. For the NES-17 team, it wasn't just an opportunity; it was a mission – a mission to capture the unaccounted Chinese man. With the ongoing tense LAC standoff, the bosses needed to be informed well in advance while acting against a Chinese man.

At 9:45 a.m., Godbole made a crucial call to Das at his office, timing it before Das delved into his daily routine.

"Good timing," Das said. "I was just thinking of speaking to you this morning. You know... the Home Ministry has some queries. They wanted feedback on the progress, mainly on two issues – the blackout on 12th October and the Chinese tech centre near the LAC."

"Sir, we have yet to get to the bottom of these issues. But we are poised to make a breakthrough... a significant one," Godbole said.

"I know that, Yash, but to the Ministry, this might seem like a routine update. They're under pressure. It's becoming a political issue. Now, the Army has become aggressive about the Chinese tech centre and wants the government to be proactive, you know..."

"Yes, Sir..."

"Listen, Yash..." Das interrupted Godbole and said, "The issue is serious. On 12th October, the same day the power failure and other incidents happened, two IAF jets flying in our airspace close to LAC in the Twang sector reported a strange navigational problem."

"Yes, sir, I remember you mentioning this," Godbole said.

"Following that incident, a joint technical team of the Army, IAF, and intelligence conducted a probe in the Tawang sector. Their technical team deployed advanced electronic signal sweepers near the LAC. Yet they did not detect anything. However, security experts continue to be concerned about the problem. As we did, some experts are also inclined to link the problem with the shadowy Chinese tech centre so close to the LAC."

"So now the Chinese tech facility is also coming into our defence experts' focus," Godbole said.

"It is, Yash. During the joint meeting, I conveyed our suspicion that Kanak Mohan's article is a Chinese attempt to condition the Indian mind to believe that a navigational glitch exists in our systems. However, the issue could result from China's deliberate manipulation of electronic signals to misdirect our guided weapon systems and aircraft."

"What was their reaction?" Godbole asked.

"The Army wouldn't like to sit tight on this serious issue. They want to take countermeasures. However, they need more information about the Chinese tech centre. They also want input from intelligence. That's why the government is putting pressure on us."

"Sir, I can understand the Army's position. These are very sensitive issues. But considering the enemy's ability and strengths, we must tread carefully."

"I am naturally on your side, Yash. But I have to face the Ministry officials. Tell me a response the Ministry is likely to buy," Das said.

"I am at a loss to explain this. Sir, see... the NES-17 team might not have hit the bull's eye yet. Even so, we have every reason to believe that the infamous Chinese network in India has now gone on the back foot. The Chinese might have taken Tsering Dorjee's rescue in October as a one-off incident. However, losing Dolma in about two weeks of the Dorjee incident would be alarming for the Chinese. They would consider it the precursor to more challenges in the offing—"

"Yash, I know," Das tried to interrupt.

"Sir, please let me complete. Regarding intelligence and spy games, the Chinese are sticklers for rules. That's why when they spoke to Mohan over the phone, breaking their own rules, I saw it as a sign of desperation. These are not ordinary strides; the Ministry should understand. Did we not risk so much while rescuing Dorjee? Was it not from Dorjee that we learnt about the Chinese tech centre? Wasn't it a grave risk we took in sending our operative Abdul Riaz into the Chinese ring? Can anyone say we were napping?"

"Yash, please calm down. I know the entire team has been on their toes since this matter started. You had to cover the ground from Delhi to Tawang, Mumbai, Rameswaram and Bangalore. Our professional constraint is that everyone only looks at the results and how fast we present them on a platter. Anyway, I will do my best to convince the Ministry."

"Sorry, sir. I shouldn't have been emotional. With Riaz stuck in the Chinese burrow, I know how tense I am."

"I understand, Yash."

"Sir, it is not that the challenges have eased. I know well that the Chinese do not give up that easily. They might be down momentarily, but they will resurrect and return strong."

"Correct, Yash. I know you are constantly reviewing the situation."

"Sir, frankly... I do not consider the progress we have achieved so far to be enough to get the upper hand over the Chinese. We are still in the dark about the person handling the Chinese operations within India. It is vital to identify and apprehend him. The only silver lining we find now is that we can get their man as he attempts to escape. This man could be crucial to taking the investigations into the Mumbai blackout to its logical conclusion. Maybe the same person could throw light on their tech centre near the LAC. Finally, the plight of the seventy-year-old Rinchin Tashi remains as a festering wound in my mind."

"What are your plans to trap this all-important Chinese man in Dove Villa?"

"Well, that's why I called you. The team is now getting ready to trail him. From what we know, the Chinese are working to smuggle this man out of India via Rameswaram. Since we have a real chance to apprehend him on his way to Rameswaram. I thought... I should notify you."

"Please go ahead. It should be a clean job without any errors or miscalculations. Should not give any opportunity to the Chinese to take diplomatic advantage out of this action."

"Sir, that's why we are not entering the Dove Villa to get this man. What if that chap has some legal document that has escaped our notice? The chances are remote, yet we have considered it in our plan. We know all those Chinese in Dove Villa have permits to stay and work in Bangalore, Karnataka, but not in Tamil Nadu. I will wait to act till they cross over to Tamil Nadu. At least there would be one violation on their part for us to stop them."

"That's perfect. We need to know who this mysterious Chinese man is without ruffling the Chinese diplomatically. When do you expect the Chinese to launch their *Operation Getaway*?" Das asked.

"Any time from now... literally anytime. Mohan messaged me this morning that he signalled the Chinese to proceed with their operation. So, we can probably expect the Chinese to make their move today or tomorrow."

"Wish your team all the best," Das said, disconnecting the call.

Godbole turned his attention to the team's preparations. Since the vehicle chosen by the Chinese to drive them to Rameswaram was an SUV, there could probably be more than one person travelling in the vehicle. Riaz, as a driver, and Abid, as a companion to the Chinese man as well, perhaps. Godbole remembered that the Chinese had hired two ash-coloured Ford Endeavour SUVs. What was the significance of the same make and the same-coloured vehicles? Was the second SUV a standby? Or was it intended to confuse the persons trailing the vehicles? Godbole was satisfied that the team had two vehicles ready to press into operation if necessary.

Godbole studied the two possible routes the Chinese vehicles were likely to take. It would be a ten to eleven-hour drive with short breaks. Both routes passed through topographies with inhabited plains and deserted hilly and wooded areas. Godbole would have to pick a suitable place to launch the team's operation. Somehow,

Riaz's mention of Mulla Malai in Krishnagiri stood out. He studied the map and found that Krishnagiri was on National Highway 48, connecting Bangalore to places in Tamil Nadu. It was roughly 122 kilometres from Devanahalli. Incidentally, National Highway 48 provided the shortest access to Madurai and Rameswaram.

Whatever the route, first, the vehicle carrying the Chinese man would have to proceed from Chittaranjan Farms to Devanahalli to head to Bangalore. From Bangalore, the vehicle must proceed to Attibele to pass through the Hosur Road Toll Collection Centre, follow the National Highway 48, and drive to Rameswaram. Therefore, Devanahalli and Hosur Toll Centre were the two exit points that the Chinese vehicles could not avoid. Keeping that in mind, Godbole planned to deploy the team's SUV with Talreja and Kamini near the Hosur Toll Centre to help them follow the Chinese vehicle proceeding to Rameswaram. At the toll centre, Talreja might get a chance to use face recognition equipment to check the Chinese passengers in the SUV. If necessary, Talreja would have the option to use the equipment to jam radio signals and obstruct automatic toll collection using the RFID sticker on Chinese vehicles. During the temporary obstruction, the vehicles would have to wait at the centre longer, giving Talreja time to peek into the vehicles.

The other vehicle Talreja hired, a navy blue Maruti car, would wait at Devanahalli with Godbole. It would be easier for Godbole to trail the SUV with Chinese passengers from Devanahalli to the Hosur Toll Centre. Talreja and Kamini could take over the chase from the toll centre. However, all those arrangements would work only if Pande gave a timely alert when the SUV or their car with the Chinese man moved out of Dove Villa.

At 4:10 p.m., Godbole's cell phone rang. Pande from the other end said, "The SUV bearing number 3189 and their white Benz car just now turned to Chikkaballore Village Road and headed towards Devanahalli. Riaz was driving the SUV. He deliberately slowed down to help me take notice. I feel it was Abid at the wheel of the other car. I couldn't look for passengers in the vehicles. It all happened very fast."

Like an unleashed spring, Godbole got up and rushed to Talreja's room. He asked Talreja and Kamini to proceed to the Hosur Toll Centre. He reminded Talreja to check their kits to ensure all equipment required for operations was stocked. Next, carrying his kit, he boarded his car and moved to the spot he had selected earlier to wait for the vehicles with Riaz, Abid and the Chinese man to arrive. He just had about five minutes before the vehicles would pass by.

The Chinese surprised Godbole by making their move before it got dark. Why did they start so early? Would the second SUV join the journey? The Chinese plans for their getaway operation were difficult to read. Godbole called Das in Delhi and apprised him of the situation.

"Go ahead, Yash. All the best to you and your boys. Please note that I have sent Amit Rao and Sneha Kumar to Bangalore with a small group of commandos. After you leave, they will take care of any residual work left in Bangalore. They will also be on standby for any emergency," Das informed.

The moment Godbole was waiting for finally arrived. The SUV, followed by the white Benz car, appeared in the distance. In a flash, Godbole switched on the ignition. Just as the vehicles passed, Godbole followed, keeping a fair distance. He hoped there would not be any more surprises from the Chinese and that they would drive to Hosur Road Toll Centre to head for NH 48. In addition, Godbole was alone on that chasing mission. It was a disadvantage. He had to watch the getaway vehicles and drive, negotiating the problematic traffic. Therefore, he called Pande and asked him to hire a taxi to reach the Hosur Toll Centre.

As they reached the periphery of Bangalore city, the traffic became dense, and they had to move at a slower pace. Fortunately, because of the traffic conditions, the chase did not turn into the typical race usually described in stories. Yet, he had lost sight of his target vehicles twice, but managed to catch up with them.

When Godbole noticed the target vehicles approaching Attibele, he knew they were going to the Hosur Toll Centre. Godbole heaved a sigh of relief and kept driving. After almost two hours, the target vehicles reached the toll centre. They waited at the end of a long queue to pass through the barricaded toll-collecting counter. Godbole stopped away from the target vehicle in another queue.

As it had turned dark, the lights at the toll centre were already on. Godbole saw Talreja and Kamini moving closer to the target vehicles in the bright light. He saw them taking positions tactfully. Since the vehicles were stationary, Godbole knew Talreja would get the opportunity to use the face recognition device. When the target vehicles approached the toll collection counter in about two minutes, Talreja and Kamini moved away and disappeared. As Godbole waited, he received Talreja's call.

"Sir... no one in the SUV other than Riaz. With his hands still holding the steering wheel, Riaz managed to show me his thumbs down."

Godbole was anxious. "What about the car?"

"Yes, one Chinese man is in the car's back seat. Our device recognized him as Zinto Lee, one of the residents of Dove Villa. He has valid documents to stay and work in Bangalore. We did not find the unaccounted fifth Chinese man in the vehicles. Oh, see, they've reached the counter. What do we do?"

Trying to hide his disappointment, Godbole said, "Keep following them. We have no other option. I hope you're on the other side of the toll centre."

"Yes, sir, the vehicle is on this side. They just passed; we, too, are starting..."

"Good. I am expecting Pande here. We'll be behind you soon. Let Kamini keep updating me."

Godbole was shocked to learn that the elusive Chinese man was not in the vehicles. Without that person, why would the vehicles proceed to Rameswaram? Godbole wondered. He reasoned that either the Chinese man was hiding in the vehicles or might join them on the way. Therefore, they needed to trail the vehicles continually. Then Godbole remembered that the Chinese had hired two SUVs of the same make and colour. Did the Chinese man leave Bangalore, travelling in the other SUV while the team was busy chasing the vehicle carrying Zinto Lee? Undoubtedly, the Chinese were playing their cards well, making the team flounder in the dark.

However, Godbole found something odd about Zinto Lee travelling to Tamil Nadu. Lee's visa permit was confined to Bangalore. On records, he was an engineer working with Tinmin Electronics and Instrumentation, a Chinese company in Bangalore. Why was he risking travel to Tamil Nadu? Probably, Lee had an intelligence background. Therefore, Godbole felt trailing Lee was the best bet under the circumstances.

Chapter – 14
The Slippery Ghats

Hosur Toll Centre
November 14, 2020
6.30 p.m.

After twenty minutes of waiting at the toll centre, Godbole saw Pande emerge from a taxi. Pande hurried over to Godbole's car, offering to drive so Godbole could focus on the mission ahead. The taxi man was good. He took a shorter route through a rural area to bring me here so fast," Pande said.

"That's good. We must catch up with Talreja," Godbole said, his voice filled with urgency.

It was already pitch dark, with visibility limited to a few metres, even with the car's headlights. There were no streetlights for long stretches. However, the stream of red and amber tail lamps moving ahead gave a rough impression of the road winding forward. In these conditions, trailing an ash-coloured SUV wasn't easy. On the other hand, it also meant that Abid and Lee would not know whether anyone was trailing them. He hoped Talreja and Kamini would make the best of the prevailing conditions.

Meanwhile, the enigma of the Chinese plans continued to consume Godbole. What were they scheming? And where was the elusive fifth Chinese man? Godbole sensed that something of great significance might unfold that night. As he noticed water droplets on the windscreen, he realized it was drizzling, which could further hinder their pursuit of Talreja.

Forty-five minutes into the drive, Godbole received a call from Kamini. She said, "We are in Krishnagiri. We parked our vehicle on the left side of the highway about two hundred metres after the Krishnagiri flyover."

"Where's the target? Any issue?" Godbole asked.

"No, no, sir," Kamini added hastily. "Instead of taking the Krishnagiri flyover and remaining on the highway, the Benz car took the service road. But the SUV went ahead, cleared the flyover and stopped on the side of the highway. We missed the car as we could not have taken the service road. We went ahead of Riaz's SUV and parked quite a distance away. Maybe Riaz's SUV is waiting for instructions. Or, maybe he is waiting for the car to return."

"We'll be there in fifteen minutes. Is Riaz's vehicle visible from your position?" Godbole asked.

"It is drizzling here. Visibility is poor. Riaz has also switched off his parking and tail lamps. We are debating whether we should approach Riaz. We can walk up to him. But we're afraid that someone might be hiding in the vehicle."

"Kamini, you said the Krishnagiri flyover, didn't you?"

"Yes, why..."

Before Kamini could complete it, Godbole said, "You know, under the flyover, there is a right turn to a small road to Krishnagiri Dam and Mulla Malai village, about ten kilometres from the highway. Maybe... You know, we have not yet seen that fifth Chinese man. What if..."

"Sir..." Pande interrupted and said, "Mulla Malai is the village mentioned by Riaz. Abid had taken Riaz there to an acquaintance's house. The Chinese also have a rented bungalow there."

"Yes, I was coming to that. Now we know why they had this break at Krishnagiri. My hunch is that the missing fifth Chinese man might appear now. The Chinese are clever. They may have secretly brought him to this village and kept him here after the engineer and I spotted him in Dove Villa last Thursday. That was why Riaz did not find him at the villa when he returned. Kamini... are you listening?"

"Yes, sir, I heard what Pande and you were saying."

"Good. Talreja, and you be vigilant. The second SUV with the mysterious Chinese man may join the journey soon. They may take about thirty minutes from the village to return to the highway," Godbole said.

"I got it, sir. What I was asking is if we should try to meet Riaz?"

"You see... since Riaz saw Talreja and Kamini at the toll centre, he would expect them to trail him. Let Talreja walk close to Riaz's parked vehicle. It is dark and drizzling, yet I hope Riaz will notice Talreja. Riaz will have a quick word with Talreja if he is alone and safe. Let Talreja try his luck. Anyway, we are reaching soon," Godbole said.

"Okay, sir. Please note that we are parked about two hundred metres beyond the Krishnagiri flyover."

*****

Braving the drizzle, Talreja walked past Riaz's SUV. The faint light from the shops near the flyover and the junction barely cut through the darkness. As he passed the vehicle, Talreja removed the hood of his jacket, hoping Riaz would recognize him. He couldn't see who was in the driver's seat, but assumed it was Riaz. Talreja glanced at the SUV, but Riaz remained still. Talreja continued walking to the flyover and turned back, passing the vehicle again. Still, no response. Either Riaz didn't see him, or it wasn't safe to acknowledge him. Was someone in the vehicle, or was the vehicle fitted with an electronic monitoring device?

By the time Talreja returned to his vehicle, Pande and Godbole had arrived. Godbole was disappointed to learn that Riaz did not communicate with Talreja. Since no new input came from Riaz, Godbole stuck to his original plans. After studying the maps,

Godbole had planned to trail the Chinese until they entered the ghats in the Mallur area, ahead of Salem town. As Godbole tried to evaluate the situation, various challenges sprang up in his mind. If the Chinese vehicles were fitted with electronic monitoring devices, it could cause problems. Devices like microphones, cameras, and location finders could be deployed in a remotely setup live monitoring mode, meaning the vehicles could be under live surveillance. Godbole considered Riaz's not responding to Talreja a strong indicator of that possibility..

Operatives always prepare for the worst-case scenario in risky operations. Godbole, being no exception, assumed that the Chinese vehicles were equipped with a live monitoring system. The same channel used for the monitoring facility could also support remotely controlled arrangements. Godbole considered this a real possibility and factored in the risk of explosives or self-destruct devices to prevent capture by Indian intelligence. Godbole gave his team a quick recap of the proposed operation, stressing the need for them to be prepared for all eventualities. Their professionalism and readiness for any situation were their best weapons in this high-stakes game.

*****

The team waited an hour for the Chinese vehicles to move. The drizzle continued intermittently, cooling the air. With no dinner break in sight, they made do with biscuits and soft drinks from Godbole's car. They had no idea what caused the delay. Godbole felt it would be better if Talreja and Kamini could hit the road before the Chinese resumed their journey.

Godbole explained, "We have to avoid two vehicles following them. If they had seen you during the journey from Hosur Toll Centre, it would be obvious if they saw you behind them. So, it would be best if you left now. Drive slowly. We can share our locations on our location devices."

Talreja and Kamini drove off while Godbole and Pande waited.

At 8:40 p.m., Pande finally noticed an SUV from the service road entering the highway. It briefly stopped near Riaz's vehicle, but no one got off. Soon, Riaz's vehicle moved first like a pilot, and the other SUV followed. Godbole expected Abid, Lee and the fifth Chinese man to be in the second SUV. Godbole informed Kamini about the Chinese resuming their journey from Krishnagiri in two SUVs.

Once the Chinese vehicles drove off, Pande and Godbole followed in their car. The drizzle had stopped, improving visibility, but the wet road limited speed. Pande kept a safe distance, with several vehicles between them and the Chinese SUVs. However, as the road got progressively drier, the Chinese vehicles picked up speed, and Pande strived to maintain a safe distance. Talreja and Kamini's location showed they were at a comfortable distance of about one kilometre ahead of the Chinese vehicles.

Approaching Salem, streetlights made driving more manageable. Godbole pulled out his kitbag and retrieved a laser gun.

"If the Chinese vehicles have satellite connectivity, they will have antennae on their roofs. We have to disable their satellite antennae before launching our operation," Godbole said to an enquiring Pande.

"Are you going to try that while we're moving?" Pande asked.

"No. I am just getting ready. We have to wait until the vehicles enter the ghat."

"Don't you think the drizzle and clouds would have already weakened their satellite connectivity?"

"Maybe, but why take a chance? We will disable the antennae rather than take the risk."

Close to midnight, they entered the Mallur forest road. By then, the drizzle intensified to rain, making the winding, steep route challenging. Traffic was sparse, with only a small pickup truck and two heavy trucks ahead. Godbole was worried that the Chinese would notice them on the empty road. In that situation, the best Pande could do was keep more distance from the target vehicles. Anyway, the tail lamps and the glow from the headlights helped determine the target vehicles' location. After about twenty minutes of driving, the pickup truck exited the ghat road and took a side road. Now, their car was directly behind the Chinese SUVs, which made Godbole uneasy.

Suddenly, Godbole saw the Chinese vehicles overtaking the trucks one by one. They found a more expansive stretch of the road to overtake. Pande also wanted to go past the trucks. However, before their car could pass the trucks, they were again at a narrow patch of the road. Godbole was concerned that the Chinese vehicles might now go faster, leaving his car behind the two crawling trucks. Immediately, he checked the position of Talreja's vehicle and found that it was still about one kilometre ahead of him. Then Godbole noticed that the cell phone network had become weaker already. He instantly dialled Kamini.

"The network is getting weaker. Communication can be a problem. After what we experienced in Dolma's case, I am averse to using our wireless communication. We have to act when we are still able to communicate."

"Understand, sir," Kamini said.

"Listen, the two SUVs were able to overtake the trucks. I think soon they will catch up with you. I think we have to act. As planned, look for the right place and block the Chinese vehicles. We are trying to join you as soon as possible," Godbole said.

While Godbole was on the phone, Pande overtook one of the trucks. Now, only one truck was in front of them. The road was still climbing, and the fully loaded truck struggled to move forward. In a short while, the climb ended, and a relatively plain stretch emerged. The truck in front of their car pulled up. Pande took the opportunity to drive past the truck. Now, there was no vehicle between them and the Chinese vehicles. When Godbole turned back to see why the truck had stopped, he saw the other truck pulling up. The trucks appeared to be together on that journey and were taking a break from the tedious driving.

Pande accelerated the car to catch up with the target Chinese vehicles. While Pande's car had been tied down by the slowly moving trucks for the past fifteen minutes, the Chinese vehicles had moved forward with incredible momentum. When Pande negotiated a hairpin curve, he saw the Chinese vehicles' headlights glow quite a distance away. Godbole feared they might miss the chance to intercept the Chinese in the ghats. He was unsure when Talreja would be able to stop the Chinese vehicles. He called up Kamini to express his concerns. Luckily, the call got through despite the poor connectivity. Kamini appeared confident. She informed Godbole that after a relatively more straightforward stretch of road, they were about to take a heavily wooded, steep portion of the road again. Kamini sounded hopeful of finding a suitable place somewhere there. Before they could speak in detail, the call got disconnected.

*****

Talreja's heart pounded as he spotted the headlights of the Chinese vehicles drawing nearer. Scanning the road ahead, he searched for a perfect spot to spring their trap. Soon, he saw a hairpin turn followed by another sharp bend. Perfect. He brought the SUV to a halt, blocking the narrow road completely. The blinking tail lamps cast a warning glow in the drizzle. Talreja opened the bonnet, feigning an engine failure, and waited.

As the Chinese vehicles pulled up, Talreja busied himself under the bonnet, acting like he was fixing a breakdown. Drenched and shivering, Kamini approached the first SUV, her eyes wide with feigned helplessness. Riaz, behind the wheel, remained impassive. He exited the vehicle and walked to the second SUV.

"There's a dead vehicle ahead," Riaz explained. Abid, initially wary, relaxed upon seeing a helpless-looking Kamini standing drenched in the rain.

"We don't have time to fix it, but we can push it aside," Abid murmured to Riaz. Riaz relayed the message to Kamini, who climbed into the driver's seat, ready to steer. Riaz and Talreja began pushing the SUV, straining against the weight and uneven road. Abid, sensing their struggle, stepped out to help. As he joined in, Kamini started steering the vehicle to the roadside.

Meanwhile, Pande spotted the stationary lights. He parked their car at a safe distance and hurried towards the action. As they approached, Godbole, using the laser gun, swiftly disabled the antennae on the SUVs. With the antennae out of commission, they rushed to the SUV, where they expected to find the Chinese men and Abid. Pande positioned himself on one side of the Chinese SUV while Godbole moved to the other. Just as Godbole reached his spot, one of the Chinese men inside the SUV shouted a warning. Abid, who was pushing the vehicle, instantly turned and was startled to see someone trying to open the door of his SUV. Realizing it was a trap, he drew his gun and fired at Godbole, but missed. Riaz sprang into action, striking Abid's hand and causing the pistol to slip. Abid's shock turned to fury as he saw Riaz siding with the enemy. Just as he prepared to strike back, Talreja charged, tackling Abid. A scuffle ensued, with Riaz and Talreja eventually subduing and handcuffing Abid.

As they secured Abid, the left rear door of the second SUV flew open. A Chinese operative leapt out, attacking Pande. Pande struggled, but Godbole rushed over to assist. The Chinese man bolted into the woods with Godbole in pursuit. Meanwhile, Pande overpowered the second Chinese man attempting to flee. Kamini quickly handcuffed him, and they shoved him into the backseat of their SUV. Pande pinned the captive down and searched him, finding only a leather wallet.

Next, Talreja restrained Abid while Riaz searched him, finding nothing. They shoved Abid into the front seat, with the Chinese man secured in the back. Abid shouted at Riaz, calling him a traitor. Talreja and Riaz quickly gagged both captives and tied their legs. Then, grabbing a torchlight, Talreja sprinted towards the bushes where Godbole had pursued the fleeing Chinese operative.

As Kamini stood guard, Riaz pulled Pande aside and whispered, "I got a good look at the captured Chinese man. He's the one they want to send to Sri Lanka."

"Good that we got their mysterious guest. He looks devastated. I didn't have much of a problem subduing him. The one who ran into the bushes was tough... he is Lee, isn't he?" Pande asked.

"I don't know. I did not get a chance to see his face. I was alone in the vehicle."

"Riaz, if your vehicle was not to be used, I wonder why they employed your services?"

"It's not merely a standby vehicle. It's fitted with electronic gadgets. I couldn't even speak to Talreja at Krishnagiri."

"We also suspected something. Godbole disabled the antennae of both vehicles."

"I am relieved to know that. You know, before getting out of the vehicle, I disconnected the battery power to their equipment in the SUV."

"That is smart of you... Now, do we go to look for the fellow in the bushes?" Pande asked.

"I think Godbole and Talreja are enough to tackle that man. But this is a difficult terrain so I'll join them. You and Kamini guard these two captured chaps. Please park these vehicles on one side of the road," Riaz said, rushing in the direction the torchlight was visible in the thick greenery.

When Riaz reached Godbole, he shared the news: their captured Chinese man was indeed the mysterious guest they sought, but Lee had vanished into the forest. Godbole felt a mix of relief and concern. The steady drizzle and pitch-black night compounded their difficulties. Tracking Lee amidst tall grass and thick foliage seemed nearly impossible. Yet, Godbole knew Lee's options were limited. Shivering in the cold and wet, the team began combing the bushes and tall grass.

"Keep the flashlights on and look for the foliage and grass getting ruffled as he moves. He cannot hide for long in there. Let's spread out in a semi-circle formation," Godbole told his men.

"We need to be vigilant. He might be armed," Talreja warned.

"If he had a gun with him, he would have shot Pande when Pande tried to stop him. I think only Abid had a weapon. The Chinese wanted to look like genuine travellers if they happened to be checked at any of the checkpoints," Godbole replied.

Twenty minutes passed, but there was no sign of Lee. Lee's confrontation with Pande and escape showed he was a formidable operative. Godbole was frustrated that even though they had apprehended one Chinese man, they couldn't leave the place without getting Lee.

The team would have to leave that place before 4 a.m. because traffic would start by then. Godbole didn't want the media to get even a whiff about the incident. Abid and the detained Chinese man also needed to be taken away securely for interrogation. Godbole wished he could get some additional help to speed up the search. Even if he wanted to request help, it wouldn't be possible then as there was no mobile network in that jungle.

"Buck up, guys," Godbole told Talreja and Riaz. "No chance of getting any help; we must catch the fugitive ourselves."

Chapter – 15
Hide and Seek

Mallur forest road
November 15, 2020
1.40 a.m.

It was 1:40 a.m., and except for the unrelenting monotonous buzz of the drizzle and the occasional clatter of the insects and frogs, the forest was calm. The hilly terrain, known for its wild animals and poisonous snakes, was eerily silent. Even the animals preferred to remain in their burrows and hideaways. Only Godbole and his team had no choice but to bravely search for Lee.

Godbole, Talreja and Riaz tried to move forward through the tall grass, bushes and trees. Their wet clothes got caught in the thorny plants, and they received pricks and scratches as they struggled to go forward. For a moment, Talreja stood briefly sweeping the terrain with his torchlight. He realized he was at the beginning of a slope that went down, undulating a few metres to meet a large water body. With the lake ahead, Lee would have to veer left or right to escape. The team decided on a triangular formation: Riaz to the left, Talreja to the right, and Godbole at the third point, trailing behind.

If Lee had moved, they would've noticed a disturbance in the bushes with the moving wet leaves reflecting the light from their torch. Was Lee sitting tight amongst the undergrowth, waiting for an opportunity to escape? At one place, Riaz noticed trampled grass. He turned his flashlight there and saw a grove formed amidst tall grass, indicating that Lee had hurried through. He called out Godbole and Talreja, and the trio followed the grove, which led them back to the road. On the road, Lee's boots had left slush that was beginning to wash away in the drizzle. He might have just crossed to the other side of the road.

"The Chinese fellow is a clever chap," Godbole said. "He knew we'd be looking in the direction he had run away. So, he quietly made a U-turn and went in the opposite direction."

"But he crossed the road only a few metres behind the parked vehicles. Was he trying to get back to the vehicle?" Talreja asked.

"We may have to wait to figure it out. Now stay on his trail," Godbole said.

The trio fanned out in the direction Lee crossed. The trail soon disappeared as the patch of trampled grass ended near thick bushes. Nevertheless, with the flashlights, they kept combing every inch of the area.

It was already 2:30 a.m., and they had detected no movement. Suddenly, an idea struck Godbole. Why not switch off the lights for a few minutes? To avoid detection, Lee might be waiting for the lights to go off to make his move. They switched off the flashlights and remained immobile with bated breath.

As a few minutes passed, Godbole suddenly switched on his flashlight, catching the movement of wet leaves of a low-level plant. The team rushed to the spot. On the way, Riaz stumbled over a shoe lying in the slush near a bush. As they looked around, they saw a thoroughly drenched and exhausted Chinese man lying on the muddy ground. His shoes had come off in the mud, and his feet were severely hurt and bleeding. His shirt was torn, and his body was bruised.

As Talreja lifted Lee from the mire, he did not resist. His battered body had no strength left to put up a fight. His eyes mirrored the profound dread that had haunted him throughout his covert career. Being captured was the nightmare of any spy, a moment feared above all.

Aware of what was going through Lee's mind, Godbole remained vigilant. He knew the dark clouds in Lee's mind could vanish instantly if he saw an opportunity to flee. In the blink of an eye, the fallen spy could spring back to life, desperate and dangerous. So, their team stayed on high alert, their eyes never leaving Lee for a second.

Talreja and Riaz carried Lee to the vehicle and laid him in the backseat of Abid's SUV. All the while, the team maintained a studied silence. No questions and no instructions were given. Despite Lee's condition, Godbole handcuffed him. Godbole would have offered Lee some hot beverage had it been available.

Godbole checked his phone, but there was still no network. The team wanted to leave the ghats and reach Bangalore immediately, so they had to move. Before leaving, the team searched for the third captive, too, but found no cell phone, purse, or other items. The two travel bags in their vehicle contained personal clothes, undergarments, and essential toiletries in small kits. They were travelling clean.

Godbole asked Talreja to drive the SUV with the handcuffed Abid and the Chinese man in the backseat. Although their hands and legs were tied, Godbole could not take Abid for granted and decided to travel in the front seat of that vehicle. Pande drove the SUV with Lee in the back seat. Lee was exhausted, weak and had vomited quite a few times. Unsure if Lee was genuinely unwell, Godbole had his legs loosely tied as a precaution. Kamini drove the car, and Riaz drove the SUV he had driven from Bangalore.

The convoy of the four vehicles left the ghats at 3:30 a.m. The team had been on their toes since the previous afternoon. Action in the inclement weather was doubly challenging. Now, without food and sleep, all were dog-tired. But there was no scope for rest until they reached Bangalore after a four-hour drive. As soon as their phones began to work, Godbole asked Talreja to stop the vehicle. After alighting, he stood away from the vehicle and dialled Das's number.

"Waiting for your call all night, Yash. I've been checking your location continuously. We lost you as you reached the Mallur ghats. Are you all safe... is everything fine?" Das asked, clearly worried.

"Everything is fine, sir. We're now on our way back to Bangalore. The good news is that we picked up Abid, Lee and their mysterious guest."

"Oh good," Das said.

"Now, sir, we'll reach in another three hours. What are your instructions?"

In some time, our men, led by Amit and Sneha, will meet you. They're in a seventeen-seater minibus."

"Really?" Godbole asked in surprise.

"Well, Yash, when I lost your location around midnight, and you did not get back to me even after an hour, I was concerned. I dispatched them from Bangalore after 1:30 a.m. Please call up Amit or Sneha and coordinate. The detainees and all four of you can board the minibus for the rest of the journey. They have enough food, water, and flasks with hot beverages. I have also sent a few T-shirts and trousers. Come back relaxed."

For a moment, Godbole thought of Das. He might not have been with the team physically, but he was always there for support. A captain should be like that. For Das, the team members were like his children; otherwise, how could he have considered packing food and even clothes for the team?

Feeling grateful, Godbole said, "Thank you, sir..."

"That is okay, Yash. I know what it means to be in the field."

"Sir, what about the four vehicles with us? The Chinese vehicles have to be searched."

"The commandos will drive those vehicles back to Bangalore. We will search them there. Now let me appraise the Chief. I'll call back." Das ended the call abruptly.

Godbole returned to the vehicle, and they resumed the journey. Fifteen minutes later, Das called again. Godbole told Talreja to stop the vehicle to attend to the call away from the two captives.

Spoke to the Chief. The bus will take you straight to the HAL airport. An Indian Air Force plane will be waiting to carry the apprehended men and the team to Delhi. I have instructed Amit and Sneha. They said they are aware of your location... should meet you in about thirty minutes."

"Noted, sir."

"How are the Chinese men and Abid behaving?"

"Abid is the toughest of all three. The guest seemed shell-shocked and not as agile as the other two. Lee appears to be the real operative. But for now, he is exhausted."

"Well, it is not Zinto Lee. Lee is back home in Dove Villa."

"What?" Godbole was astounded.

"Yes, Lee is in Bangalore. I deployed Amit and Sneha as backup when you left Bangalore. At around 10:30 p.m., Lee returned to Bangalore in the same Benz car. Amit and Sneha spotted him entering Bangalore at the Hosur Toll Centre."

"Oh, then who is this guy with me?"

"We will have to find out. He must be important."

"This is crazy. Now there are two unaccounted Chinese men." Godbole wondered what was happening. That would mean those two Chinese men were hidden in Mulla Malai village in Krishnagiri. They boarded Abid's SUV from there, and Lee returned to Bangalore.

Godbole said, "The Chinese-rented bungalow in Mulla Malai will have to be identified and searched."

"You are right, Yash. I was waiting for the outcome of your operation. Now, I will initiate the necessary action. Dove Villa will also be under our scanner."

Chapter – 16
The Chinese Play

New Delhi
November 15, 2020
11 a.m.

Das hurriedly settled in the back seat of his office car. Why was the Agency Chief sending him to the Ministry of External Affairs to meet the Deputy Secretary at 11:30 a.m.? The timing was inconvenient, disrupting his packed schedule. Just an hour ago, the NES-17 team had landed in Delhi with three detainees. After dispatching Godbole and his team for some well-deserved rest, Das had finished a thorough search of the detainees and their belongings. Then, the Chief's sudden directive came. Das wanted the detainees interrogated immediately without giving them time to relax. Reluctantly, he handed over the three men to a team of expert interrogators and quickly left for the MEA meeting.

Usually, MEA meetings were held at the MEA office at South Block. However, since it was a Sunday, the meeting was being held at the Ashoka Hotel, where the Government of India had two full floors for official use of various kinds. As the car entered the Ashoka Hotel gate, Das's phone buzzed. It was a text message from the head of the team assigned to interrogate the three detainees. The message read:

> *Before we could conduct the customary medical checkup ahead of the interrogation session, the bruised and weak Chinese fellow collapsed. We shifted him to the clinic to provide medical help. For info.*

Das felt worried. He instantly replied, *'Please ensure he gets full medical care.'*

Since their arrival in Delhi, Das had observed that the Chinese man appeared visibly fatigued, requiring assistance to walk from the aircraft to the waiting vehicle. Das was uncertain whether the man's condition was genuine or a ruse.

Raghav Tripathy, the Deputy Secretary handling the China desk, waited in the lobby. "Please sit down, Mr Das. I'm glad you are on time. I have just ten minutes before the Chinese diplomat arrives here," Tripathy said as they entered his room.

Hearing his words made Das uneasy. The Chinese seemed to be in overdrive, their actions hinting at a hidden agenda. Requesting a meeting on a Sunday was highly unusual, underscoring its importance.

"Sorry you had to come on a Sunday... at such short notice," Tripathy continued, "But we have a small issue here. This morning, the Chinese Embassy requested an immediate meeting. They said they have intelligence input to share and discuss related developments in person. We have no clue what they have to share. We don't want to be caught off guard. That's why we spoke to your Chief, and now you're here. Any developments on your end?"

Instantly, Das became alert. Were the Chinese trying to pre-empt any fallout because of last night's operation by the NES-17 team? If that was the case, their reaction was swift. The Agency did inform the Home Minister's office orally earlier that morning, but a formal report was yet to be sent. There was no chance for anyone outside the system to learn about the incident. The only way for the Chinese to know about the operation could be by tracking their vehicles via satellite. They lost the signals at the ghat and never regained them because the team disabled the antenna on their vehicle. That was enough for the Chinese to infer that there was trouble. The capture of their three men would expose their assets and plans in India. The Chinese might be attempting damage control.

"Mr Das, is there anything... any development? There is no harm in letting me know. You see... I have to tackle the diplomat," Tripathy pursued.

"Yes, there was an incident late last night... rather early this morning. We have yet to report it to the government formally. Before I could do that, I had to come here," Das informed Tripathy. Then, he narrated the incident that culminated in the detention of two Chinese and a Pakistani ISI agent. He also mentioned the possible links between the captives and the Mumbai blackout and the issue arising from the Chinese tech centre near LAC in the Tawang sector. Tripathy's face grew serious.

"If that is why this diplomat is coming, then the matter is grave," Tripathy said, his tone reflecting the gravity of the situation.

"You are right. The Chinese are in an awkward position. They might be concerned that the cat might get out of the bag. They would want to pre-empt the consequences of this serious setback," Das said.

"I agree, Mr Das. The Chinese always try to take us by surprise. They know how to play such games with near perfection. Good that I consulted you. I will try to handle it as best as possible. While narrating the incident, you said you did not recover anything from the detainees. Are you sure they are the real culprits?" Tripathy asked, raising his concern.

"Yes, there was nothing in their possession. And you know, that itself becomes the main reason for our suspicion. Does anyone travel without a basic thing like a cell phone?"

"I get it, Mr Das."

As Tripathy was speaking to Das, an attendant entered the room and informed him about the arrival of the Chinese diplomat. Tripathy immediately got up to proceed to the meeting.

"Mr Das, can you please join this meeting in the guise of my assistant to take notes of the meeting? These Chinese people wouldn't speak straight. They have a roundabout way of speaking.

You may quietly sit there and watch his body language, choice of words, and tone. You are from intelligence; perhaps you can read him better."

Led by Tripathy, Das walked to the room where the Chinese diplomat was waiting. He was all smiles as he shook hands with Tripathy warmly and exchanged pleasantries.

"I know... unfortunately... our countries are going through a challenging period. Luckily, we are still talking to each other. However, some forces are bent upon creating more rift between us," the Chinese diplomat said, glancing at Tripathy and looking serious.

He continued, "We have a reliable intelligence input that two or even three men are planted in India by this unscrupulous outside power with a label that they are Chinese spies. It is disconcerting, but we should not fall into this trap. Our government instructed us to forewarn India about this betrayal by this outside power." The diplomat stopped and waited for Tripathy's response.

"We are surprised to learn this. We have no such inputs. By the way, which outside power are you mentioning?" Tripathy asked.

"We have an idea, but it is inappropriate to name it now. We are doing further work on this. Once more information is available, we will share it. In the interim, please be vigilant and do not get swayed by the designs of the power I mentioned."

"Do you have more information about the two or three men you said are planted here?"

"We are not sure about their full identities. We gathered that one is an Indian, and the other two are of the Tibetan lineage, but are shown as Chinese nationals. That is why we are worried."

"Oh, I see..."

"If you apprehend them, we will cooperate with your investigations."

"With only such sketchy information, I do not know how we will apprehend the culprits. However, if ever we come across these men, we will inform you after due vetting."

"Thank you so much for agreeing to this meeting on a Sunday. We always assure India of our highest consideration and cooperation. Looking forward to further strengthening our age-old ties," the Chinese diplomat said, raising to leave.

Das looked at the Chinese diplomat, slowly walking away, amused by the world of diplomacy. Even at the height of tensions on the ground, diplomats behaved as if everything was fine. Their words were ornamental, standard or hollow. Through those words, they conveyed what they meant. It was not what they said but what they did not say that often mattered.

"I am convinced that the issue is critical to the Chinese. What could you make out of his words, Mr Das?"

"It was obvious that he was referring to their three men in our custody. He seemed to say that if you have arrested those three men, do not assume that they are Chinese spies. He wanted to ensure there wouldn't be any scope for us to go and tell the Chinese that we caught their men. Their stance would be that they have already warned us that it will happen. It's like a chess move. The Chinese are ready to disown their men."

"Mr Das, you are right. Whether it is diplomacy or intelligence, they are ruthless players. They believe in saving the situation, not the men. That is the difference between us. Anyway, I know you will find a way to proceed from here."

"Whatever he said, he knows the game has just started. As we do, they, too, would keep their fingers crossed. Their next attempt would be to know the extent of the damage caused to their operation. They would be more concerned about their tech centre near the LAC getting exposed. Expect him to request further meetings," Das said.

"I know he will. In this, we may have to work together. Anyway, I will send an official note to your Chief about today's interaction with this Chinese diplomat. Thank you for coming."

Chapter – 17
Rising Challenges

New Delhi
November 15, 2020
3.30 p.m.

A four-hour sleep did Godbole a lot of good. Therefore, when he reported to the NES-17 office at 3:30 p.m., he was fully charged. Before plunging into work, he met Das to learn how the three detainees behaved and if there had been any further development. He was aware that in the morning, Das had arranged for three separate teams of experts for the preliminary questioning of the three captives.

When Godbole entered, Das was alone in the cabin. Although he sent his team to rest, Das was still relentlessly trying to organize all the requirements so they could quickly return to work.

"Yash, you could have relaxed today," Das said, smiling. "But I admit I am relieved to see you back in the office. Here, the pressure is not easing."

"I have rested enough. You know I can't stay away when an operation is in progress. I am eager to get updated about our three guests," Godbole said.

Das's expression darkened. "Well, Yash, things are bad." When Godbole anxiously leaned forward, Das said, almost whispering, "That Chinese chap is dead. The one who had tried to escape is dead."

Godbole was taken aback, but before he could speak, Das said, "As we always do, we brought a doctor for their medical checkup.

Before the doctor could begin the checkup, Tsering Wangchu... collapsed. He was taken to the hospital but died. The doctors said it was a case of poisoning."

"This is a disaster. Tsering Wangchu... was that his name?" Godbole asked.

"Yes, Tsering Wangchu. He muttered that name when we took down their details upon arrival here. It might be fake."

"So, he was not acting. He had vomited a few times. He appeared unwell from the time we apprehended him. That means he consumed poison before he fell into our hands. It is a terrible setback to me and my team," Godbole said, lowering his head and clasping his hands in disappointment.

"Yash, I understand. I tried explaining the situation to the Chief. It was a tough operation. Things did not go perfectly well in our favour in the darkness of a rainy night in a remote, inhospitable jungle. Yet, we have the other two culprits in custody."

"All that is true. A living Wangchu would have been a powerful bargaining chip. I'm sorry we lost someone who could have provided critical answers."

"Yash, now look forward. We have to march on from here."

"What was the poison he consumed? Why did it take that long to work?"

"Maybe even the Chinese-made poison is substandard," Das laughed. He added, "Yash, the doctors said they could answer all these questions only after the autopsy and chemical analysis of the viscera," Das said.

"I wonder why only Wangchu had the poison with him. We didn't find anything on the other Chinese chap. Does that mean Wangchu was the key player, and as we expected, the other chap was the guest... the guy brought to rectify the technical issues?"

"Possibly. Only professional operatives and spies would have the heart to end their lives."

"You're right, sir. We now have only one Chinese to take the probe forward. Abid might help only to a lesser extent. Sir, did they reveal anything in the questioning?"

"The Chinese man now with us is Lobsang Pema. Again, it could be a fake name. Before I speak about Pema and Abid, I want to inform you about the visit I paid to an MEA official. The detention of these three men seemed to have sent the Chinese scurrying for cover," Das said and narrated the Chinese diplomat's meeting with the MEA Deputy Secretary that morning.

"It looks like the Chinese are desperately attempting to contain the damage. But I do not think that they would sacrifice their men. My mind says they would want at least the tech fellow, Pema, back. That diplomat will come back on some pretext. This is turning into a chess game. The diplomat may have made only his first move," Godbole said.

"Yes, we have to remain watchful. Returning to the two guests, they are in separate cells. From the time they were brought here, they were questioned and continuously kept engaged without being allowed to rest. However, Lobsang Pema is not showing any signs of cracking. He claims that he is a Tibetan from Lhasa. His Mandarin isn't strong. He crossed over to India through Tawang. We do not buy that. Despite his physically drained condition, Pema is sticking to his story. We've found some holes in his statements. Let us give him a long rope till we devise a strategy to deal with him," Das said.

"So, we have to do a lot of work on this fellow. What about Abid, sir?"

"I must say, while the fragile-looking Chinese man is proving to be a hard nut, tough man Abid appeared shaken. After a hard grilling, Abid admitted that he is Pakistani. Surprisingly, he is a graduate from Lahore who chose to work for the ISI to satisfy his father. His handler, Major Jamal, sent him here in July 2018 to help the Chinese. A few months after he came to India, another Pakistani, Arshad Gulam, joined him in Delhi. Arshad assumed the name of Hemant Khanna and started liaising with the Indians for the Chinese."

"Did he reveal who his handler was in India?"

"All instructions came from Major Jamal, who used Dubai phone numbers. Initially, Abid never met or communicated directly with any Chinese operatives. Only after he came to live in Dove Villa did he meet Zinto Lee and the other three men. But they were not the ones running the show."

"Did he reveal who the two Chinese men we apprehended are?"

"Abid also says the person who tried to escape into the forest was Tsering Wangchu, and the other chap was Lobsang Pema. He says he doesn't know Pema closely. But Wangchu had told him that he was a resident of Himachal Pradesh, working in Bangalore as a marketing agent for hardware manufactured by Zinto Lee's company for power generation equipment such as turbines, transformers, and so on. Abid believed that both Wangchu and Pema were Chinese because he had heard them speaking Mandarin."

"I also suspect Wangchu and Pema are Chinese men," Godbole said.

"Abid said he met Wangchu and Pema for the first time at the Chinese-rented bungalow in Mulla Malai village in Krishnagiri. They were taken to Dove Villa only once... a few days ago. It was for a homely Chinese meal. The following night, they were taken promptly back to Mulla Malai," Das informed.

"I think that was when I saw one of them," Godbole said. "On 12th November, when I had accompanied the electrical engineer to restore electricity at Dove Villa."

"Oh, yes, I know," Das said.

"However, I wonder who the one I saw in Dove Villa is. I had only a fleeting view of that person. I believe it was Pema. What else did Abid share?" Godbole asked.

"Well, we did a bit of coercing, and he admitted to killing Arshad, that is Hemant, in his flat in Mumbai on orders from Major Jamal. He said Arshad had made the grave mistake of hiding the laptop used to carry out his personal secret work related to their operations in India. He had used it to send mail to his family in Pakistan. The laptop had programmes that could harm Chinese interests if Indians discovered it. So, they had to eliminate him as he was no longer trustworthy. Arshad also wrongly delivered some important items, which angered the Chinese."

"We, too, suspected that. What was Abid's main assignment?" Godbole asked.

"Abid was to provide security to the Chinese, drive them around and so on. Since he was educated and could speak English, the Chinese felt comfortable with him. You know it was Abid whom we saw at the library when we had gone there to pursue Mohan. And he was the one Talreja encountered near Hemant's apartment. He, too, had come to retrieve the missing laptop and other devices. He said the Chinese expected to conclude their work in India in about a month or two, allowing him to return to Pakistan and join his family by December or January."

"It seems the Chinese took care to keep Abid away from their core work," Godbole said. "Arshad was the one they depended on for their critical work. Since Arshad and Wangchu are dead, we must focus on probing Pema to get to the bottom of the case."

"Yes, we have to start because the government is in a hurry," Das said.

"I hope we have the recording of Pema's interrogation."

"Yes, we do. We also have Wangchu's short-duration interaction. I have already transferred the voice files of the interrogation via our internal mail. Luckily, both spoke English. But it may take three or four hours for you to listen to the complete recording."

"Doesn't matter. I'll start listening right away. I'll be ready to interrogate the Chinese man tomorrow morning," Godbole said, rising to leave.

When he reached the door, Godbole turned and added, "Sir, now that I am here, please, why don't you rest? I can imagine how gruelling the past twenty-four hours have been for you." Das smiled as Godbole left the cabin.

Back in his cabin, Godbole switched on his desktop computer and saw three voice files titled 'Abid-1', 'Lobsang Pema-2' and 'Tsering Wangchu-3' already in his inbox. Before opening the voice files, Godbole tried to focus on the case. The team already knew Kanak Mohan, Kesang Dolma and Arshad, the deceased Pakistani. Now, they had to work on Abid, Lobsang Pema and the Dove Villa resident Zinto Lee to get a clearer picture. Pakistan's involvement in facilitating the Chinese operations in India took the case to a new dimension, which worried the policymakers. Therefore, Abid and his handler, Major Jamal, assumed importance. More questions would arise from the establishment of the Pak-Chinese collaboration against India.

Initially, Godbole went through Lobsang Pema's voice file and then the short voice file of Tsering Wangchu. He finished scrutinizing the files at 9:15 p.m. After reading the notes he prepared while listening to the Chinese men's responses, Godbole dialled Amit Rao.

"Buddy, where are you?" Godbole asked Rao.

"If you are in the office, can I be home?"

"Good," Godbole said and laughed. "Look, Amit, can you run the pictures of our two Chinese guests against our social media database?" Godbole asked.

"Oh... the database is so huge that it might take over twelve hours to complete one cycle. Can you give specific parameters, like social media, location, or period, to make the search easier?

"You know, Amit, besides running against the database, you must also run it against live data."

"Oh my... that'll be a colossal job? If it is live data, I must scan one segment after the other."

"Please do it, no matter how difficult. When you run Lobsang Pema's picture... do it particularly against the US segment. I have reason to believe that we can expect something from this exercise," Godbole said.

"I'll do my level best, Yash."

"Amit, please remember that I need the results by tomorrow morning. Pema isn't cracking. I need something to needle him tomorrow during his second round of questioning." Godbole disconnected the call.

On his way home, Godbole thought over the responses of the two Chinese men to the interrogator's questions. Lobsang Pema said that he was thirty-three years old and educated in Lhasa. Then, like every bright student in Lhasa, Pema moved to Beijing for a college education and became an engineer in advanced electronics. He started working in a Korean electronics manufacturing unit in Hong Kong. Three years ago, he was detained for attending a meeting of the Tibetan Youth Forum, a cultural organization tainted in the eyes of the Chinese government. He was sent to one of the corrective camps for two years as a punishment. When he returned, he continued facing harassment from authorities, so Pema crossed over to India to live with the Tibetan refugees.

Tsering Wangchu, too, gave a similar statement before he died. Wangchu also claimed to be a thirty-eight-year-old Tibetan refugee in India. He was a resident of Lhasa. He graduated in business administration and served in a Shanghai company as a manager for nine years. Four years ago, Wangchu was detained by the Chinese authorities for alleged linkages with a banned Tibetan organization and sent to a corrective camp for two years. After his detention, he lost his job and underwent harassment. Wangchu crossed to India through the Tawang route in search of better prospects. Pema and Wangchu met in Shimla. Since they could not fulfil the legal criteria, they were not accepted into the camp there. Then, they thought of trying their luck in the Tibetan camp near Mysore in Karnataka.

Their stories were riddled with inaccuracies. Pema could not convince the interrogator about the source of his funds to roam around in India. He also could not explain why he and Wangchu proceeded to Tamil Nadu when their destination was Mysore. Their excuse was that Abid had misguided them. The problem was that they could not have spun a better story. Unlike resident agents and spies on long-term missions, floating operatives on a brief mission could not present a flawless cover story. Their best bet would be not to get caught.

Thus, the information available from the interrogation was of no use. But Godbole was not merely looking at the content of the interaction. He also concentrated on how they spoke, their chosen words, etc. The recording of what Wangchu said was not enough to make a study. Both spoke English, but the level of Pema's spoken English surprised Godbole. He spoke in a typical American style. Godbole also noticed quite a bit of American slang in Pema's conversation. Pema must have lived in the US for years to pick up that style. It was the only clue Godbole could dig up.

Pema's engineering background and possible US connection made Pema more relevant to the probe. Even Chinese living in the US have a presence on social media. It was unavoidable in the US. That was why Godbole insisted that Amit Rao examine the Agency's social media database, particularly the US segment, and compare the photographs of the detainees with images available there.

When Godbole was preparing to go to bed, his phone rang. It was Kanak Mohan calling.

"Mohan here, sir. Sorry to disturb you. The Chinese party has not yet arrived here. Rolex and I have been waiting since last night. We have not heard from the Chinese. What to do? Any instructions?"

"Good that you called, Mohan. You stay in Rameswaram. Keep Rolex in good humour. Maybe the cops will soon arrive and take Rolex and his men into custody. You need not worry. You will be allowed to return to Delhi."

Chapter – 18
The Tech Game

New Delhi
November 16, 2020
8.30 a.m.

Godbole entered his cabin at 8:30 a.m., eagerly looking for any sealed envelope or file folder kept on the table. Disappointed to find nothing, he reached for the phone to call Amit Rao when the control room officer walked in.

"Good morning, sir," the officer greeted Godbole and handed over an envelope. "Mr Rao has sent this."

"Good morning. Where is Rao?" Godbole asked.

"Rao was here the whole night. He left at 5 a.m."

Godbole instantly opened the envelope and found eleven sheets of printed paper. There was also a note from Amit Rao. He keenly read the note:

> *Photographs of Wangchu and Pema were run against our database and live data. There was no strike against Wangchu's picture. I found several social media accounts associated with the name Tsering Wangchu, but none of those accounts seemed to have anything to do with our suspect. Those accounts' photographs, age, location, and usage patterns did not tally with those of our detainee Tsering Wangchu.*
>
> *Lobsang Pema's picture got eight strikes in the US segment of our database. The first was a photo of him and his*

mother, Chun Yang, taken at the time of his convocation at MIT, USA. Chun posted this picture on 21st December 2010 on her Facebook account. Tracing of Chun's account helped to track Pema's account. Pema's real name is Shoi-Ming. He was active on Facebook and Twitter till January 2018. Most of his posts were on his visits to various places in the US and his engagement with his friends. After January 2018, Shoi-Ming disappeared from social media altogether. One smartphone and two laptops he used to access social media are no longer in use. At the same time, no new social media account has come to notice for being associated with Shoi-Ming. His mother, Chun Yang, has a Facebook account that is still active, and her location is in California, USA.

The printouts of some of Shoi-Ming's posts, photographs, and details of his social media accounts are pinned to this note. I have also sent you a soft copy of these papers via internal mail. Please call me if any more clarification is required.

Godbole studied the attached sheets meticulously, appreciating the thoroughness of Amit's work. It was evident that extracting these results had consumed the entire night. Although the results were not exhaustive due to the limitations of the Agency database, what Amit had unearthed was substantial. Shoi-Ming, with a degree from MIT, was a tech guy – a crucial detail considering the case's background. It also emerged that Ming and his mother, Chun Yang, resided in the US. The lack of information on Tsering Wangchu suggested he might have deliberately avoided leaving a social media trail, indicative of a spy's caution. Ming's disappearance from social media after January 2018 hinted at his enlistment by Chinese intelligence for technical work.

Godbole quickly wrote down his observations and the points he needed to grill Shoi-Ming. He devised a plan for the interrogation, deciding to use a separate photograph of Ming's mother to pressure him. Using the computer's editing option, he isolated her image from the convocation photo. By then, his team had entered his cabin.

Godbole briefed them on the latest developments. The death of Tsering Wangchu cast a shadow, but Godbole urged them to focus on the task ahead. He assigned Talreja and Riaz to interrogate Abid while he and Pande prepared to confront Shoi-Ming.

*****

Since Shoi-Ming was the only person left with the team to understand the Chinese game's full dimensions, Godbole knew he had to prepare meticulously for the questioning. There was no standard interrogation technique; the tactic was tailored to the case and the person being questioned. Approaching a spy, facilitator, or informer varied, and these individuals usually had a higher level of intellect and determination, making their interrogation a mental tussle. Hence, getting them to talk was a challenge, and extracting the truth was another matter entirely. Ming was well-educated and knowledgeable. What was his role in the Chinese scheme of things?

The preliminary interrogation, done a day earlier to gauge him, indicated that Ming might not be just a peripheral person. He claimed to be a Tibetan and remained firm. His withdrawal from social media since 2018 hinted at his involvement in Chinese clandestine operations. Godbole anticipated a tough opponent.

Considering what he knew about Ming, Godbole decided against questioning him in the dingy, dark, scary interrogation cell. He would use that room only if Ming refused to cooperate and coercion became necessary. Instead, Ming was brought to an ordinary office cabin.

Godbole was pleased to see Ming without handcuffs, wearing clean pyjamas and a white T-shirt provided by the detention warden. He also wore a nice pair of white canvas shoes. It was clear that Das wanted Ming to feel comfortable, which was a tactic to make him fear losing those little privileges. Godbole expected Ming to recognize Pande and him as the people who detained him the day before. However, when they entered the cabin, Ming didn't react. Before sitting in a chair facing Ming, Godbole fetched a glass of water from a jar on a table near the window and placed it within Ming's reach.

"Good morning, Mr Lobsang Pema... I think that was the name you gave to the officer who spoke to you yesterday," Godbole said.

The interrogator's insinuation that Lobsang Pema was not his real name worried Ming, who silently avoided looking at Godbole and Pande.

Nevertheless, Godbole continued.

"So, you claim to be a Tibetan?"

"It is not a claim. It is a fact," Ming replied firmly.

"As a Tibetan, what do you want in India?" Godbole asked.

"Is it not clear that I want to live here as a refugee?"

"You're sounding irritated. Somehow, it does not suit the situation, Mr Ming."

"Why... why I ask?'

"Because my mind says that a person from a foreign country who has come here to seek refugee status would be a bit more polite to a government officer. Instead, you sound upset. It looks like you're frustrated," Godbole said calmly.

Ming didn't respond, possibly realizing he had erred in his response. He might be a trained operative, but he was still maturing. Meanwhile, Godbole continued, "The truth is that you are not a Tibetan. I am certain about it."

"How can you say that?"

"Do not waste my time. Please say who you are and why you are here."

"You want me to say I am Chinese, right?"

"I want you to tell me the truth, that is all."

"Whether you like it or not, I am not Chinese," Ming asserted.

"My question is what you are, not what you aren't," Godbole said firmly.

Ming momentarily glanced at Godbole, perhaps assessing his interrogator to plan his responses. Ming was silent for almost a minute. Godbole did not want to lose the momentum of the interaction. Therefore, he decided to come to the point without delay. He pulled out Ming's mother's photograph.

"You know this woman?" Godbole asked.

Ming's face showed shock. It might have shaken a brick of his mental firewall. Yet, in moments, he regained his composure. "No. I do not know her."

"Well, you do not know? You do not know Chun Yang?" Godbole asked loudly. "I thought you would get up and say... no, she is not my mother!"

Godbole's sarcastic way of questioning needled deep into Ming's bones. Godbole could see that his youthful subject was labouring to contain his frustration. So, to stir him further, Godbole shot another arrow.

"How was your life at MIT?"

As Godbole kept pricking Ming with his questions, Ming's defences crumbled. Those questions were an indication enough that the Indians had a fair idea of his background. Godbole delivered yet another blow.

"Sorry, Mr Shoi-Ming, you missed that boat to Sri Lanka," Godbole said and chuckled.

For Ming, it was a thunderbolt. He paled because there was nothing more left for the Indians to know. His interviewer touched on his life in a few short and clever sentences. There was no scope to stonewall the interviewer. Ming shuffled his legs and lowered his head.

Godbole waited. He was not sure what was going on in Ming's mind. Was he considering giving up or planning something? His body language suggested he was short on defences. However, in such circumstances, the detainees might make one last bid, so giving Ming time to think was not prudent. Godbole resumed his interaction.

"Look here, Mr Shoi-Ming," Godbole said. "I have done my homework. We have seen through your game."

Ming looked up slowly and said, "Yes, I am Shoi-Ming. Chun Yang is my mother, and I have a master's from MIT." Saying so, Ming hit the desk with his fist, and the water in the glass almost spilt. He quickly added, "You must be happy now."

"Not yet, brother. I want to hear everything," Godbole said.

"By the way, please know that I am not a Chinese citizen. I am an American citizen. I was born and raised in the US," Ming said emphatically.

Was Ming saying it as part of his new strategy, or was it true? Godbole also remembered Das informing him about the Chinese diplomat's claim that a big power was behind planting men in India to complicate India-China relations. 'Big power' was a Chinese jargon for the United States of America. Godbole could not dismiss Ming's claim.

"Where is your passport? We did not find it with you or in your bag. Even if you are a US national, that does not make any difference. For me, you are a foreign national who entered India illegally."

"As a US citizen, you are bound to notify my country's mission in India. I can explain I lost my passport... or say I was abducted and brought to India."

"It does not work that way, Ming. I should be convinced that you are a US national; only then will I consider contacting the US mission."

"My country will not be pleased."

"Now listen, Mr Ming, you may be a US national. But I know that you are a trained Chinese intelligence operative. You came here on an intelligence mission," Godbole said, raising his voice.

Ming instantly retorted, "That is preposterous!" Ming's voice trembled, and he breathed heavily.

"I repeat... you are a Chinese operative," Godbole asserted.

"How could you say that?' Ming demanded to know.

"I have reason to believe so... I know the Chinese intelligence recruited you in early 2018." Godbole lowered his voice and added, "I feel for you, Ming. In just about two years of your joining them, they sent you on this dangerous mission."

Ming looked shattered. He glanced at Godbole, wondering how the Indians knew all that! They knew even the precise time of his joining hands with the Chinese!

Godbole continued, "You see, as long as there is no record of your entering India officially, you are not in India. I need not tell you of the implications. I am at liberty to deal with you the way I want without being accused of harming a US citizen."

It was a veiled threat. But Godbole was aware that threats or torture would not be enough to make an operative speak. As an interrogator, he might have come closer to realizing the first of the two objectives – knowing the detainee's identity. The second objective of unravelling the detainee's mission remained a tricky proposition. Spies and operatives rarely opened up about their mission, fearing reprisal from both their own and the enemy's sides. In such circumstances, Ming would open up only if he could gain something in the bargain. Godbole would have to come up with something worthwhile.

Godbole leaned forward and said, "Ming, you are educated, a qualified tech guy. You are only thirty-three – yet to marry – yet to see the world. Do not think that the Chinese will rescue you. The truth is that they have already disowned you. Yesterday, when they understood that you and your two friends were apprehended, a

Chinese diplomat met us to say that you are US stooges, planted to harm India-China relations. Do not be surprised if they come forward to share your details with us."

Ming looked shocked. It was beyond logic that his masters would be ready to sacrifice him. Now, it looked as if there was no distinction between his master and enemy; both were looking to take advantage of his situation. Ming grabbed the glass of water on the desk and gulped, his hands trembling. Godbole watched him keenly in a mental brawl, which was the moment the interviewer could use to gain an upper hand over his subject. Godbole had always believed that it was not force but a proper tactic that helped to establish dominance over the prisoner.

Bending forward, his gaze locking with Ming's, Godbole said, "This is a cloak-and-dagger game. In the shadows of uncertainty, even allies can become adversaries. You must learn to navigate this treacherous terrain alone. Tough, isn't it?"

Godbole continued, "See Ming, the two years you have spent in this profession so far are not enough to learn the ropes of this complex game. Your masters, the Chinese, have deserted you, knowing that you are trapped by the enemy. Now, you stand at a crossroads, with only your own interests to guide you. The time has come for you to take control of your fate. Forget everything else, and keep in mind your interest, yours alone. If you are reasonable... if you behave, I might examine what I can do for you. But for that, I, too, should benefit. I am blunt on this... do you want to cooperate?"

Ming was in turmoil. Cooperating with the Indians would be a gamble. But was there any other worthwhile option to consider? Ming knew well that his fate hinged on the Indian sitting before him.

Seconds passed, but Ming was silent. For Godbole, it was precious time slipping away. However, he was willing to wait a little longer because he knew that the subject's silence could mean consent in such a situation.

Godbole got up, picked up the glass jar, and filled Ming's glass with water. Godbole pushed the glass towards Ming and said, "I will order lemon tea for us. In the meantime, have some water..."

Ming promptly picked up the glass. He now looked less stressed. Godbole sensed an opportunity, but Ming needed to be slowly nudged into speaking.

"You are a US national, that is all right. Where is your passport?" Godbole asked.

"It is not with me now," Ming said.

"Okay, where is it now?"

"I have kept it in my hotel room in Hambantota."

"You mean in Sri Lanka, Ming?"

"Yes, I was not permitted to bring the passport. I was told I could come here without any problem and return. They said using the ferry service was safe."

"Who was with you when we detained you in that forest?"

"I knew him as Tsering Wangchu. I don't know who he is. I met him at that village house in Mulla Malai, and he was with me to assist me with my work."

"We will discuss this man Wangchu and your assignment in India in detail. Before that, tell me, how are you a US citizen?"

"Before I speak more, may I know your plans for me?" Ming appeared to have gathered the confidence to ask a question for the first time.

"My plans for you will depend upon your willingness to come clean on all aspects of the Chinese intelligence operations in India and the role you played along with Wangchu and Abid," Godbole said.

"Suppose I am truthful; to what extent can you save me from trouble?"

"To the extent possible, is what I can say. Tell me, are you trying to bargain to save yourself from our laws?"

"It is not your laws alone... nor me alone. I have many concerns..." Ming said and closed his eyes.

Godbole noted Ming's words. Something was bothering Ming. "I did not get you, Ming. Can you explain?"

"But can I trust you?"

"Look here, we may be enemies, but we always respect our commitment once given. If you are truthful, I shall do my best, but it will also depend on the nature of your involvement."

"I do not disbelieve you that the Chinese double-crossed me. Wangchu had already warned me of such a possibility if the operation got exposed. But Wangchu also had told me something else... is Wangchu alive?" Ming asked.

"Why? Please forget Wangchu and come back to the point."

"I think Wangchu has ended his life..." After a pause, Ming said, "What I am worried about is not me, but my mother in California. I did not know this would end up in such a horror. I did not just shatter my mother's dream, but I am putting her in danger, too. Now, the Chinese have turned against me. But the bigger issue is that I am supposed to rejoin work on the twenty-third at my company in Seattle. If I fail to return, US intelligence might start looking for me. My mother will also come under pressure from both the Chinese and the FBI. I don't know if you can do anything for me or her..."

"This sounds too cluttered. First, let me hear what you have to say. I can discuss this with our team and the higher-ups. They should feel convinced that what you said is worth our intervention," Godbole said.

"I know that I am screwed... anyway, India is not my enemy. I shall share with you something precious from your point of view. See what you can do for me."

Godbole knew that Ming was willing to speak now, but he had to answer the questions to get a complete picture of the Chinese network.

Resuming their conversation over lemon tea and biscuits, Ming spoke about his background and role in the Chinese operation. Although the hidden recorder was switched on, Pande kept noting the details for quick reference.

Ming was the child of a struggling Chinese immigrant couple in California. He lost his father when he was only five years old. His mother worked hard to educate him, and he ended up at MIT. In 2010, his master's degree in advanced electronics fetched him an excellent job in the R&D section of Futuristic Dimensions, an American firm based in Seattle, collaborating with the US government's Defence Department. Gradually, he built a good reputation and was selected to work with a team, developing new technologies for use in the defence field.

The Chinese intelligence somehow learnt about the research Ming's company was doing for the US Defence. The Chinese secretly approached Ming. They tried to impress upon him that he was obliged to the land of his origin. They kept bugging Ming for a few months. Finally, in January 2018, he fell for the money they offered.

"What did the Chinese want you to do?" Godbole asked, steering the conversation to get crucial information.

Initially, they did not give me any tasks. The first thing they did was arrange a ten-day vacation for me in Istanbul. A Chinese guy met me on the second day of my vacation there. He visited me all the remaining days of my vacation and gave me a crash course in intelligence functioning, especially communicating secretly, dodging surveillance and exchanging parcels securely. This was the first intelligence training I received."

Oh, I see..."

"On my last vacation day, the Chinese man asked me to get two pieces of UNX26181C. That shocked me because what he uttered was the secret technical code of a critical component manufactured by Futuristic Dimensions exclusively for the US Defence Services."

"What is that component?" Godbole asked.

"Component UNX26181C uses highly advanced technology. It is a tiny but critical electronic component in signal-swapping devices."

"What kind of signal?"

"Any electronic signal. It can substitute any genuine signals with doctored signals."

"Did you give them that component?"

"Yes, after three months of effort, I handed over two pieces. It was a difficult task because these components are accounted for and guarded closely."

"Then how could you get two pieces?"

During the development stage, we had manufactured such pieces for testing. They were lying in the lab unaccounted for. I picked up two such pieces, rectified and upgraded them to suit the Chinese requirements."

"Did they tell you what they were doing with those components?"

"No, but they had to consult me twice. They were facing problems because they had deployed the equipment in freezing temperatures. From what they discussed, I could figure out that they were using our technology to swap GPS signals. I also could gather that they deployed that equipment at a high altitude in the mountainous region bordering India."

Godbole straightened up, trying to absorb what Ming just said. He remembered the Chinese tech centre in Tangma near the LAC and the GPS testing carried out by Arshad in the Tawang area. At last, they were getting closer to resolving the secret behind the Chinese tech centre.

Godbole said, "Ming, you see, we know of a Chinese tech centre in the Chinese village of Tangma, close to our border. We have been trying to sweep that area with electronic signal sweepers without any results. Why was it so?"

"The Chinese are very wise. Once they tested and found that their signal-swapping equipment was working well, they switched it off. They planned to use the tech facility only during a border conflict or war. However, they mentioned to me that they had switched it on the day of the blackout in Mumbai last month, fearing fresh border tensions. They were happy that the tech centre could successfully swap the GPS signals and misguide two Indian Air Force jets that flew in the area on that day."

Godbole was aware of the potential for the Chinese tech centre in Tangma to damage Indian defence manoeuvres. Having obtained a picture of the Chinese tech facility, Godbole probed further.

"What were the other demands from the Chinese?" Godbole asked.

"After I gave them that component, they did not demand anything for a few months. Then, in December 2018, they arranged another vacation for me in Egypt, where they imparted intelligence training. They enquired about SSTIS, PBS and DFP technologies being developed at Futuristic Dimensions as well."

"Ming, the abbreviations you just uttered are hard to grasp. What is this SSTIS...?"

"These are very sensitive micro technologies not yet known to the world. SSTIS stands for Short-Span-Targeted-Intelligent-Signalling. PBS indicates Piggy-Back-Signalling, and DFP is Deep-Frozen-Programme. Separate internet or Wi-Fi connectivity is not required to send these signals. Instead, these signals can travel in piggyback mode on any other signals, crisis-crossing the area. It is a path-breaking technology."

"That is something to learn! What is the application and use of SSTIS?"

"Briefly saying, it is not the conventional electronic signalling. It is a revolutionary technology that sends a hybrid signal lasting only a fraction of a nanosecond, making it extremely hard to notice or detect. An SSTIS micro signal can carry only specially written short commands that can be contained in a few bits. Besides, this signal can be received only by a designated or targeted receiver, which remains passive till the signal hits it," Ming explained.

"Can you explain it in simpler terms?"

"It is like a TV set and its remote. SSITS technology is used to tamper with or remotely disrupt a programme in an enemy system. It involves two main components: a remotely based sender circuit in a chip and another chip with a receiver circuit and a tiny programme to be planted in the target's system. The advantage of SSTIS technology is that both the sender and receiver circuits can remain undetected in a system because they are always at rest. It can remain frozen or stay dormant in the system till it is activated."

"I think this would be hard for any nontechnical person to understand. After we finish this session, you must write down all the details so our technical experts can evaluate them. Did you also pass on these technologies to the Chinese?"

"No, not the technology. But I did help them with programming tiny SSTIS sender and receiver chips. They wanted at least twenty pairs of those chips, but I could manage only seven."

"Why did the Chinese want them?"

"Initially, I did not know, but three months ago, I received an urgent request from them for a meeting to discuss something. When I met them, I realized that they wanted the chips to disrupt the power supply in major cities in India, especially Mumbai. They planned to plant those chips in the grid's substations and network monitoring equipment supplying power to Mumbai."

"Do you know how they planted the chips in the equipment in the power grid to which they had no access?" Godbole asked.

"I think they did it through a company... Tinmin... something.... This company has been supplying hardware for a public sector company that manufactures network monitoring equipment, transformers, switchgear, and other items for the power grid in the Mumbai region," Ming said.

Godbole turned the pages of his notepad and found the mention of Tinmin Electronics and Instrumentation, where Zinto Lee was working. So, Godbole thought, the curtain over the Chinese secret agenda was rising.

"You mean Tinmin Electronics and Instrumentation is hand-in-glove with Chinese intelligence?"

"That is what it looks like," Ming said. "At first, when Tinmin was manufacturing the equipment using the component I gave the Chinese, they consulted me. Well, that is how my chips found a place in the equipment installed in the Mumbai region's receiving stations and substations of the power grid."

"Ming, if the Chinese were managing, why did you come here?"

"The Chinese faced a problem. Since they got only seven pairs of chips from me against the twenty they needed, they copied the circuits, fabricated thirteen more chips in China and smuggled them to India via Sri Lanka. Subsequently, they found that four of the fabricated and planted chips were malfunctioning. There was fear that more Chinese fabricated chips might also work erratically. Either there was an error in the copied chips, or the person who collected the smuggled parcels from South India caused damage to the chips while delivering them. Whatever that problem, it was enough to spoil the Chinese plans."

"So, that is why you had to come?"

"Yes, they arranged my travel to Sri Lanka as they thought it risky for me to travel to India directly," Ming said. "It was difficult to resolve the issue remotely. The best way was to deactivate the malfunctioning chips. If not deactivated, it could affect the entire system and result in power tripping. Since I couldn't leave my work and go immediately, I tried instructing them on how they could do it. Tinmin engineers tried to train Wangchu to do that work without the knowledge of the power grid staff. One of the chips malfunctioned before they could access the hardware, and the blackout happened."

"You mean the blackout that happened on 12th October was accidental?"

"Yes, it was an accident. As in the case of the GPS signals swapping operation, the Chinese plan was to trigger a blackout only if a war broke out. The Chinese wanted to remain prepared. If war happened, they could quickly incapacitate India. Remember, a complete power breakdown would paralyze your communication system, radars, missile launchers, rail and air traffic. During a war, that would have a crushing effect on your ability to defend your nation."

What a strategy, what planning, Godbole wondered!

"What about the other chips? Could you deactivate the other planted chips?"

"I could deactivate the seven pairs of genuine chips I had given them. The others remain planted in the systems of the substations in the power grid. Even though all the fabricated chips will not malfunction, at least a few may cause problems."

"What?" Godbole shouted. "It is a dangerous situation. We have to get all of them deactivated soon. You have to help me."

"The best way for that is to go to your power company and find out where all the equipment they have installed is supplied by the Tinmin company."

Without waiting to hear more, Godbole rushed to speak to Das about the potential danger of the power grid going through another disastrous blackout. After listening to Godbole, Das assigned a team of officers to the electric company supplying power to the Mumbai region. The company would be asked to identify the equipment provided by Tinmin Electronics and Instrumentation expeditiously. A separate team of technical experts, including Professors Singh and Farook, would be assigned to examine and study the components and their circuits in the equipment supplied.

"Yash, I will brief the teams and ask them to do their work quietly so Tinmin or the Chinese are not alerted. Today, the MEA also received a message from the Chinese Embassy enquiring if there had been any development."

"Sir, the Chinese worry is not about the men, but about their secret operation getting exposed and we getting to know about the new technology."

"You are right. Because of this, I have decided not to arrest Rolex and his men in Rameswaram for now. We will maintain a close watch on them and act only when it is safe," Das said.

"I agree, sir."

"Yash, I know you are eager to brief Inspector Ghorpade about the Hemant, aka Arshad Gulam's murder. However, it must be deferred to a more suitable time."

"Sir, I will wait until it is safe to do so," Godbole said.

"Similarly, we will wait longer before investigating Zinto Lee or other Dove Villa residents. We will also not search the Mulla Malai house yet. This is required to keep the Chinese guessing," Das said.

"That is fine, sir, but the Chinese would wonder what happened to their men in the Mallur forest. There is no word about their three men and the two vehicles. I wonder whether we could plant a story in the local press that the police recovered two vehicles abandoned in Mallur forest, and that it was a suspected case of smugglers abandoning their vehicles, noticing police presence in the area."

"It sounds good. I will check with the local police."

As Das and Godbole continued their discussions on the information divulged by Ming, they realized that the case would have to be kept under wraps for another reason, too. Das wanted to sound out the department about the desirability of developing Ming. However, there was also a nagging feeling that if Ming remained missing, US Intelligence would soon start looking for him as he was associated with developing sensitive technology for the US Defence. The Americans would not want their new technologies to fall into the hands of the Chinese or the Indians. If the US happened to step in, the case might become a three-cornered tug of war.

Godbole and Das wanted to discuss the issue in detail. But Godbole had to return to continue Ming's interrogation. He had many more questions to ask Ming.

Chapter – 19
A Triangular Tussle

New Delhi
November 18, 2020
6 a.m.

Godbole's morning started with the intrusive ring of his cell phone, disrupting the silence of the early hours. He guessed the caller to be Das. Usually, no one else called him.

"Good morning, Yash," Das said. "I know after yesterday's marathon interrogation session and equally demanding discussions with me, you could not have hit the bed before 1 a.m. So, I didn't want to disturb you this early. But we have an important meeting this morning at eleven. Our Chief will discuss the points that emerged from Ming's interrogation. Later in the afternoon, the Chief has a joint meeting with officials of the Home Ministry, MEA and the Army to understand the issues in formulating their strategy."

"So, you already reported our findings to them?"

"After you left last night, I had to brief the Chief because he was waiting for feedback. I went to his residence since the discussions could not have been over the phone. We had discussions till midnight. A while ago, he called to inform me that a meeting was scheduled at his office. Yash, this allows us to speak to him about the other action plan we discussed last night," Das said.

"That is true. I will be there on time."

A meeting with the Chief of the Agency, Amareshwar Vohra, would always be a serious affair. Vohra was known to be a hard-boiled 'intelligence man' and a meticulous analyst. Officers had to be well prepared to meet him. However, Godbole did not need any special preparation because every word Ming uttered was fresh in his mind.

Later, upon arriving at the office, Godbole found himself in the company of Das, ready to face the formidable Amareshwar Vohra. Sporting a broad smile, Vohra warmly welcomed them and switched on the no-disturbance sign at the door.

"Sorry, I had to call this meeting hurriedly. First of all, I appreciate the efforts made by Mr Godbole, his team, and you, Mr Das," Vohra said in his opening remarks. "The Chinese actions took us aback. The government is highly concerned. The question is whether the power outage and the Chinese tech facility are just part of their usual signalling... or they are signs of China preparing for a war?"

"The Chinese actions are always meant for signalling. Even then, the blackout and their tech centre have exceeded the usual and revealed their intentions. We better take note and make our preparations," Das said and sat with his hands clasped.

"You mean the Chinese are preparing for a war?" Vohra asked.

"Sir, the point is... signals have to be in the open... should be seen. However, the blackout preparations and the tech centre were kept under a veil of secrecy. So, it was not for signalling. I think the Chinese see a possibility of a conflict," Das said.

"What does that mean? They see a possibility of war... or feel it is unavoidable?" Vohra asked pointedly.

Das released his clasped hands and said, "The Chinese will not do all that just for signalling alone. They have a definite plan. They are already smarting after the Galvan incident, in which they lost twice as many men as India. Indian soldiers also audaciously occupied the Kailash ranges in eastern Ladakh, which forced the Chinese to climb down from their adamant stand. My question is… after that setback, are the Chinese plotting something to instil confidence in their men? To show their men they still have the upper hand."

"Of course, there is merit in your view," Vohra said. "Since the blackout and the tech facility were set up stealthily, they might not be meant for signalling. The Chinese may be preparing for an eventuality. In case a war happens, they want to be ready. Well… Mr Godbole, you are closer to the ground. What are your comments on this?" Vohra asked, turning to Godbole.

"I think China was trying to keep its powder dry… just in case a war happened. However, there is another aspect to Chinese actions. I do not think they are preparing for a full-fledged war. Both countries realize that a prolonged war would be detrimental to both. So, if a war happens between China and India, the expectation is that it will be a short one, lasting a few days. Therefore, it is important to make early gains and take a quick upper hand in the war before both countries come to a ceasefire. The advantage they take before the ceasefire usually remains frozen for the future… just like the LAC was decided just after the 1962 war ended."

"You mean, their tech facility and the preparations for the blackout are part of their quick upper hand policy?" Vohra asked.

"Primarily, yes. Ming informed us that the Chinese plan was to switch on the tech facility or engineer the power outage only if there was a war," Godbole pointed out.

"You have a logical explanation," Vohra said. "Anyway, what do you think we must do now? The Army is also evaluating the situation and drawing a plan to counter China's strategy by strengthening the defences and scaling up the vigilance at the LAC," Vohra said.

"Sir, now that the setup they built both for the power outage and the GPS manipulation stands exposed, we need to send a tough signal back to the Chinese," Godbole said.

"What kind of signal is there in your mind?" Vohra asked.

As Godbole hesitated to answer, Das intervened and said, "Last night, Godbole and I discussed this in detail. Godbole believes that some proactive action is warranted, not just defence. The fact is that I, too, feel it is necessary."

"I need specifics," Vohra said.

"We are already neutralizing the Chinese plan targeting our power grids," Das said. "We are trying to know the power stations and grids in the country that use equipment sourced from China-connected companies. Now, what is left untouched is the tech facility in the Chinese village of Tangma, just across the Tawang sector. Currently, China does not suspect that we know about it. We feel India should plan a stealthy attack on the tech centre and destroy it. India has to upstage the Chinese. That will be the biggest signal we can send to China."

Vohra could not hide the streak of dismay on his face. After a minute, Vohra looked at Godbole and asked, "Do you know the consequences of our crossing the LAC?"

"Yes, sir, I do," Godbole said. "If the Chinese can breach our boundaries and come to Bangalore and Mumbai, we should not ponder on breaching their boundaries, and go to Tangma. Yes, they did it stealthily; we would also do it stealthily."

"I do not comment on an issue like this in an instant. You know... we in the Agency are not averse to taking risks or tough challenges. Look here; even if it is done sneakily, there are many concerns. The danger of failure is too high."

"Sir, admittedly, there are odds," Das said. "But I feel the significance of the Tech Centre built so close to the state of Arunachal Pradesh, which China claims as theirs, should not be lost."

"I know what you mean, Mr Das."

"Sir, we see a chance," Das said, taking a deep breath. "Their tech centre is only under four kilometres from the LAC. The place is within our reach on foot. The trenches where the tech facility is installed are isolated and away from the village. So, there is no scope for attracting the villagers' attention. To top it off, no PLA men are deployed there to guard the trenches. It is unmanned."

"I have seen the satellite images sent to us by the Army. Yes, no PLA deployment is seen. But then, the place itself can barely be made out. Such is their precaution. So, can we be sure the place is not guarded?" Vohra asked.

"We learnt about the site from Dorjee, whom we rescued last month. So, his information is the latest. Dorjee has seen the place since it was built two years ago. Keeping the tech facility in the trenches is intended to prevent the US and Indian satellites from picking up the images."

"Well, what kind of attack do you propose?" Vohra asked.

"It will be a passive action carried out quietly. So, we will not use explosives. Instead, we can burn the centre silently using timer-triggered inflammable gel. It should look as if a short circuit occurred, causing the fire. We expect the fire to destroy the equipment and, more importantly, the sensitive component given by Ming. Since Ming will not be available to them, the Chinese will not get that component again. The action could be carried out under darkness... at night. A joint team of commandos from the Agency and the Army can do it and safely return. Dorjee and Lote will serve as our guides," Das explained.

"Let us assume the Army, and we are ready for this operation – Operation Tangma. The question is... will the government be open to taking this risk? The final clearance will rest with the National Security Adviser. Anyway, please write down your action plan, give all the details and mail it to me by 2 p.m. "

"I shall send the note," Das said. "If we plan to proceed with the operation, we should hold back our action against Zinto Lee,

Rolex, and others for a little longer, and postpone the search of Dove Villa and the farmhouse in Mulla Malai."

"I can understand. But in the interim, please keep a watch. Now, what have you done to stop the publication of that article?" Vohra asked.

"The writer, Kanak Mohan, himself has asked Banerji to hold on till the article is updated and revised," Das said. "Speaking of Mohan, can we know the official reaction to our proposal to protect him from legal troubles?"

"Well, the Joint Intelligence Committee has no objection to your proposal for Kanak Mohan. However, their view of Kesang Dolma is different. The external intelligence wing conducted a thorough enquiry in Kathmandu and found that she is one of the key Chinese operatives in Nepal. She might have shouldered just a peripheral role in their India operations, but in Nepal, she has developed a deep reach in the policy-making quarters. For that reason, we will take time to decide on her. However, there is no objection to us treating her well and keeping her in good humour," Vohra said.

"Yes, sir, I agree," Das said. "Sir, I also wanted to speak about Ming. He has agreed to work with our tech experts on the new technologies being developed in the US."

Vohra raised his head. Tapping the desk, he said, "There is a development concerning Ming. I deliberately kept it as the last item for discussion." As Das and Godbole sat with raised eyebrows, Vohra continued, "A two-member FBI team has arrived in Delhi looking for Ming."

"That was fast! Are they on Ming's trail?" a surprised Godbole asked.

"Ming's company somehow found out about Ming's liaison with Chinese intelligence a few weeks ago. They also realized that some electronic components were missing. The company notified the FBI. By that time, Ming had embarked on his tour to Sri Lanka. The FBI men promptly arrived in Colombo and tracked his trail up to Hambantota. After that, they have drawn a blank," Vohra said.

"Then how did they land here?" Das asked.

"They worked on a simple intuition. They knew Ming was recruited to put to use the lethal technology. Sri Lanka couldn't be the place to deploy such harmful technologies. In this part of the world, India could be the Chinese target. So, they guessed Ming's destination correctly," Vohra said.

"That is logical, indeed," Das said.

Vohra continued, "The FBI team felt that the Chinese operators might have abducted Ming to India. So, Ming could not be held for entering India illegally. It is a subtle argument to get Ming's custody from India easily. The US Embassy has formally approached us, requesting that Ming be located and handed over to them. Ming is now wanted by China, India and the US."

"Do the Americans know that Ming is in our custody?" Das asked.

"They certainly suspect that Ming is in India. However, there is nothing to suggest that they have proof of Ming's presence here. Now that they have given all their details, we must respond to them. After all, he is a US citizen," Vohra said.

"What would be our response? Since he entered India illegally without a passport and got associated with sabotage activities for Chinese intelligence, we have the right to arrest him and send him to trial. We can keep him with us for some time. We need him at least till he explains those critical technologies to our experts," Godbole said.

"You see, the critical technologies are the problem. Ming is important, and they may have even started looking for Ming in India. If they learn that Ming is in our custody, they will try to scuttle the legal process by putting pressure on the government. They say he was abducted and would not like Ming to remain in our custody for long. The only way to hold him would be to arrest him formally and start the legal process. After the legal process starts, the Americans would have to wait till the case is decided in the court," Vohra said.

"But we can't arrest him at this stage. We cannot allow this to go public till we carry out Operation Tangma," Das said.

"I know. That is the difficulty. Anyway, I will do my level best," Vohra said. After a brief pause, he added, "Meanwhile, please encourage Ming to start working with our experts."

"Noted, sir," Das said.

"About Operation Tangma, from your side, keep everything ready. But please remember that we plan to proceed with this operation based on certain assumptions. We assume that Tangma is easily accessible from the LAC in the dark and in freezing temperatures. We assume that the village is far away from the tech centre and that the place is not guarded. Please put your heads together and do your homework. Whatever the plan, you will not carry any destructive weapons into China. I want a foolproof proposal that can work even in the worst-case scenario. This is not the green signal; it must come from the government," Vohra said, signalling that the meeting was over.

Chapter – 20
The Mountain Bats

Zemithang
November 25, 2020
3 p.m.

Three nights of strenuous practice drills with Maj Bakshi's ten commandos were exhausting for Godbole and his colleagues, Talreja and Riaz. The night training sessions in the darkness and the freezing weather at the high-altitude Zemithang camp pushed them to their limits. Considering the time and place of the operation, the team of commandos and the NES-17 men were named the Mountain Bats. Yet, the intense training sessions fuelled their spirits, prepping them for a frigid night operation. Their gear was ready: night vision goggles, thermal imaging equipment, enemy communication jamming devices, and special protective clothing. The Mountain Bats awaited only the final orders.

Despite the hectic schedule, Godbole was happy to return to Zemithang. He particularly liked Maj Bakshi's company. The bond he shared with Maj Bakshi might be just four weeks old, but it felt like they were lifelong buddies. Godbole admired the Major's ability to remain calm even in the most challenging situation. The way he handled the Tenzin Lote episode and the rescue operation of Tsering Dorjee in mid-October was enough to underscore the quality of his leadership. So, when he learnt that Maj Bakshi had been chosen to lead the ten-member commando team, Godbole was confident and relieved.

Amidst a lot of follow-up work pending, it was difficult for Godbole to leave Delhi. However, the NES-17 team worked overtime. Amit Rao and Pande looked after the work, that included keeping a watch on Rolex in Rameswaram, Zinto Lee in Bangalore, and the farmhouse in Mulla Malai. They also kept communicating with Dolma and Kanak Mohan. Sneha Kumar and Kamini Dube were on duty, helping technical experts work with Shoi-Ming.

Since their arrival in Zemithang, Godbole and Maj Bakshi had meticulously planned every step of the operation. Godbole also took the initiative to talk to Dorjee and Lote, gaining valuable insights about Tangma village, the Chinese tech centre, and the route from the LAC to Tangma. Godbole even drew a detailed map, marking the location and distribution of the villagers' houses, PLA quarters, and the three main streets of the small village. Dorjee and Lote would serve as guides and required separate conditioning. Godbole spent additional time with Dorjee to learn about the house where Rinchin Tashi, the long-lost Indian intelligence operative, resided.

On the fourth day of training, Brig Kedar and Anand Kumar Das arrived around noon. At 3 p.m., they met Maj Bakshi and Godbole for a final operation review.

"Major, are your preparations complete?" Brig Kedar asked.

"Yes, sir, we are fully prepared," Maj Bakshi said.

"In that case, will it be okay if we launch the operation tomorrow evening?"

"It will be fine, sir. The Mountain Bats are charged up; they are raring to go," the Major said confidently.

"Then let the boys rest today; no need to train tonight. You start marching to Janung early tomorrow. As per your schedule, the Bats should be near the LAC by late afternoon, isn't so?" the Brigadier asked.

"That is the plan, sir. If we reach the LAC before dusk, we can rest for a couple of hours before moving ahead at 8.30 or, at the latest, by 9 p.m.," the Major explained.

"So, the plan is that only ten of our members will cross over to the other side?"

"Yes, sir. The Bat team will have ten members: Godbole and his two men, Dorjee, five commandos and I. The remaining five commandos, Lote and Sub Rameshwar Gupta, will wait at the LAC as stand-by," the Major said.

"I saw the route map prepared by Godbole. I think it should serve our purpose. Although we cannot see the tech centre in the satellite imagery, its location, which relates to the Tangma village, has been somewhat accurately marked," the Brigadier said.

"Yes, sir. Besides, Dorjee will guide us," the Major said.

"Okay, Major. Once you cross over to the other side, you are alone. We cannot help you there. So, remember, failure is not an option. You have to come back victorious," the Brigadier said, looking at the Major and Godbole.

"Sir, we are committed. We will succeed in our mission."

"Good, that is the spirit. All the best," the Brigadier said. After a brief pause, he added, "One more thing, we are not moving troops to the Tawang sector to bolster our defence. If we venture moving troops, the enemy may have informers on this side and will find out. No top Army brass was sent here to review the operation. They did it from Delhi. The movement of a senior Army officer to this place will also attract attention. And that is also why we told you to pick up commandos from your men rather than sending men to join you in Zemithang."

The Brigadier paused for a brief while and continued, "Please remember that in case of any hostile manoeuvres by the Chinese at the LAC following your operation, you will have just your men in Zemithang... sixty of them, I think, to fend off the Chinese at the LAC. So, move those men to Janung tomorrow afternoon and keep them ready. If the Chinese try to escalate the situation further, then, only then, we will airlift men from Tawang to the LAC.

"Yes, sir."

"I did all the talking because Mr Das told me to do so. He said he conveyed all that he wanted to say to me. I see even Mr Godbole sitting here quietly. I think the intelligence officials do not speak out in public," the Brigadier joked, laughing loudly. Everyone there smiled, and it relieved some tension that had built up.

The Brigadier said, "Well, this is a joint operation. Mr Das and I will stay put here to monitor the developments. Please keep us informed using the wired phone you installed near the LAC. We have a hotline to the Delhi Army Headquarters and the National Security Adviser's office. They, too, want live feeds. Tomorrow, before you move, please gather here. Mr Das and I will meet the entire team of Mountain Bats to wish them success."

"Noted, sir," Maj Bakshi said.

"Now, concentrate on your goals and no deviation from the plan under any circumstances. Be vigilant and execute your plans so that the possibility of our men getting trapped in Chinese territory is zero. Jai Hind!" the Brigadier concluded.

"Jai Hind, sir!"

Chapter – 21
Red Glow on the Horizon

Crossing point at the LAC, Arunachal Pradesh
November 26, 2020
5 p.m.

Dusk had already enveloped the landscape at 5 p.m. when the Mountain Bats reached near the crossing point at the LAC. Sub Rameshwar Gupta, five commandos, and Lote were already at the LAC as the support-cum-standby team. The Mountain Bats and their support team settled at a spot eclipsed by a small hill on the Chinese side. Yet, they did not venture to switch on lamps or torches. They silently had some refreshments and tried to relax, leaning on rocks. Once they set out, they would have to forget refreshments and rest until they returned to the Indian side after about eight or nine hours.

In the oppressive darkness, silence reigned. The Bats were mentally preparing for their roles in the operation. The temperature had plummeted to a bone-chilling -2 degrees Celsius, worsening by the hour. The still air was a cruel reminder of their vulnerability as they sat exposed without physical movement.

In the stillness, Maj Bakshi suddenly got up and said calmly, "Bats, it is thirty minutes past eight. It's time to move."

The Bats got up in a flash. They couldn't see each other's faces but instinctively took their positions from practice drills. They formed a ring, hands on each other's shoulders, silently praying. They were about to enter a dangerous battle with no guarantee of return, each inwardly pleading, 'Oh God, when we venture in this darkness, in the biting cold, in an unfamiliar land over twelve thousand feet above sea level. Kindly guide us every step of the way. Kindly help us to make our nation proud.' They remained motionless, praying for over a full minute.

Maj Bakshi's voice broke the silence, his words carrying a weight of unwavering dedication. "We must focus solely on our mission today. We owe this to our motherland and will not relent until we succeed. Jai Hind."

"Jai Hind," everyone repeated softly.

As Subr Rameshwar Gupta and his team saluted, the Bats moved towards the crossing point with their kits on their backs. Godbole and Dorjee led the team, followed by two commandos. Maj Bakshi, Talreja, and Riaz, with the remaining three commandos bringing up the rear. All had night vision goggles, while two commandos wore thermal vision imaging equipment. When the team entered the enemy territory, Sub Gupta picked up the hotline to Brig Kedar.

Meanwhile, in Delhi, the National Security Adviser was in his office keenly waiting for updates from the field. His hotline rang as he impatiently began to sip his third cup of coffee.

"Sir, as planned, the team has crossed over... at 8:30 p.m.," a voice said.

"Well, Brigadier, since you have already told me it will take at least four to five hours for the next feedback, I am going home. But I will be waiting. The moment you come to know something, please call up."

The landscape from the LAC to Tangma was plateau, mostly plain ground, with a few stretches of climbing up and down. Guided by Dorjee, the team made steady progress. Maj Bakshi checked the compass frequently to ensure they did not lose the general direction. They walked steadily, mindful not to increase speed to avoid breathlessness in the rarefied air. The clear sky above prevented the landscape from turning pitch dark, and they were relieved not to encounter the mountain dogs and foxes said to be abundant in the area. During the arduous trek, some team members started chewing hard cubes of yak cheese to prevent their throats from drying.

After an hour and a half, Godbole asked Dorjee, "Have we not got closer to the village?"

"Tangma is about three kilometres from the LAC. We may be closer, sir. Let me see," Dorjee said. But he sounded tentative. In the darkness, he was trying hard to find landmarks to help him identify the place. The team had no other choice but to bank on him entirely. After all, Dorjee had lived in Tangma for a few years. He had also walked a few times from Tangma to the LAC to see off Tenzin Lote. Yet, Godbole was fearful of losing his way in that barren wilderness.

After walking for some time, Godbole wanted to ensure they were on the right track. He asked Dorjee, "We know the trenches are about two kilometres after the village. So, the team has to go past the village, doesn't it?"

"Yes, sir."

"Hope you will avoid going even to the village's periphery."

"Yes, sir. We are walking far away from the village. I think we have already crossed it. We do not see the village because everyone is asleep, and there are no lights. The houses do not have electricity," Dorjee said.

The walk appeared unending, and everyone waited for Dorjee to say they had reached the spot. At last, just before 11:40 p.m., Dorjee spotted a rocky patch and a steep elevation that he instantly recognized. He softly declared, "We are on the right course... the trenches should be down there." Soon, he took the team down a gentle downward slope. Dorjee described the trenches as being at the bottom of a funnel-shaped depression.

Maj Bakshi asked everyone to stop before approaching the tech centre. He activated the electronic signal sweeper, ensuring the area was free from any electronic signals. Finding none, he instructed everyone to lie down and crawl forward to minimize the risk of being captured by laser or infrared surveillance devices. The team had to come sufficiently close to the spot to realize something was hidden underground. The team identified the outline of four large square trenches through the night vision goggles. There were no guards – just two barbed wires held by two-foot-tall rods encircling the trenches as the perimeter protection. The roof of the trenches was only one and a half feet above the ground level, with ventilation holes at regular intervals. The entire roof was covered with sturdy steel sheets on which soil and stones were scattered for camouflage.

The Bats sprang into action. They had just fifteen minutes to finish the operation per the drills they practised. Initially, four commandos took positions with their back towards the trenches, each looking in four different directions. They then lay on their bellies, scanning the area far and wide. Dorjee sat by one commando while the remaining commando kept a vigil using thermal vision imaging equipment. Godbole, Maj Bakshi, Talreja and Riaz quickly went around the trenches to find an opening to enter. At one place, there was a small pathway covered with a metallic sheet. The path had steps going down, probably leading to an underground entrance. They decided not to use that path as it could have had security measures. Their guess proved right when Godbole's device detected an infrared light screen covering the entrance. Godbole asked Talreja to step back and stand guard near the pathway.

Maj Bakshi, Godbole, and Riaz continued looking for a suitable place to enter the trenches. Since they did not find one, they explored all six ventilation points in the trenches. They did not detect any infrared security screen protecting the ventilation. However, there was wire mesh protection. The ventilation points were also not wide enough to let a person slip in. Since there was no other way, the team selected a ventilation opening. First, Godbole cut the wire mesh. Then, using a metallic tool from his kit, Riaz dug the ground along the edges of the opening and made it broader to allow them in.

One by one, the three entered the trench. The ceiling was too low, and the air was stuffy but pleasantly warmer. The flooring was wooden. A thick, round cable went into a switchboard on the wall. A few wires from the vent were connected to two pieces of equipment that looked like servers, having incessantly blinking tiny green lights. The system was in running condition. There were two more such pieces of equipment in the second and third trenches. However, they seemed to be switched off. In the fourth trench, there were two medium-sized dish antennae. Interestingly, the bases of the dish antennae were attached to a solid metallic zig-zag-shaped system with levers. It looked like an arrangement to pop the antennae out of the trench into the open whenever required. Many more wires, clipped in separate bunches, ran from one trench to another. All four trenches were interconnected with narrow passages.

In the trench where the antennae were housed, there were two single cots in the corner. A few sleeping bags were kept rolled on the cots. Godbole found a bunch of rectangular cardboard packets on a desk near the cots, with sides varying from about 4 to 3 inches and about 8 to 6 inches. All the packets were empty except one, in which a broken piece of circuit board was present. He quickly picked up the packets and stuffed them into his backpack.

Godbole video-recorded all the equipment once they finished searching the trenches, using the night vision recorder. Meanwhile, the Major and Riaz started planting the inflammable gel and the timers on each server-like piece of equipment and the elaborate wiring work at the base of the dish antennae. To ensure that the equipment would be destroyed entirely, they injected a good amount of gel into the equipment cases through their tiny air vents. Soon, they activated the timers and came out of the trenches.

The Mountain Bats completed their mission in less than twenty minutes after entering the trenches. It was already a quarter past midnight, and they needed to make a quick retreat. The team felt relief and jubilation for completing the mission. They focused more on a fast and safe return journey to the LAC and maintained the same formation as during the approach, with Godbole and Dorjee leading. Meanwhile, the temperatures might have dropped to -18 degrees Celsius, and a damning wind made their progress hard. After covering some distance, Godbole asked, "When do you expect the timers to go off?"

"Two hours. That is the maximum time we could set," Maj Bakshi said. "But do not worry, two hours is a good time to be in a safe zone. About three hours from now, we will be rejoicing on our side of the LAC."

"Well, for now, celebration is far from my mind. You know, there is unfinished work in Tangma," Godbole said.

"What are you saying?"

"Major, I have to go to Tangma."

"But why?"

"To take Rinchin Tashi back to our motherland."

"Mr Godbole, it is too dangerous. Even if you get him, how do you take him with you? He is seventy years old; he has severe arthritis. That is what Dorjee had told us."

"I can do this. My colleagues Riaz, Talreja and Dorjee are there with me."

"You know, Mr Godbole, there cannot be any deviation from our approved plan. That was the order from the top."

"Major, you and the commandos can keep walking to the LAC. We will join you soon."

"This is just crazy... just crazy."

"We have worked it out. Do not worry; we will be back. Until then, you can keep walking."

"This is just impossible!"

"Major, let me just ask you... if one of your soldiers gets stuck here, will you walk away, leaving him to his fate... without even trying once? Just because you have no orders?"

Maj Bakshi was in a dilemma.

"Major, Tashi was one of our finest operatives. We shudder to be on this side of the LAC for a few hours. Tashi often came here on duty alone... many times. Unfortunately, he was caught. Now that we have come to this place, how can we return without trying our best to rescue him? If we could pull off today's operation at the tech centre, it is because of Tashi. Had Tashi not cooperated selflessly, Dorjee could not have returned to us to tell us about the tech centre." By then, he was panting. Talking while walking at such an altitude was almost impossible. Godbole stopped walking.

"Mr Godbole, are you sure you want to do this?"

"Yes, because I see a good chance of us succeeding in rescuing Tashi. Tashi's house is on the outskirts of the village. Dorjee would help me get there. If everything is fine, we will bring him with us. I have a thick sheet of cloth in my backpack to carry him. Riaz is carrying warm clothing for himself. We have hot drinks too."

"I will come with you to do this," Maj Bakshi said.

"No, Major. In case of danger, we should not all perish. At least you and the commandos should be back. And... please keep your compass handy. We will catch up soon."

"I respect bravehearts. Please remember that our timers will ignite their tech centre in just one and a half hours. Achieve your goal and try to get as far as possible from Tangma. All the best."

Godbole, Talreja, and Riaz followed Dorjee as he marched to Tangma. The village was not far, but after the tech centre operation, they were all exhausted. Their feelings for a long-forgotten colleague were the only factor that kept them moving. It was a calculated risk. Godbole was conscious that several things had to go right for them to succeed. The time was ticking for the fire at the tech centre, which would alert the Chinese. So, the question was how swiftly could they get Tashi and rejoin Maj Bakshi.

At ten minutes past one, Godbole and his men entered the village. Everything was quiet. The only light came from a shed-like structure at the far end. Dorjee whispered that it was a PLA office. Would someone be awake there, Godbole wondered. Through the night vision goggles, the village area appeared surreal. A narrow gravel road passed through the middle of the village. There were a few houses on both sides of the road. The houses were built wherever they found plain land, not in a particular order. As the team passed the third house on the left, Dorjee hesitated. He stared intently, moved forward, then returned and scanned the area again, clearly confused. "What is the problem?" Godbole asked softly.

"I am looking for the small pathway leading to three small dwellings, one of which is Tashi's house. But I can't see the pathway. The path should have been there after the third house along the left," Dorjee whispered.

Godbole felt concerned. Maybe Dorjee had a problem seeing through the night vision goggles. He eagerly asked, "Are you sure the path was near the third house?"

"That was my impression, sir. Maybe the problem is that we entered the village from the back."

The walkway would not disappear. Dorjee might be looking for it in the wrong place. As tension started mounting, Godbole and his teammates decided to search for the pathway. There were no trees or bushes to stay hidden, so they had to move openly, risking exposure.

Five minutes later, Talreja approached Godbole and said, "There is a sidewalk after the fourth house and another closer to the fifth house."

Godbole quickly moved forward and spotted both pathways a little distance from each other. Immediately, Dorjee came there, stood thinking briefly, and led the team through the walkway near the fourth house. There were three houses at the end of the path, all similar-looking ones. As the team waited for Dorjee to show them Tashi's house, Dorjee looked confused again.

"Sir... the problem is that I rarely come to this part of the village. But I can say that this is where his house was. One of these three houses should be Tashi's," Dorjee said nervously."

Godbole could not blame Dorjee. He was not thoroughly familiar with that part of the village and was under the pressure of the risky operation. However, checking all three houses for Tashi was out of the question.

The team was in a miserable situation, not finding a solution to the problem. Time was running out, and the fire at the tech centre would alert the sleeping Chinese guards at any moment. As disappointment and frustration caught up with the team, Godbole struggled to keep calm. Would they be compelled to return from there empty-handed? Godbole was hesitant to retreat. He instinctively thought of going around the three houses. All three houses were stunningly alike. The walls of the houses were made of corrugated metal sheets. The houses had one main entrance door and two windows. The doors and windows were tightly closed from inside to secure the house from the freezing temperatures outside. Godbole did not find anything in particular to help him identify Tashi's house.

As Godbole started walking back to join the team, he noticed a stick leaning on the wall near the entrance door of one of the houses. It appeared to be a walking stick. Godbole slowly examined the baton and put it back in its place. As he was about to go, he remembered Tashi's arthritis and difficulty walking. Was it Tashi's walking stick?

Asking Talreja and Riaz to remain on guard, Godbole and Dorjee evaluated the house from outside. Since the door and windows were closed from the inside, entering the house was difficult. However, they noticed that the corrugated metal sheets were unevenly fitted in some places. Trying to breach the sheets was dangerous as it could create sounds. So, they tried to find loose sheets to dislodge easily. Luckily, Godbole found that one of the windows was not correctly bolted. Instead, the window shutter was kept in place by tying it to a hook with a string. Working with night vision goggles at close range was difficult. Somehow, Godbole managed to cut the string. Taking care not to scare the occupants of the house, Godbole and Dorjee entered the house through the window.

The house had just one room with a kitchen area on one end. It was warmer than the outside, as a few pieces of the coal in the hearth were smouldering. Two low-level cots were close to the hearth. Both cots were occupied. The people sleeping were covered in thick quilts, so it was difficult to identify who they were.

Godbole removed a small plastic pouch from his backpack, opened its seal and slowly pulled out a piece of cloth soaked in anaesthetic liquid. He then slowly pulled the quilt to uncover the face. It appeared to be an aged woman. Godbole signalled Dorjee to take a look. When Dorjee showed his thumbs down, meaning the person was not Tashi, Godbole let the lady smell the wet cloth. He then covered her face with her quilt.

After that, Godbole and Dorjee moved towards the other cot. Dorjee removed his night vision goggles and carefully lifted the quilt. Godbole switched on his tiny torch to help Dorjee identify the person. Just as Dorjee showed his thumbs up, the person woke up startled. Fearing that he might shout, Godbole tightly covered his mouth. By then, Dorjee bent forward and whispered something into Tashi's ear. Tashi recognized Dorjee, but he still looked alarmed. Dorjee explained what they were trying to do.

After almost two minutes, Tashi understood what was going on. Godbole opened a flask from his kit and poured a hot chocolate drink for Tashi.

While Tashi sat sipping the drink, Godbole opened the door and called in Talreja and Riaz. Once they were in, Godbole quickly spread the sheet he had brought to serve as a cloth stretcher. Meanwhile, Dorjee helped Tashi to wear the special protective clothing they had brought. Soon, they asked Tashi to lie down on the improvised stretcher. They held the four corners of the sheet and moved forward. After they came out of the door, Riaz pulled the door and closed it tightly. Godbole was happy that the operation was so swift, taking only about ten minutes.

The walk back with the personal kit and the stretcher was strenuous. Godbole was sure that the temperature might have fallen further. As he checked the time, he felt concerned. It was 1:50 a.m., and the timers were set to ignite the fire in the tech centre by 2:15 a.m. The concern that the Chinese would get alerted and come to check the fire incident was genuine. Nevertheless, jubilation fuelled their exhausted bodies to keep moving forward.

Barely out of the village, they saw some people sitting on the ground ahead. The team froze. Godbole recovered instantly and once again peered through his night vision goggles.

"Those people are only about five-hundred metres away from us. They do not seem to be in combat mode," Godbole said.

"Yes, sir," Riaz said.

"I can see six of them. How many can you count?" Godbole asked.

"I also see six of them. What should we do?" Riaz asked.

"Hold on, Riaz. If they are six... and relaxing, they should be the Bats. They did not go. Oh God, they are waiting for us!" Godbole said.

"I think they have seen us. They are waving," Riaz said.

Godbole and his men waved back and tried to move faster to meet the waiting Bats. However, walking fast and carrying Tashi made them feel breathless. Finally, they saw that the waiting team was coming towards them. When the two teams met, it was like a reunion of long-lost friends! Nothing could reinforce one's willpower in grave adversities as the sense of togetherness could.

"We welcome Tashi," Maj Bakshi said. "And... hearty congratulations, Mr Godbole. I salute your determination, fearlessness and solidarity with your men. But you misjudged us. How could you think we would leave you and your men behind?"

Sensing that Godbole was speechless, the Major said, "You were modest... trying not to force others into your trouble. But Tashi lying in here is not your soldier alone. He is a warrior of our country."

Maj Bakshi stopped to take a deep breath. He added, "We came up to the outskirts and waited there. Had we sensed any trouble, we would have intervened. We moved out only when we saw you coming back."

He continued, "You said we all should not perish if you got into trouble in the village. But we came here together. If you get into trouble, it would be our trouble, too. So be it if we all perish trying something worthy, like saving a fellow warrior. After all, the aim of our mission was achieved when we successfully planted the combustible material in those trenches."

"Major, it is my turn to salute you. I am glad and lucky that I got an opportunity to work with an officer like you. When it comes to such life-threatening assignments, I do not ask my men to join me to sacrifice their lives. If they join me, it should be because their hearts tell them to do so. You came to help me because your inner voice told you. That is the character of the warrior. Warriors come to the field not to run away."

Godbole, too, was getting breathless, but he continued, "Major, I knew you would come. That was why, when my colleague spotted some men ahead of us, I confidently said it would be the Bats waiting for us."

"True, Mr Godbole. There is so much to learn from you. Anyway, we have to get away from here. The fire might start in the trenches in about twenty-five minutes. We have to double up."

"Why don't we have our chocolate drink and eat some dry fruits before we start? It would help us move faster," Godbole said.

"Do you know why you are suggesting having refreshments rather than rushing to the LAC?" Maj Bakshi asked. "It is because of this newfound confidence. We realize that we are a solid team, having each other's backs."

The Mountain Bats and Tashi quickly sat down and emptied their flasks of hot chocolate drinks. Some ate dry fruits, too. The ten-minute break recharged them. They were back on their feet and resumed their march. Every fifteen minutes, the Bats carrying Tashi's stretcher were replaced by a new set of Bats. As they kept walking, one of the commandos said, "I think the trenches are now burning. I can see the red glow on the horizon."

"We have done it!" Maj Bakshi said. "Keep walking, friends; we have one more hour to reach the LAC."

Long hours of exposure to the cold and physical fatigue slowed down the Bats' movement. Carrying Tashi was an additional challenge. For the Bats, a battle between their will and bodies was on. The worry of the PLA men detecting their presence kept pushing the Bats forward. The horizon appeared somewhat brighter as the time inched close to 4 a.m. They were concerned that the visibility might get better soon, making them vulnerable.

Most of the Bats exhausted the yak cheese cubes given to them to chew while walking. It prevented their throats from going dry. Godbole saw a commando desperately checking his bag. He understood the commando was searching for something to chew to keep his throat wet. Godbole had just one cube left, which he would need. Yet, without hesitation, he gave it to the commando. The grateful commando grabbed the precious piece instantly.

As the team kept tugging itself, suddenly Dorjee, who was leading the pack, shouted, "We are there... we are reaching home!"

His words injected fresh energy into everyone. Many let out a loud sigh of relief. Before long, Sub Rameshwar Gupta and his men came rushing. A few took over Tashi and carried him. Some from Gupta's team collected the backpacks from the Bats to make them feel lighter. When they were sure they were on their home ground, the Bats let them fall on the ground one by one. They had no energy to sit, let alone celebrate their hard-earned victory.

While the Subedar's men looked after the fatigued Bats and served hot drinks, the Subedar picked up the receiver of the hotline in the improvised tent and shouted, "Jai Hind, sir, the Bats are back. All are safe. Just that... they are eleven now because they have brought Rinchin Tashi with them!"

Responding to a query from the other end, the Subedar said, "Yes, sir, they said he is Rinchin Tashi."

"Correct, sir, he is an old man," the Subedar reiterated.

The Subedar answered another query. "Both Major Saheb and Godbole Saheb are lying in the makeshift tent. They are all exhausted. We are waiting to take them to Janung."

"Yes, sir. I will tell them to speak to you as soon as possible," the Subedar assured.

"No, sir. We have not yet seen any movement from the Chinese side. But the day is just breaking," the Subedar informed.

"Noted, sir. Jai Hind, sir!" the Subedar said and hung up the receiver.

*****

New Delhi
December 3, 2020

After spending four days in Zemithang to recoup from the fatigue of the strenuous operation, Godbole returned to Delhi late at night.

As he lay in bed, reluctant to get up, his eyes fell on the bright red roses on the balcony. The soft petals, glistening with dew, sparkled in the early morning sun. With so many flowering plants, Radha had transformed their small balcony into a mini Mughal Garden! He slowly sat up, savouring the sight, but guilt gnawed at him for overlooking his wife's efforts. He knew their bond was strong enough to withstand such neglect, yet he regretted the toll his office duties had taken.

"I knew you were awake," Radha said, entering the room.

Godbole was happy and surprised to see Radha dressed up formally. He was raring to catch up with Radha and indulge in small talk, but she said, "I think you have to get ready. Your boss had called."

"Das called?" Godbole was surprised.

"He will be here by nine, about an hour from now. He is coming anyway. So, I told him to join us for breakfast. I even finished making *kande-pohe*, alu-paratha, and a banana pie."

Godbole looked blankly. Why was Das coming? After all, he was to report to the office by noon. However, the boss was the boss. It would be better if he got ready to welcome him. He is a stickler for time. Godbole reluctantly proceeded to the washroom.

As always, Das had an electrifying presence. His smile and energy were admirable, even at that age.

Settling at the breakfast table, Das said, "Radha, with so many mouthwatering dishes on the table, I won't regret gatecrashing into your house," Das said, laughing loudly. In his civil avatar, Das was a conversationalist.

After finishing breakfast, when Das and Godbole settled in the drawing room, Radha withdrew into the kitchen. She knew the men would soon delve into office matters.

"Well, Yash, you said you had found a broken piece of the circuit board in one of those rectangular packets you collected from the tech centre's trenches in Tangma. I dropped in to collect it. We need it. It has to be handed over to the Americans by this afternoon," Das said.

"Oh, yeah. In one of those packets, there was a broken piece. Why do the Americans need it?" Godbole asked.

"I will explain everything leisurely."

"It is in my luggage securely," Godbole said, disappearing into his bedroom. He promptly returned with the small packet. Das kept it in his bag and prepared to go.

"I should thank Radha for the fabulous breakfast," Das said. "Yash, you'd better take ample rest. See you at the office tomorrow."

"Sir... I feel odd that the Americans are in the picture. Have they been told of the Shoi-Ming episode? You also have not mentioned anything about the other detainees, especially Dolma."

"Listen, Yash, matters take their own course at some point, and we are left with making the best of what we can do in the circumstances. But believe me, we have managed to take good advantage of the developments to the extent possible."

"You are too cryptic, sir..."

"Look here, we are moving at a fast pace. We started our action soon after you completed Operation Tangma a week ago. First, Rolex and his accomplices were taken into custody," Das explained.

"Sir, I know, we can build strong cases against Rolex, Abid and even Zinto Lee. That is fine. I want to know about Dolma and Shoi-Ming. What are we going to do with them?" Godbole asked.

"Dolma is in a pathetic situation. We took the Nepali Intelligence into confidence. You won't believe it; even before we spoke to the Nepalese, the Chinese had made oblique enquiries about Dolma. However, when it became obvious that she was trapped in Delhi, the Chinese suddenly went silent about her. They've abandoned Dolma. She could not even hope for an exchange programme. That is the plight of a spy who was a big player in Kathmandu."

“Oh, that is too bad,” Godbole muttered.

“The Nepalese are happy that she was caught in Delhi. In Kathmandu, with her high connections, she was a big source of trouble. Against our wishes, they are now planning to frame charges against her. The NES-17 can’t hold her in custody indefinitely,” Das said.

“Very sad how some operatives end up hopelessly,” Godbole remarked. “Now, how is Shoi-Ming placed?”

“We needn’t worry about Ming anymore,” Das said.

“I did not get you...” Godbole said, staring at Das.

“We handed over Ming to the Americans yesterday.”

“What?” Godbole almost shouted.

“It was a government decision. But don’t worry, everything has been taken care of.”

“Can you be more precise, sir?”

“We needed Ming’s custody to acquire those innovative technologies, right? We have achieved that. When the Americans insisted on getting back Ming, our negotiators skillfully insisted on the technology. At last, they agreed, and we did too. This arrangement serves us both well,” Das said and smiled. “Rest assured, for Shoi-Ming, it is the end of the road. He will be in the US jail for a miserably long period.”

“But, just an assurance about technology? What if there is no action on the ground?”

Das opened his bag and took that day’s *Times of India* newspaper. “Yash, you may not have had time to glance through today’s newspapers. Look.”

Godbole grabbed the newspaper from Das and read the headlines of a short news item: ‘India and US sign MoU for joint development of innovative electronic signalling technology.’

“Yash, a few researchers and experts from India are leaving for the US next week. Things are moving that fast. The Chinese wanted to use that technology against us. Paradoxically, we could use that technology against the Chinese at some point. In this complex game, they never realized they could be shot with their own gun," Das said and chuckled. Godbole could not curtail a gentle smile adorning his face.

Epilogue

The Chinese might have known that the Indians had outsmarted them, but they maintained a tactical silence. Perhaps they were biding their time for another opportunity to strike. Yet, the Indians, with their unwavering resilience, had settled a score smartly. However, the celebrations of this spectacular victory were muted in the official circles of Delhi. Any public announcements and celebrations would have exerted pressure on the Chinese to retaliate and could have sparked an adverse public reaction in their country. This is why, not just the failures, but even victories, are kept under shrouds. Intelligence is not allowed to run on emotions. Tactical tussles are always a part of the intelligence games adversaries play. The aim is not as much to defeat as to keep up the pressure on the enemy.

The Indians achieved significant victories – they brought back Tashi, solved the Mumbai blackout mystery, and destroyed the Chinese tech centre in Tangma. However, NES-17 did not accomplish all its goals. The most crucial operator, Tsering Wangchu, remained unidentified. This was his ultimate aim when he took his own life. He was the critical figure overseeing the Chinese intelligence operations in India. With his death, a wealth of details and secrets about many Chinese operations were buried. This event underscored a fundamental truth – intelligence operations often do not achieve one hundred per cent success.

The return of Rinchin Tashi had a profound emotional impact on his relatives and the villagers in Arunachal Pradesh. It also had a positive ripple effect on the rank and file of the Intelligence community and the Army. It sent a powerful message to the men of the security establishment that the sacrifices of warriors would always be cherished, not forgotten, and that their collective efforts were not only recognized but also deeply appreciated.